ANDY ROBB

GEEKHOOD

MISSION IMPROBABLE

Stripes

"I think of Sarah. The rest is easy."

Jim Gordon, *The Dark Knight Returns*
by Frank Miller

ONE

I hate being late. Especially when I don't have a choice in the matter. Don't get me wrong, I don't mind a Wednesday trip to the dentist. In Geek terms, it's the closest you'll ever get to the thrill of bunking off school. There's even something vaguely satisfying about lying back in a chair, with a mouth full of fingers and looking up a man's hairy nostrils, knowing that your mates are up to their *oreilles* in French. And given how much I *brosse mes dents*, there's little or no chance of Mr Morgan whipping out anything remotely like a drill.

It's the going back to school at the wrong time of day that puts me on edge. When you walk to school with your mates, you all plug in to the same mindset. For me, Matt, Ravi and Beggsy, it's usually a discussion about an upcoming game of Dungeons & Dragons, maybe a mobile masterclass from Beggsy on new miniature-painting techniques or a highly intellectual appraisal of the Ever-Expanding Assets of Kirsty Ford, The Sexiest Girl in the School™. But, today, I've got to go without that – it feels like skipping breakfast.

By the time Mum drops me off at the gates, the school seems big and empty, without the usual melee of faces and mid-morning chatter. The corridors, usually the hunting ground of Grunts like Jason Humphries, echo with the sound of my footsteps and the stairs to 3B are uncomfortably open and spacious.

IM: *It's called being alone. Get used to it, Geek Boy.*

I guess I should explain something: I've developed a couple of coping mechanisms that get me through my daily routine. The first is my Exterior Monologue, or EM. I'd love to say that it's a well-trained fusion of controlled body language and psychological camouflage that allows me to keep my thoughts hidden beneath a veneer of cool indifference, but it's not that reliable. Occasionally, it responds to my commands like Bruce Wayne's Batmobile. More often than not, it reacts like a clown car, betraying my mood with the honk of a metaphorical horn.

The other piece of weaponry in my self-protective armour is my Interior Monologue, or IM, which works completely independently from whatever my EM is doing. It's the voice that no one else gets to hear, the voice that keeps me rooted to the ground, narrates my day, cheers me on when I'm being cool and berates me when I'm being a jerk. Which feels like most of the time.

IM: **Takes a bow to thunderous applause**

I knock tentatively on the door of 3B and go in. This is the bit I really hate – the moment where you go in late to a class and everyone looks at you. Being a Geek means you don't want to be singled out; you want to fly under the radar. But, right now, all radars are on me as I hand my note in to Mrs Moor and I can almost hear the questions bouncing around the thirty or so brains that ought to be applying themselves to quadratic equations: "Why's he late?" "Where's he been?" "What's he been up to?"

IM: *You're assuming that you are somehow interesting to other people. I hate to break it to you...*

Flushing an enigmatic crimson, I head to my seat, trying to ignore the silent stares and sit down next to the one person who looks more irritated than interested: Beggsy.

"Dude!" he hisses, exasperation written all over him. "Where've you been?"

"Dentist," I mutter, getting my books out for what will be a fairly fruitless final fifteen minutes. "What's up?"

It takes nanoseconds for the irritation to leave Beggsy's system and he's back to his hyperactive default setting. But that's Beggsy all over; he's sort of like Tigger, but with a voice that can go from sounding like the cry of a mandrake to Russell Crowe.

IM: *With Attention Deficit Disorder.*

"You know I got that job at the Hovel...?"

Of course I do. We all know. The Goblin's Hovel,

run by the Geek Lord, Big Marv, is the local gaming shop. It's where we Lesser Geeks hook up on a weekend to check out new rule books for games or browse through the racks of miniatures, deciding which ones we're going to paint. Big Marv always has awesome window displays: dioramas showing heroes battling unspeakable monsters or battalions from some fantastical army. Mostly, he paints them himself, but, occasionally, one Acrylic Acolyte™ is honoured with the task of painting up a new display. For real, live money. And Beggsy has been accorded that honour.

Beggsy's appointment sent ripples of envy through our little group; it confirmed his long-suspected status as Best Painter™. Me and Ravi were the first to grudgingly congratulate him, but Matt seemed to take it as a personal slight.

IM: *But then, Matt takes everything as a personal slight.*

"Yeah. How's it going?" I murmur back, half-heartedly trying to work out the value of x.

"Yeah, it's awesome – but that's not the important bit!"

"So, what's the important bit?"

"Dude…" he breathes, obviously on the edge of a full-blown Geekgasm, "LAAARRRP!" At this point, someone in his Voice Department has deleted the

Russell Crowe file and replaced it with one of Alvin and the Chipmunks. It kind of takes the gravity out of whatever he's trying to tell me.

"What the hell's LAAAARRRRP?" I really wish he'd just tell me what's going on.

"Total immersion, dude! Total immersion!" His hushed, helium tones are riddled with an unbearable excitement.

"All right," I snap. "But what is it?"

Whatever Beggsy's about to tell me is drowned out by the piercing ring of the new school bell – one of those electronic ones that make it sound like the school's on self-destruct. Which I kind of wish it was; I've got Art to get through after lunch.

"Dude!" *Conveys disappointment* "I can't tell you now; I need you all together!"

"Well, let's get to the canteen, then. The guys'll be there."

"Can't. Got me a Physics assignment to research. I'll tell you at the gates, after school. But it's big! Laters!" And he gathers his gear and bounces out through the door: Tigger in a school uniform. Although it's kind of frustrating to be dangling on a string about whatever he's got to say, it's completely understandable – we're Geeks. Geeks love order and we love rules and if the school bell tells you you've got to be somewhere else, then that's where you've got to be. We're like the crew of the *Enterprise*: reliable and efficient.

IM: *Except the girls don't wear those tight uniforms. Just sayin'.*

Shaking my head, I gather my books, grab my jacket and make for the canteen, quickly anonymous as a tumble of school bags and the jostling of careless elbows surge around me.

Lunch with Matt and Ravi kind of helps me get back into the school groove, but it's overshadowed by the feeling of Imminent Doom. Every mouthful I eat takes me a swallow closer to double Art. Even trying to guess what Beggsy's Big News is going to be doesn't shake it. With a malicious finality, the bell rings for the end of lunch and I traipse resignedly to the Art room.

IM: *Think you'll find Mordor through the second door on the left. It's the black one.*

The second door on the left fills my stomach with a feeling like I've had too much Coke – a bit fizzy and sick. Sarah, The Most Beautiful Girl In The World™ is going to be there. Art is the one lesson we share and it sucks. About two weeks ago, I asked her out.

IM: *That's not entirely accurate, is it?*

OK. About two weeks ago, I set a new standard for making a fool of yourself. Think bursting into tears in her bedroom, think getting into a fight with Jason

Humphries, think selling off all my gaming gear in an attempt to de-Geekify myself, disowning my friends and pretending to have some latent psychic abilities and you're just scratching the surface.

Unsurprisingly, she said no and, since then, I just haven't known what to do whenever she's around; the rule book is devastatingly blank.

IM: *Not entirely accurate, either. Look: on page one, in very small print, there's a single word: "Apologize". Whatever can it mean?*

It means that I know what I really *ought* to do, but I just can't bring myself to. So I need to try and think of something else to get back on track with her. *Anything* else.

IM: *Grow a moustache. All girls love moustaches, everyone knows that.*

But even my top lip seems to have joined in on the conspiracy. Despite a blood-spattered shaving attempt, just before I asked Sarah out, there's not even the glint of stubble. I fleetingly entertain the idea that I might be a eunuch.

IM: **Writes memo to Kleenex, preparing them for bankruptcy**

I drop back a bit, hugging the walls and trying to watch who's going into the classroom between the various heads and shoulders. If this was a game of Dungeons &

Dragons, I'd be rolling against my Initiative like a lunatic and feeling the wall for secret doors.

IM: *Come on, Iron Man, time to suit up.*

My EM comes online.

Air of indifference: check.

Casual walk: check.

Look on face as though lost in thought: check.

IM: *Thundernerds are go!*

I take a deep breath that my lungs don't seem to have room for and head upstream to the Art room, catching up the last of the stragglers. Without even raising my head, my scanners pinpoint Sarah's position: second row, third seat from the left. She's sitting next to Caitlyn, who seems to have become her "BFF". Just as I pass her line of sight, out of the corner of my eye I see her look up. The beta-particle generator I wish I had installed in my chest suddenly loses all power and my EM reverts to Sullen Mode; I can't even look back at her.

IM: *You, sir, are a jerk.*

I am and I know it. Why can't I just smile/nod/wave/make conversation and all those other things that normal humans do? What's wrong with me?

IM: **Produces list* Right then, where shall we start…?*

Luckily for me, I find Art almost as soothing as I do painting miniatures; it's an environment where I can let out the constant tumble of images and thoughts that seem to fill up my head during the day. Just after Sarah rejected my ham-fisted advances, Mrs Cooper set us a project, entitled "The Future". While the rest of the class busied themselves with pictures of technology and computer-graphic-style drawings, I took my inspiration from the scene in *The Lord of the Rings* where Pippin gets hold of the Orthanc-stone and sees the destruction of Minas Tirith. The result is a picture of a solitary tree on a hill. Personally, I'd like to have drawn something fresh out of my brain, but Mrs Cooper insists that we do research and I had to use reference material of real trees. Apparently "even fantasy has to have a basis in reality".

IM: *You never seem to complain when you're fantasizing about Kirsty Ford…*

Given my mental state when I started it, the picture looks pretty bleak, but I've grown to like it.

IM: *It looks like a depressed ent. Just sayin'.*

And I'm even getting used to the dust and smudge of charcoals, which I wasn't very good at to begin with.

Just as I'm adding some depth to the background, there's the clatter of a chair being pushed back. I look up and see one of the girls, Aisha, running for the door, her hand over her mouth, in that "Don't look at me, I'm crying" kind of way. So we all look.

This is a Girl Thing™ that I don't understand. We all

get down now and again, but surely the last thing in the world you want to do is draw attention to it? You never see boys weeping and wailing in the school corridors; we grit our teeth and soldier on, like Warriors of the Teenage Wastelands.

Suddenly Sarah stands up and goes to follow Aisha's fading sobs.

"Just leave her," Mrs Cooper says, like she's seen it all before. And given that she has the complexion of a walnut, she probably has.

"I just want to make sure she's OK," Sarah replies. She isn't rude or defiant or anything, just matter-of-fact. And then the door closes behind her, and they disappear off to the alternative dimension of the Girls' Toilets, which seems to be the Nerve Centre for all Female Activity.

I find myself glancing at the door, just a bit too long, before I spot Caitlyn staring over at me. She has a sort of pitying look on her face, like the one you get off your mum when you explain that you'd much rather stay in and watch *Doctor Who* than go to the school disco. I bravely face down the situation by turning red and dropping my charcoal.

IM: *"There he goes, the Warrior of the Teenage Wastelands! That's him – the one who looks like a fragile beetroot!"*

For the rest of the lesson, I find myself glancing at the door every ten seconds. But Sarah doesn't come back. Whatever girls talk about in these situations is obviously a threat to the fabric of time and space and demands their full attention.

IM: *Periods, then.*

Finally, the bell goes and everyone around me starts to collect their stuff together. But I just sit there, staring at Sarah's empty chair out of the corner of my eye, feeling that some Golden Opportunity is about to pass me by. Luckily, Caitlyn's on hand to let me know what it is: she comes over to my desk and gestures at Sarah's coat and bag.

"D'you want to take them to her?" she asks from behind her glasses.

IM: *Bingo! The perfect opportunity to restore balance and harmony to the universe!*

And there it is – the chance to rebuild the bridges with Sarah that I've been so determinedly torching. But the fact that Caitlyn's made this gesture lets me know that she knows about what happened. This realization only serves to increase my level of humiliation and causes a major argument between my brain and my mouth, who mutually agree to part company at the Vital Moment.

"Yeah… That's not a good idea, is it?"

IM: *Way to go, Archie. Why didn't you just squirt a tube of paint in her face? Patronizing Purple perhaps?*

I honestly didn't mean it to sound the way it did, but now that I've committed, I can't take it back. It's like the hyperdrive's locked me into a panic-powered collision course with the Planet of Sarcasm. To complete the picture, my face joins in, doing one of those dry, world-weary smiles like the Emperor did whenever he was being threatened by Luke. But without the humour.

It's not the answer Caitlyn was expecting, judging by the look of disdain that scrapes the concern off her face.

"Well, you don't have to be so immature about it!" she snaps, before turning on her heel, gathering up Sarah's belongings and strutting out of the room.

IM: *BOOM! Right between the eyes! Game over!*

There's a distinct feeling of salt being rubbed into a wound – but the offending sodium chloride seems to be in my own hand. Although I'm not going to admit it, Caitlyn's right, there's not an ounce of maturity in the way I'm dealing with any of this. A wiser man would just go up to Sarah, do the apology thing and get on with the job of being her friend. But I don't seem to have levelled up that far just yet.

My head feels heavy as I get dragged along by the growing swarm of students as they burst out of classrooms and head towards the various exits. The hive-mood is always brighter at the end of the day, and there are playful jostles and shoves thrown into the mix as the school rules loosen their grip for another few hours. But we Geeks enjoy that particular straightjacket; we like the security of rules and regulations. It's when we're left to our own devices that the world gets that bit more scary.

IM: *Red Alert: threat detected!*

My Grunt Detectors™ pick up something ahead. On a conscious level, I don't know what it is; it might be a change in the collective body language of the crowd or a new rhythm to the apparently chaotic chatter around me. It's like Spider-Man's spider-sense – you just know something's wrong.

IM: *Oh, crap.*

Crap, indeed. A school-bully-sized pile of it. Every time I see Jason Humphries, I'm astonished that we're in the same year. OK, I'm a bit young-looking for my age, but you'd at least guess I was in my teens. Humphries could be way older; he's built like the Hulk and has a face with more scars than skin. Acne pits and battle wounds seem to have eradicated any evidence of youth from his face. Those and the dark, dead eyes that burn out from under a brow that has more muscles in it than my right arm.

IM: *And that's well-exercised.*

Luckily, he's got his back to me. Unluckily, he's with

his mates and Fellow Grunts, Lewis Mills and Paul Green. Weirdly for three guys who seem to spend most of their time trying to get out of school, as soon as the final bell goes, their walking speed slows down to an absolute minimum. At some point, the crowds are going to force me past them and I'll be spotted: a Lone Geek in a Sea of Normality. Like being a hobbit at an orcs-only party.

IM: *Commence evasive manoeuvres!*

There aren't many, but I do have options. I can assume the standard Geek Stance: stooped shoulders, eyes down and just try not to get noticed. Trouble is, this often seems to have the same effect as when Frodo put on the Ring: while you're invisible to everyone else, you somehow light up like a beacon to the Great Eye of Humphries. I could opt for doubling back and finding another exit, but I don't want to be late to hear what Beggsy's LAAAAARRRP thing is all about. On top of that, struggling against the flow of hungry students might attract unwanted attention. But the crowd's moving me closer, so I've got to do something soon.

IM: *You could just wet yourself.*

As I'm dithering between options, something else grabs the attention of the lumbering Pack of Grunts™. As one, their heads swing left, as though they've picked up a scent or can hear something that the rest of us can't.

IM: *It's a mating call – pheromones or something.*

Ambling equally slowly, clacking out their dissent with their too-high heels, are three girls. They're sporting recently applied lipstick that would put the Joker to shame and more 'chood than sense. Humphries and his mates lope over and the two groups fall into a grinning, barking imitation of conversation.

IM: *No doubt they'll be grooming each other for fleas shortly.*

I take my chance and speed up – not into a run, more of a determined walk. But a fast one. I throw a quick glance over my shoulder to check that I'm out of range, and trudge towards the school gates.

By the time I get there, Beggsy is in a state of near-spontaneous combustion, pacing, hopping and slapping his hands against his thighs in frustration.

"Dude!" he squeaks. "Where've you *been*?"

My EM powers up a smile and goes into Everything's Cool Mode. "Hey. What's happening?"

Ravi, whose voice has broken far more than it ought to, rolls his eyes and sighs, like a benevolent earthquake. "Thank God you're here! He's been bugging us all day about his 'Big News'!"

"Yeah? Well, you'll be chowing down on humble pie in a minute!" Beggsy replies. He watches too much American TV.

"Well, what is it, then?" I can't help but notice that there is a darkening shadow on Ravi's upper lip and, in my current mood, it only serves to remind me of my worthless glands.

Taking the mobile stage, Beggsy moves in front of us, walking backwards as we join the exodus from the school gates.

"Gentlemen," he begins, "I give you: Live. Action. Role. Play." There's a dramatic pause, before he adds "LARP" in a much deeper voice. It's like he's occasionally inhabited by the spirit of someone with testicles.

IM: *Big ones.*

Unfortunately, he doesn't quite get the reaction he's looking for: me, Matt and Ravi exchange a quick succession of confused shrugs.

"'K. So what does that mean?" I like the word "role play", but I don't quite get the rest.

"Dude," Beggsy begins in his Serious Voice. "I took some vampire lords into the Hovel last night and Big Marv told me to put them out the back. There was a flyer on his painting desk for something called 'QuestFest'." There's another pause, while he tries to calm the storm of hyperactivity that's obviously raging in his head. "Turns out there's this bunch of people who play Dungeons & Dragons but, like, for real! They meet up in a field, dressed as their characters, and there's a

Games Master and a team of bad guys, all dressed up as monsters, and they do an adventure – but *for real*! Big Marv says it's like 'total immersion', like you're living your favourite fantasy film!"

Our confusion vanishes in a puff of smoke. This is Big News for a number of reasons. First off, it's a ridiculously imaginative take on our Games Nights. Usually, we're sitting round a table, rolling multi-sided dice and arguing about the finer points of the rules, but this would be taking it to another level. My mind is suddenly awash with images of shining armour, clashing swords and living, breathing monsters – we can do this for real! Secondly, it means we're not alone. By their very nature, Geeks are hard to sniff out; we like to keep our profiles as low as possible, in case it attracts unwanted attention. But they are out there. And we might get to hang out with people for whom debating *Star Trek* versus *Star Wars* is something to be taken seriously. Thirdly, it means I've got something else to think about instead of Sarah.

Matt and Ravi look at me expectantly, as though they're seeking some sort of approval.

"Sounds awesome!" I declare and see three Geeks visibly relax.

"There's one next weekend and," Beggsy continues, back in *Alvin and the Chipmunks* territory, "Big Marv says we can go with him! He says if we're interested, to come to the Hovel today and he'll talk us through it!"

"Cool," I reply. "Let's do it. To the Hovel!"

Big Marv isn't ashamed of his Geekhood; he wears it like a big, shiny, unconventional medal. From his tousled brown hair and scruffy beard to the waxed tips of his moustache, Big Marv, like most Geeks, appears to have been born in the wrong time. If it wasn't for his penchant for bright yellow T-shirts (usually referencing *Doctor Who*), his glasses and the cut-off jeans he likes to wear, he'd remind me of Volstagg out of the *Thor* comics. And we won't even talk about the sandals.

"Ha-haa!"

And Big Marv is always laughing in a Friar Tuck kind of way for no apparent reason. Because of this and the extra weight he's packing, it's hard to put an age on him, but I'd guess late thirties.

"Ha-haa!" he chimes again. "So, my bold adventurers, you want to know more about the fabled world of LARP!" I love the way he speaks.

The cool thing about Big Marv's apparent madness is that because he doesn't seem to care about how other people see him, in his company, we don't, either.

The shields we all keep in place for our parents and other grown-ups are silently dropped and we just behave like we do with each other.

IM: *But without the willy jokes.*

"Can you explain it, Marv?" Beggsy rasps.

"Be seated, good fellows!" Big Marv booms, pulling up a painting stool round a wargaming table that depicts the Battle of Weathertop. We all follow his lead and soon have something that looks like a council of war – five generals seated round a three-dimensional map.

IM: *Or five Geeks sat round some tin soldiers. Pick one.*

With Big Marv kicking off in his weird patter, this feels *really* Geeky; like, *über* Geeky.

"Well met, fellows!" he begins, before lowering his voice to a Serious Level. "LARP is the gaming experience taken to the next level: Total Immersion! For two days, you live and breathe the character of your choice! There is a quest to be undertaken and there are foes to be slain!"

IM: *If he broke into a few "fol-de-rols" here, you'd be sitting with Tom Bombadil.*

"And what are you?" I ask. "In the LARP thing."

"Ha-ha! I, Archie, am a necromancer! I can raise the dead, create poisons and wield magic, according to the Dark Arts!"

"How does it work?" I ask. "What about the rules?"

IM: *Ah, the comfort-blanket of parameters…*

"Slowly, slowly, young Quester – there is much to learn!"

For the next half-hour, Big Marv gives us the lowdown on LARPing. And the more he tells us, the more awesome it sounds. It's one thing to sit round a table and use miniatures and D20s to work out how a fight resolves itself, but to actually wield a sword and smite the forces of evil in man-to-man combat is a Geek dream come true. Especially as you can't get hurt.

IM: *Bravely spoken, Sir Runalot!*

Even Big Marv telling us that all the weapons are made from foam doesn't dampen our enthusiasm. In fact, when he shows us some pictures of past QuestFests on his laptop, it only stokes us all the more: the weapons look real, the armour is ornate and the costumes are brilliant.

IM: *Doesn't sound Geeky at all. No, really.*

And the rules aren't that far off Dungeons & Dragons; all the usual Hit Points and Magic Points and stuff. As Big Marv explains the rules a bit more, I take a quick glance around Weathertop; although the guys are listening, I can see that their minds are doing the same as mine – conjuring pictures of bloody battles, encounters with warlocks and, most importantly of all, a world in which WE CAN BE HEROES.

IM: *Gonna take a lot of imagination.*

Big Marv suddenly produces a rule book and slams it down on the table, knocking over a Ringwraith in his excitement.

"All you need to know, you will find in here!" he declaims, like he's Gandalf or something. "But the question is: is LARP for you?"

"Dude!" Beggsy affirms, conveying *Most definitely!* with a single syllable.

"I'm in," Ravi agrees. "Sounds awesome."

Matt waits for my response; he always likes to go with the majority. The responsibility of making an individual decision is way too much for him. But I'm in. There's no way I'd miss this.

"Let's do it," I nod. "Matt?"

"You shall have my sword," he replies, and, for a moment, he's not my nerdy, ginger-haired friend; he's a noble warrior, bristling for battle.

IM: *In his school uniform.*

Big Marv hands round some consent forms for our parents, and then we take our leave and wander through town, checking out the Book of Rules as we go. We're all excited and there's a feeling that Something Good is happening; it's like we're no longer part of the real world, but are already set apart from the mortals that scurry around us. Today, we are gods.

But these gods have to go home and ask for their mums' permission. So, at the corner of Hamilton Road we all separate, with glassy-eyed smiles on our faces as we dream of the adventures to come.

Even coming into the kitchen and finding Mum and Tony obviously pretending that they weren't just having a smooch doesn't dampen my warrior's spirits. It does make me feel a bit funny, but my EM boots up an expression of blissful ignorance.

"Hey, guys. What's for tea?" I'm using diversion tactics; the pan of bubbling bolognese and the simmering spaghetti kind of give it away. Just to let me know that I'm still her little boy, Mum detaches herself from Tony and glides over to me for a hug.

"Spaghetti," she smiles, ruffling my hair. "Your favourite. Tony's making it."

"Thanks, Tony." It's a simple offering, but it lets him know that I know that he knows that spag bol is my favourite and it must be a big thing for him to be making it, what with his new-found healthy regime.

Tony's changed since he came out of hospital. But so have I, I guess. We've both been trying really hard with each other and it has made life a bit easier. My contribution has been to actually engage him in something like conversation, rather than skulking up the stairs to my Lair. And, in return, I get something like conversation back. I think we might be getting to know each other.

His biggest change has been stopping smoking, but it's been replaced with something else. Something that has more far-reaching effects for the rest of mankind: Tony has become something of a health guru.

IM: *Dun-dun-duuuuhhh!*

The thing with my sort-of-stepfather is that he doesn't do anything by halves. When he smoked, he smoked like his life depended on it.

IM: *There's irony in action.*

But since he's been told to embrace a healthier lifestyle, he's turned into a fully paid-up member of the Food Fascist Society. I've started to miss the smell of his Sunday-morning fry-ups, and the tutting that goes on when I hit a packet of biscuits or open a Coke is really starting to grate. However, in the interests of honouring our unspoken agreement to cut each other some slack, I have to keep swallowing the comments that threaten to leap out of my mouth.

But there's a problem brewing: Tony's diet has had an effect on the way his body processes food. It builds up more gas than a North Sea oil refinery. And that gas has to go somewhere or he'll simply explode. Which would be the end of civilization as we know it.

IM: *Fartageddon?*

The trouble with Tony is that he appears to have no idea about social graces. It doesn't matter where he is or who he's with, when he feels the urge to Float An Air Biscuit ©Beggsy, he just fires it out there, like he's on a one-man mission to dismantle the ozone layer, one quack at a time. I don't know how Mum can stand it and I don't know how he can do it in front of her in the first place. If I was with Sarah, I'd never fart.

IM: *And who said romance was dead? That's …*
beautiful.

As Tony tests a piece of spaghetti to see if it's ready, I open the fridge and grab a Coke. Given that everybody seems to be in such a good mood, now might be the time to sound Mum out over the LARPing thing.

"Mum … there's a thing on next weekend that the guys are going to… Can I go?"

"What is it?" Mum asks, flicking the switch on the kettle.

IM: *Let's see you explain this…*

"Well, it's like a Games Night, but it's happening in a field. Loads of people turn up in costume and have an adventure." It sounds even more stupid than when Beggsy first explained it. "It's a camping thing and Big Marv said he'll take us," I finish lamely.

"What, like LARPing?" Tony throws over his shoulder, as he drains the pasta.

IM: *Sound of two wet thuds as eyeballs drop from sockets in amazement*

"LARPing. That's what it is." How on earth does Tony know what LARPing is?

"Oh, you'll have a great time. I used to LARP a bit, back in my uni days."

IM: *WhoawhoaWHOA! Back up there, buddy! Let's have that again?*

"You used to LARP?"

"Yeah. Not seriously, though." He spoons the bolognese sauce on to three plates and plonks them on the kitchen table. "Although there were a few…"

IM: *Geeks. Just say it!*

"…more hardcore types who used to do it a lot. We just used it as a chance to get drunk and have a laugh. One of the organizers had access to an old asylum and we used to play there. Cthulhu stuff, you know – Lovecraft."

I sit down at the table, and scoop up a forkful of spaghetti.

"What *is* LARP, exactly?" Mum asks.

As Tony launches into some "hilarious" tales about his experiences, I find myself getting annoyed. Why can't something be just *mine*? Why does everybody else seem to have done it *first*?

IM: *And why does this bolognese taste funny?*

"What meat's this?" I ask, interrupting Tony explaining how many Sanity Points he lost at his Lovecraft LARP. And probably never regained.

"Aha!" Tony grins, gesturing at my plate with a fork. "What does it *taste* like?"

IM: *If I can just stifle my gag reflex, I'll let you know…*

I'd really rather not get into this game but, in the interests of maintaining the Peace Treaty, I chuck in a couple of guesses.

"No and no," Tony chuckles. "What you're eating there, my friend, is a soya-bean substitute! Incredible, isn't it? Tastes just like the real thing!" And just to show me how incredible it is, he shovels an incredible amount into his incredible mouth. "And," he splutters through his mouthful, "it's fat-free!"

IM: *Inedible.*

"Great," I smile as sincerely as I can without splitting my own head in half. Everything in my life keeps changing – even the spaghetti.

"Like it?"

"Yeah," I lie. "So… Mum. What d'you think about me going LARPing? Everyone else is going."

"O-K…" Mum frowns, obviously concerned that her son hasn't quite left the joys of the dressing-up box behind yet. "And where's it happening?"

"Don't know. But I've got a consent form."

"Well, let me read it over and have a chat to Marvin and we'll see." While the idea of my mum sitting down over a cup of tea with Tom Bombadil is a funny one, it also feels a little weird; Big Marv's part of my Other World, one that is quietly reserved for me and my mates.

"Thanks, Mum."

"I haven't said yes, yet," Mum says, in a way that suggests she's probably going to anyway. "What are you going to wear? *If* you're going…"

"Dunno. I'll have a think."

"Elves are cool!" Tony announces, leaning sideways in his chair and letting out the First Fart of the Evening.

IM: *Noise of air-raid siren*

It's time to beat a hasty retreat before the barrage gets any heavier.

"Yeah. I like elves. Anyway, I've got homework to do. Thanks for tea, Tony. It was nice."

IM: *"Nice": the most non-committal word in the English language.*

"Pleasure, mate." As I exit the kitchen, I hear the beginning of the second bombardment.

Up in my Lair, I kill my English homework: *Twelfth Night*. But it's not like an instant execution, it's more like drawn-out torture; the more I write about Orsino, the more I see of myself in him. Maybe, like the love-sick duke, I'm just in love with the idea of being in love. Could I be that much of a jerk that all this humiliation I seem to be putting myself through is just the empty posturing of vanity? Am I actually enjoying it, in a weird way?

IM: *"Some are born Geeks, some achieve Geekhood and some have Geekhood thrust upon 'em."*

A squeak from my laptop heralds the arrival of an incoming missive through the portals of Facebook. It's Beggsy, sending me a link to something called the Larper Colony and telling me to ring him afterwards. With nothing else but my own self-damnation for entertainment, I click on the link.

IM: *Whoa…*

This site just reeks of Geek, from the Middle-earth-style logo to the gnarly, wooden background. How could I not "Enter Site"?

IM: *By going out and getting a life? Just sayin'…*

Much as I'd love to read "About Us", my eye is instantly drawn to the "Armour" and "Weapons" buttons. I go to "Armour".

IM: **Sound of a Geekgasm**

This is Geekarrific. You can buy armour! And not just your standard knight plated mail – here you can buy leather armour, chainmail and full suits constructed to look like they walked off the Pelennor Fields. You've got Dragon Helmets, Skull Helmets, Elvish Armour, Orc

Armour, Devil's Head Shoulder Plates – the list is endless. My Vanity Department does a quick promotional trailer in my head of me striding around a battlefield in black armour covered in Elvish runes, carrying the severed head of Jason Humphries.

IM: *Swords! Swords! Look at the swords!*

I do and it's just as exciting. The selection is mind-blowing: there are bastard swords, longswords, rapiers, scimitars, broadswords and even a claymore that has to have been made from finely sculpted Awesome. The hilts are ornate and decorated with eagles' heads, skulls – you name it. They might be foam, "with a polycarbon core", but these things look like the real deal. I pick up my mobile and call Beggsy.

"*Dude!*" Yep. He knows I've seen the website.

"Mate – look at this stuff! Just look at it!" I'm still scrolling through the pictures of foam-rubber instruments of death.

"I know!" he squees. "But look at the price tags, dude!"

I take a look. Wow. Real-deal foam rubber comes at real-deal sterling-silver prices. I can't even begin to afford the Blade of Chaos that looks like I was born to wield it.

IM: *You could glue a few sponges together…*

Silencing the disappointment that threatens, I take charge – there's no way I'm going to let an opportunity this epic pass me by.

"Beggsy. It doesn't matter. We'll get the money, somehow. Or we'll find a way of making them ourselves. We're Geeks; it's what we do. Remember your Halloween costume last year?"

Beggsy made himself a Jawa outfit. The eyes even lit up.

"'K. But check out 'Masks and Prosthetics'."

I click it.

IM: *No WAY!*

Way. These guys have thought of everything. Here, I can buy Demon Horns, Orc Masks, Devil Chins, ears and beards. Even the Elf Ears come in different types: Standard, Deluxe, Long, Night Elf or Blood Elf.

"What're you looking at?" Beggsy's excitement is threatening to snap his upper register.

"All of it! It's just ... *awesome!*"

"Hit 'Beards'."

Despite the fact that this is a sentence I never thought anyone would ever say to me, I hit "Beards". It's Face-Fungustastic: Celt Beards, Barbarian Beards, Musketeer Beards, Dwarf Beards and Wizard Beards. There are more beards here than at a *Lord of the Rings* convention.

"Got 'em."

"Guess which one I'm having."

It doesn't take too much guessing. At our Games

Nights, Beggsy plays the role of Damli, Lufur's son – a Dwarven Warrior with a grim disposition. And if we're to believe everything that J.R.R. Tolkien tells us, then dwarves have beards. Even the girl dwarves. But will it be the Dwarf Warrior Beard (brown), the Dwarf Lord Beard (black) or the Mountain Dwarf Beard (grey)?

IM: *He's either going to look like a miniature Hagrid or a young Santa.*

"Dwarf Warrior."

"You got it, dude! I am going to be bearded-up to the max! Damli, Lufur's son will be the most beardacious dwarf there! And what about you? What're you gonna be?"

IM: *You could go as a regular member of society. That'd be fantasy in action.*

Good question. In the past, I was a Level 5 Mage, going under the name of Luscus The Betrayer, but, when no one else fancied being the Dungeon Master, I just sort of stepped in and have done it ever since. So I've got a blank canvas on this one, I can be who I want to be.

"An elf," I say, clicking back to the ears section. "I want to be an elf." I've always liked elves.

IM: *Probably because they're everything you're not: handsome, athletic, inscrutable…*

Probably. They've got that whole aloof thing going on and it seems to win them legions of girls wherever they go. I think it's the ears.

IM: *Logical, Spock.*

"Dude!" Conveys *Enthusiastic approval* "Look, I gotta go, but we'll talk more tomorrow, yeah?" There's no way I can resist a "yeah?" of that intensity. It's like a tractor beam from the Death Star.

"You got it."

"Later."

"See ya."

The sheer joy Beggsy generates about stuff is like a sort of Happiness Virus. Sarah and the question of What To Do fades into the background, like I don't have to think about it right now; even the shadow of Jason Humphries seems a little bit shorter. I decide to treat myself to a little painting session before bed. I've started rebuilding my collection – but I'm going for quality, not quantity. I've got this superb ogre that's calling out for me to test my new paints on it. But, while I'm lovingly applying a second wash of Fuegan Orange to my base colour of Tallarn Sand, part of my mind is dedicated to one glorious thought:

Next weekend, we shall be heroes.

TWO

When I wake the next morning, I spring, Legolas-like from my bed, full of elvish enthusiasm for what the day will bring.

Even Tony preparing a fresh fruit salad with probiotic yoghurt doesn't dampen the Spirit of the Eldar coursing through my veins. And even though my heightened elvish hearing picks up a couple of predatory parps from Tony's Trouser Trumpet ©Beggsy, I don't really care. Mum picks up on my mood, saying that it's nice to see me so happy and I can tell by the twinkle in her eyes that she thinks there's a girl at the bottom of it.

IM: *But that would be ridiculous! Why would there be a girl involved, when there's the prospect of dressing up as an elf? Madness.*

The walk to school is bright and full of hope. I am one of the Elder Races, an otherworldly figure walking through the dominion of Man.

IM: *You are a twat.*

Maybe. But it seems like forever since I last had something to really look forward to and I'm going to milk it for all it's worth.

"Archie!" A voice so low it could bring down the

walls of Mordor rolls down the pavement at me. Ravi. I up my pace, breaking into a light-footed elven trot, and greet my LARPing comrades by their True Names.

"Damli! Jh'terin! Praxxus! Well met!"

Beggsy, Ravi and Matt look at me like I've turned up in a dress. Which is fair play, given I've just used our Games Night names in public.

"Sorry, guys," I grin. "Just excited about the LARPing thing."

"Yeah?" Ravi booms. "Well wait til you hear this: we're going to a party!"

IM: **Computer voice* Insufficient data! Does not compute!*

"We're what?" This might be too much for my head to handle. This doesn't happen. Geeks do not get invited to parties. It's outside the rules.

IM: *Hold your horses, Legolas! Let's just find out a bit more. You could be talking jelly and ice cream here!*

"Dude! We're. Going. To. A. Par-*tay*!"

"Yeah, OK. But *whose* 'par-tay' are we talking about?" I ask, trying to keep the irritability out of my voice.

The look Beggsy gives me is the visual equivalent of a drum roll. Thankfully, Matt knows me well enough to spot the cloud forming over my head and cuts in.

"Kirsty Ford. It's Kirsty Ford's party."

IM: **Sounds of shattering as everything Archie*

40

perceives to be real crashes around him to reveal an alternative universe where all he knows to be impossible is suddenly entirely feasible*

"What? *Kirsty Ford* invited you? To *her* party? When is it?" The reason I'm whispering is that Kirsty Ford lives in the Forbidden Zone; we don't approach her, we don't look at her directly and we don't talk about her, unless we know no one else can hear. If Jason Humphries is violence incarnate, then Kirsty Ford is sex. It's all you can think about in her vicinity, like the first time you see Princess Leia when she's chained to Jabba and wearing That Outfit. Most of the girls our age are getting Bumpy Bits ©Beggsy and their legs are suddenly long and shiny, but Kirsty Ford takes it to a whole other level. When I started to really like Sarah, I realized I couldn't imagine her with nothing on. I wish I could say the same about Kirsty Ford.

IM: *No, you don't.*

"It's tomorrow," Ravi grins, like some invisible weight has been lifted from his shoulders. "It's her birthday."

Somewhere on a cloud, the Gods of Fate laugh mockingly.

"Oh, maaan!" My head rolls to one side, while my eyes roll in the other direction – it's multitasking in the face of despair.

IM: *It IS the face of despair!*

41

"What's up?" Matt always manages to ask questions without there being any emotional commitment to his words. In a weird way, it makes it easier to answer.

"I can't go," I groan. "I'm visiting Dad in York." And here it is: the first Major Impact on my life from my dad's decision to move away. Right now, all the missing him that I've been through over the last few weeks pales into insignificance. It's like my mates have all got Golden Tickets to meet Willy Wonka and my dad's just torn mine up. The silence that haunts the next few minutes of our journey is punctuated only by me muttering the word "great" or sighing loudly.

IM: *Not that you're the indulgent type…*

"So," I finally say, "let me get this straight: Kirsty Ford came up to you guys, just now, and invited you to her party? What was *that* like?"

But instead of the round of sniggers and boob jokes I'm expecting, the silence just gets even more awkward.

"What?" I snap. "What's going on?"

"It wasn't Kirsty who asked us…" Ravi valiantly starts a sentence, but it seems he's no match for the end of it.

"It was Sarah," Matt explains. "Sarah asked us." And then, just to make me feel even more despondent than I already am, he caps it off with a cranky "OK?" But my despondency quickly turns to outrage.

"So, she invited *you* guys, but she didn't invite me?"

"No," Matt says, turning to me slowly and fixing me with one of his "don't be such a dork" stares, "she invited *all* of us. She was here just a moment ago, but she saw you coming and decided to head off."

"Why?" I sometimes wish I was in control of my mouth.

IM: *Because you're such a weirdo whenever she's around, that's why.*

Matt, as if he's picked up on the musings of my Interior Monologue, decides to throw his thoughts into the mix. "You really ought to sort it out, Archie. Sarah's all right."

"Why? Because she gets you invited to parties?"

IM: *Insert Tab A (foot) into Slot B (mouth) and hey presto! You've built your very own idiot!*

I can feel my friends flinch as soon as the words tumble out of my mouth, and I know I've overstepped the mark. When me, Matt, Ravi and Beggsy were hanging out with Sarah, before Cupid started using me for target practice, it was like we'd all suddenly gained an Invitation to Normality. Which felt completely *ab*normal – but in a good way. It was exciting and it stoked our failing Fires of Hope. And I can see that they don't want to give it up; they're completely cool with her, like she's an honorary member of the gang. The only spanner in the works is me.

"Sorry, guys. I didn't mean it. It's just..." I fire off

another sigh, while I search for the right words.

IM: *Honest ones generally fall into that category.*

"…it's just *hard*. I do need to get it sorted, but I just can't. I just feel like such a—"

"Tosser?" Matt intercepts the word that I was trying to avoid and throws it at me with some force.

"Cheers," I scowl ruefully. But he's right.

"Dude! You can't avoid her forever. Just go and talk to her! She's cool; it'll be fine."

But even Beggsy's advice niggles me a bit; it's like my mates have now got some sense of ownership over her, like they know her better than I do. Which they might.

"Yeah, I know. I will. I've just gotta find the right time."

IM: **Gets out 500-year diary* Which century did you have in mind?*

What I need to get my head around is that Sarah wants to be just friends. But I'm still not ready to do that. It would mean admitting the truth of the situation and retracing my steps to become part of a club that I don't want to join.

"So, anyway, Archie, what about the LARP? What're you going as?" Ravi's Empath-O-Meter must be firing on all cylinders as he gallantly swerves the conversation out of oncoming depression. The Sarah-shaped fog in my head starts to part, revealing me, dressed as…

"An elf! I want to be an elf." It's the first thing I've

said today that I'm sure about. "But I need a name."

"What was your Game Name?" Beggsy toots.

"No good," I frown. "I need a new one." It's a challenge and it's a Geeky one. For the rest of the journey to school, my mates pepper me with suggestions, ranging from obscure *Lord of the Rings* characters, like Radagast, to Non-player Characters who've turned up in our Dungeons & Dragons campaigns, but "Crystalbeard" just doesn't seem to cut the mustard. As we reach the school gates, the crowds chop our party in two. As Beggsy and Ravi go on up ahead, Matt flicks me a tentative look and his body stiffens with the effort of asking a personal question.

"Sarah; you still like her, then." It's a hybrid of question and statement.

"Yeah…" I reply and my entire body erupts into one big blush. I look like the red man on the traffic lights. Matt doesn't say any more, so neither do I, but I think I see his jaw muscles flex, like he's trying to work something out. As we separate, the Sarah-shaped fog fills my head again and I go after Beggsy and into registration.

Biology morphs into Geography and neither get my full attention; I'm too busy thinking about Sarah.

The Sméagol in my head knows what I ought to say to her, but the Gollum that lurks within doesn't want me to go through with it. I'm torn in two; I *want* to speak to her but, at the same time, I really don't.

By the time the lunch bell goes, the chatter in my head has filled every available nook and cranny. And Gollum wins: there's no way I can face seeing Sarah today, so I head to the library rather than joining my mates in the canteen.

I love libraries and, as libraries go, the school one's pretty cool. I don't know if they put special glass in the windows or something, but you can't hear what's going on outside like you can in the classrooms. And, if you're a Geek like me, if you can't hear it and you can't see it, you can pretend it doesn't exist. So, for sixty glorious minutes, I can just be me. On my own. With myself. And the other silent members of the Order of the Hopeless™.

IM: *Let the party begin!*

I browse the Sci-fi and Fantasy shelves, looking to see if anything new's turned up. Which it hasn't, so next I start working my way down towards the biographies and pick up a brick about J.R.R. Tolkien. I'm just flipping through when the faint smell of perfume announces the arrival of Miss Doyle.

"Archie. This arrived today; I kept it back for you.

I thought it might be the kind of thing you'd enjoy." It's a sad indictment of my life that the librarian actually knows me by name.

In her hand is a glossy-covered book, with a blue background. In the foreground, a figure squats, hunched and malevolent, balancing on a wire. His features are blacked out by avaricious shadows, but two, piercing white eyes glitter in the darkness. A flash of lightning behind the figure lights up just enough of his form that we can pick out a few details – the hooks on his gauntlets, the cut of his cape and the slightly demonic ear-tips on his cowl whisper his identity.

IM: *We're talking Batman!*

"Thanks!" I say softly, not wishing to break the Spell of Silence the library seems to be under. We go to Miss Doyle's desk, sign the book out and I hit my usual spot, tucked just behind a bookshelf, so that even if Sarah were to come in, I'd see her before she saw me.

I open the first page of *The Dark Knight Returns* and an invisible, blue-gloved hand pulls me into another world.

Bruce Wayne is old; he's in his fifties and he hasn't put on the tights for about a decade. All around him, Gotham collapses into corruption and violence as crime becomes the new law. But something twists and snarls in his belly – the spirit of something else, something vengeful and dark. Much as Bruce tries to resist it, Batman needs to come out and play. And when Batman comes out to play, all his old enemies want to join in.

The artwork is brilliant. On a first look, it seems scrawly or unfinished. But it speaks to me and, as I drop slowly into the story, I suddenly get it: this is *angry* artwork, like the artist has got an axe to grind. Right now, it's just what I need. Each picture seems to ignite a seething flame in my gut, fuelled by the knowledge that I'm not going to make the only real party I've ever been invited to.

All the characters look jagged and twisted and ugly, which is kind of how I feel. I feel like Batman.

Gotham's Gothic skyline dissolves, slowly replaced by the streets and houses of my home town.

It is night. A storm threatens; dark clouds gather over the town, weighing heavy and oppressive. I wait, cloaked in darkness, perched on the gargoyles of St Martin's Church in Park Road. A party is in full swing at Number fifty-two, the hideout of Kirsty Ford – sounds of carefree revelry pumping out on to the pavement. The front door swings open and suddenly my senses are heightened, primed, ready for action.

IM: *If you need a wee, you're going to be a bit stuck in that costume…*

Jason Humphries staggers into the front garden followed by a girl whose beauty threatens to douse the burning flames that crackle in my belly. But the flames still burn; I will always be alone – a silent, brooding, solitary figure of vengeance. The girl's voice cuts through the claustrophobic night like a beam of light.

"Archie! Where are you?"

"See? I told you he weren't gonna come!" Humphries's appalling use of grammar is just another crime to add to his rap sheet.

"But he wouldn't let me down! I secretly wanted him here, so I could tell him my true feelings! I ... I didn't give him the chance he deserves!" As her voice cracks, an old wound in my heart threatens to re-open, but I cauterize it with the heat of the rage I feel for her antagonist.

"You need a real man in your life," Humphries sneers, flexing a pumpkin-sized muscle.

"No! I can't betray him! He'll come back to me one day! I know he will!"

Humphries's reply is a cold, harsh bark of laughter.

I've heard enough. Leaping from the face of the church, I land between Sarah and her harasser, my arrival heralded with a flash of lightning and a KRAAAKK! of thunder. I draw myself up to my full height, my obsidian cape draping over my muscular shoulders like a shroud.

Fear melts the smile on Humphries's face and he

49

staggers back, as though the impact of my landing has shaken the very earth. He recovers enough to take a swipe at me. But he's slow, too slow. He gives me all the time in the world to duck. There are seven working defences from this position. Three of them render a man unconscious. Three of them kill. The other…

KLUDD!

…hurts. I knock him on to his back and then I'm on him, my eyes raging white beneath the cowl that hides my identity.

"Please! Please! Don't hurt me!" Humphries begs.

I don't need to hurt him. He'll never forget this moment. "Go," I snarl in a voice that's barely my own. "And stay away from the girl."

"Yes, yes! Anything! Just let me go!"

I release him from my vice-like grip and watch as he scarpers into the darkness.

"Thank you…" That beautiful voice silences the lava in my soul. I turn to her; her Dark Knight.

IM: *Dork Knight is more accurate.*

"I guess I should be frightened of you," she murmurs, stepping closer. "But I can see a vulnerability in your eyes, something deep and sensitive. Something beautiful."

I remain silent, a statue to Lost Love.

"Who are you?" she whispers, closing in for a kiss.

"I'm Geekman," I rasp, before vanishing like a ghost

*into night's embrace. But as I fade into the shadows, I hear
her plaintive cry: "Geekman! Come back!"*

Maybe, Sarah. When you're ready. Until then, I belong to the darkness.

The screech of the school bell reminds me that, actually, I belong to Mr Barker's French lesson. With an empty stomach and a heavy heart, I pack up my books and go and complete the rest of my day.

Walking home with the gang, the conversation once again turns to my elvish name. After a few more suggestions and an equal number of rejections, Beggsy suddenly becomes even more animated than usual.

"Dude! Dudedudedudedude*dude*!" he chants. "I've got it! Use your Jedi name!"

"What are you on about?"

"Duuude!" Beggsy breathes, conveying disapproval at me not knowing something that every self-respecting Geek ought to. To highlight his point, he breaks out of our little line-up and starts walking ahead of us, backwards. "You take the first three letters of your surname..."

"K..."

"...join them on to the first three letters of your first name..."

"K…"

"…and that's it! You've got your Jedi name!"

"Bararc," I say slowly. "Bararc… How does that sound?"

"No dumber than anything else that's been said so far," Ravi rumbles cheerfully.

"Bararc," I say again. "But what about my surname?"

Once again, in the comforting embrace of Geeky conversation, I feel removed from all my problems. After a debate about the nature of elvish names, we decide that it ought to be something a bit foresty. Matt suggests "Longbeam", as a deliberate joke, which starts the required round of sniggers. But sometimes humour generates creativity and, after running through a series of permutations, my name is decided. Next weekend, I shall be Bararc Darkleaf.

The guys are going to hook up at the weekend to try and work out what to do about weapons and stuff and I'm gutted I can't be there; it's a quest in itself. But nothing seems to be able to burst the bubble of excitement that surrounds us: in a week's time, we shall shed our Geekly forms and bestride the realms of another world, as champions in our own right.

We split with excited and meaningful looks at each other. The game's afoot.

The front door opens to the smell of curry. I'm praying that Mum's in charge and she's doing one of her ones with bits of pineapple in it, but the smell isn't quite right.

My bag and jacket hit the banister and I mooch into the kitchen, to find Mum stirring something in a pan.

"Hello, love," she smiles. "Good day?"

"Yeah, it was all right." Non-committal answers tend to spark the Spanish Inquisition, but I haven't got the energy to go into detail. My EM opts for Diversion Tactics, plastering a mischievous grin on my face.

"Cup of tea?" I offer. It's a bit of a joke, because Mum drinks more tea than your average builder, but no one ever makes her a cup.

"Oooh, that'd be nice," she mock-gasps, like we're talking about an annual event. I can't help but grin as I flick the kettle on; I like these cosy moments with Mum. While the kettle's boiling, I peer over her shoulder and look at the contents of the pan.

"Where's the chicken?" I ask, sounding more than a little horrified.

"No chicken. It's vegetarian."

"But why?" Now I seem to have become a whiney five-year-old.

"Because Tony's cooking and it's nice that he's taken such an interest. And it's nice that I don't have to cook all the time."

"Well, where *is* Tony, then?"

"He's gone to the loo."

IM: *Probably all these weird meals.*

I make the tea in a sulky silence, before sitting down at the kitchen table.

"But I like *your* cooking," I mutter plaintively. "Your roasts are the *best*! Nobody does roast potatoes like you!"

Mum beams at the compliment as she continues her stirring. "That's sweet of you, Archie, but it's good to try new things."

"But that's all I've been trying recently! I just want something *normal*."

IM: *Says the elf.*

"Well, maybe I'll do a roast on Sunday, when you get back from your dad's."

IM: **Fist pumps**

"All right, Arch?" As if on cue, Tony swishes into the kitchen and relieves Mum of her duties. He still calls me "Arch", which still irritates me; it's a declaration of some sort of ownership, which he doesn't really have the right to. But my EM, fuelled by the minor food victory that's just taken place, quickly cuts and pastes an appreciative smile on my face and executes an enthusiastic nod. But, I've got to admit it, the curry isn't that bad. Could probably benefit from some pineapple chunks and pieces of a dead animal in there but, otherwise, it's OK.

"I saw Marvin today," Mum says in a teasing kind of way. "We had a nice chat about this dressing-up thing you want to go to."

"LARP," Tony and I both say at the same time. Tony chuckles. I don't.

"And?" Although I'm pretty sure Mum's going to let me go, I'm all ears – just in case of any small print.

"He's a nice man, isn't he?"

IM: *Oh, come ON, woman! Stop stretching it out!*

"Yes, yes," I snap. "But what about the LARP?"

"It seems very well organized; everybody's CRB-checked, and Marvin's even a qualified first aider."

IM: *COME ON!*

"So-o?" I cast my conversational fishing line and wait with all the patience of a podracer at a red light.

"Are all your friends going?"

"Yes!" I reply, like it's the thousandth time I've heard the question.

"Then, it should be fine. What d'you think, Tony?" Tony looks as surprised as I am that he's being brought into the Final Say.

"Yep. Sounds good." He really doesn't care, it's all

about curry right now.

IM: **Punches air* Win!*

With my weekend as a hero confirmed, I plough through the rest of dinner, before scarpering up to my Lair. There's a message from Beggsy on my Facebook Timeline:

Dude! I'm in! Buy your ears!

IM: *Not a post you see every day...*

I thunder back downstairs to ask Mum if she'll let me use her credit card. Once she's got over the shock that I want to buy a pair of pointy ears and has managed to stop laughing, she comes back up to my Lair with me.

"And what do you need these for?" she asks, sitting down at my painting desk, card in hand.

"I'm going to be an *elf*," I strop, irritated that I've got to say something this stupid-sounding out loud.

"And elves have pointy ears..." Mum says to no one in particular.

IM: *Promoted to Chief of Police.*

A few clicks and some detail-entering later, the Larper Colony promises to send me a shiny new pair of pointed ears via next-day delivery. Which, for some reason, I'm ridiculously excited about.

IM: *Facepalm of biblical proportions*

I spend a while joyously imagining myself as a willowy elf, hacking at orcs with my trusty blade or bringing them down with my mallorn heartwood bow. Possibly wearing a mithril shirt.

IM: *"Mithril: Geekwear you can trust."*

While I'm starting to mix up the highlights for my ogre (a two to one mix of Ungor Flesh and Zamesi Desert), my laptop squeaks the arrival of an incoming message. But it's not, as I anticipate, Beggsy. It's Dad.

hi son lukng frwrd 2 cing u 2mrw and u cing yr new hse L u Dad xxx

Once I've deciphered Dad's attempts at text-talk, I type back a reply:

Look forward to it! Love Archie X

And then something hits me: I'm seeing him tomorrow.

IM: *And your mates are going to Kirsty Ford's party…*

I haven't seen him for three weeks and, while my eyes ought to be full of tears, they're not. They're full of resentment and I sit, staring at the screen, like I'm trying to make it explode. Tomorrow night is the first and probably only time in my life I'm ever going to be invited to a party. And not just *any* party, a party that Sarah's going to be at. I have visions of me, dressed casually in a tuxedo, standing at the bar and sipping nonchalantly at some cocktail in a Y-shaped glass and peppering the conversation with my wit and charm. Quite why I think Kirsty Ford's got a low-lit bar in her house or that she's allowed to serve cocktails I've no idea, but it's my vision and I'll have what I want in it.

IM: *Can there be pole dancers in the background, like in the movies?*

And Sarah's there and she's looking at me and I raise a rakish eyebrow and she can't help but notice the stubble on my upper lip and I tell her a joke and she laughs and everything's OK.

But none of that's going to happen, because my dad shacked up with someone else and moved to York. If he wasn't satisfied with ruining my life when he and Mum split up, he should be now. The *one* party that could have changed everything – and I won't be there.

IM: *You don't actually own a tuxedo. Just sayin'.*

I go back to my ogre for a bit, to try and stop thinking about how angry I am at Dad. But it doesn't work; I can't seem to concentrate and my hand isn't rock-steady, like it usually is. Which pisses me off even more; he's even affecting my painting. With a growly sigh, I give up and pick up *The Dark Knight Returns*.

IM: *A bit of bedtime Batman! *Repeats faster and faster**

Two-Face in the films is rubbish, but this Harvey Dent is proper bonkers. Even though he's had plastic surgery to hide his scars and his psychologists have said he's sane, he's not dancing to the same tune as the rest of us. And, although he doesn't want to believe it, Batman knows that Harvey's still intent on destroying his own life and the lives of others.

IM: *And why would you relate to that character, hmmm?*

So Batman's got to take him down and, while he's hunting him, he reflects on how similar they are: it's like his sanity depends on it. And the artwork seems to get even darker and grimmer and more sketchy, like Batman's grip on reality is getting shakier.

IM: *Same question applies.*

There's a bit of chasing and Bats does some unpleasant things to some unpleasant people, while wearing this werewolf smile. But eventually there's a showdown, where the guy we think is Two-Face jumps from a helicopter and Bats saves him, just to be sure it is Harvey Dent, and rips off the bandages that cover his face.

Batman's IM: *I close my eyes and listen. Not fooled by sight, I see him ... as he is.*

At this point, Batman sees that, deep inside, both aspects of Two-Face's warring personality are scarred. Not like the outside, which is a miracle of plastic surgery.

Dent: Have your laugh, Batman – take a look! Take a look...

Batman's IM: *I see him. I see...*

Batman: I see ... a reflection, Harvey. A reflection.

It's like Batman's hunting himself. It's like he needs bad stuff in his life to justify his existence.

IM: *Discuss.*

I try not to roll that thought around until 1.35 a.m. I fail.

THREE

Who'd've thought you could learn so much from comics? Despite the late night, I snap awake on Friday, like someone coming out of a hypnotic trance; I'm full of resolve. It's time to do what I should have done all along – it's time to say sorry to Sarah and just get on with being her friend. Simple as that.

IM: *Excuse me for butting in – but isn't this what I've been saying for the last few weeks? Me and the rest of the world?*

It's like Batman: he has a code he lives by, he's made a decision in his life to walk tall, no matter what. I know that whether or not Sarah sees me as her Batman, I need to draw a line in the sand. My line. A line that I'll swear never to cross.

IM: *I give it five minutes.*

I know it's going to be tough and I know I'm not going to like it, but it's The Right Thing To Do. My mission, should I choose to accept it, is to get over Sarah and become her friend.

IM: *Mission: Improbable. *Sings* Bom-bom-BOM-bom…*

I feel determined and resolute and I eat my breakfast

with renewed focus. In complete contrast, Mum buzzes around me like some tea-powered bluebottle, twittering on about all the things she's packed for me for my trip to York and how she'll pick me up from school at four o'clock. Only part of me's listening; the other part's steeling itself for Mission: Improbable.

IM: ...*bom-bom-BOM-bom*...

I stroll to school, running through the various ways this could pan out. It'd be a lot easier if I had a utility belt or some of Ethan Hunt's gadgets, like if I could suddenly drop down out of her bedroom ceiling on a wire, apologize and then zip back up to the ceiling and scamper away across the rooftops.

IM: *Doo-di-doooo... Doo-di-doooo... Doo-di-doooo...*

But people tend to get arrested for that sort of thing.

And, I suppose, once it's all been said, that's where the hard work really begins. For me, at least. No more furtive glances at the back of her neck, no more daydreams about saving her from threats of danger...

She has no idea what I'm giving up.

IM: *Dah-dum!*

And I wish I could get that damn tune out of my head.

IM: *Bom-bom-BOM-bom*...

"Archie!" Ravi's voice booms somewhere behind me. I turn, to see him, Matt and Beggsy walking along the pavement. It only takes a few seconds after our morning round of hellos before I get the sense that there's something that everyone's not saying. I don't know *how* I know; everybody's acting pretty much like they normally do, with the usual wisecracks and sarcasm, but there's an almost-tangible feeling of "something's going on". And I think I know what it is.

IM: *...dressed casually in a tuxedo, standing at the bar...*

"You guys looking forward to the party?" The tension in my buddies' faces tightens for a few seconds, before suddenly giving way to smiles of relief.

"I *so* am!" Beggsy bubbles, clenching his fists and doing some sort of excuse for a boxing move.

Ravi admits he's looking forward to it, but Matt's not sure if he's going. I'd love to report that it's out of some ridiculous sense of loyalty to me, but it's not: Matt is an Olympic-level Geek. He's muttering his almost-excuses darkly and looking at the ground, which tells me that he kind of wants to go, but it's so outside his Comfort Zone that he's not sure he could handle it. Having said that, his Comfort Zone is about as big as an Ewok's purse. But I know Matt, and I know that inside he's already damning himself for his weakness.

IM: *It's like a self-help group for the emotionally bewildered.*

"You ought to go, mate," I offer, taking the tauntaun by the horns.

"What for? I won't enjoy it." It's like he's already decided not to.

"Dude! There might be some *hotties* there!" Beggsy's boxing hands turn into invisible-piano-playing hands on the word "hotties". He's so excited, it's like he's got lemonade for blood.

"And?" Matt scowls. "What am *I* going to do with them?" Where Beggsy's brain is playing a montage of him being hilarious and chatting up girls with all the cool of Captain Kirk, Matt's is playing him a trailer of *Cast Away*.

IM: Sans *basketball*.

"But we're gonna be there," Ravi rumbles. "And we don't know what we're doing, either."

"You ought to go," I say again. "Treat it like a mission."

IM: *Bom-bom-BOM-bom…*

"Dude! You can be my sidekick! The good-looking one always has an ugly friend…"

"And which one are you, Beggsy?" Matt deadpans. I can sense his mood lightening. "I'm just not sure…" But this time it's an invitation for us to tell him it's OK; it's like he needs permission from the rest of us to join the human race for an evening. We cajole and reassure him all the way to school. As we pass through the gates, he sighs and rolls his eyes. "OK... I'll think about it..."

IM: *Translation: "Don't pick me up too early; I'll be doing my hair."*

"And make sure you text me if anything happens," I say. "I want the lowdown."

"Dude!" Beggsy exclaims, looking crestfallen. "You'll be missed!"

"Thanks," I sigh.

"Maybe there's a beautiful Yorkshire lass with your name on her," Ravi says, always trying to keep the mood up.

"What – a girl called Archie?" Matt quick fires. It's a lame gag, but I know the guys are just trying to make me feel better about things.

"There'll be other parties," Ravi counters with a smile, as we head inside.

Me and Ravi discuss the party through Biology and I offer handy fashion tips to Matt during English.

IM: *Like wearing clothes from this century?*

But, through all of this, that stupid tune is playing in my head. Lunchtime's getting closer and I know I've got to complete the first stage of my mission: apologize to Sarah.

IM: *Bom-bom-BOM-bom...*

The bell cuts through Maria writing Malvolio a fake love letter from Olivia. The *Mission: Impossible* theme tune is now almost the only thing I can hear. I tell Matt I'm off to the bogs but, instead, I head off to the Maths block. Not that I'm a stalker or anything, but I pretty much know where Sarah's going to be at any point in the day.

IM: *And probably before she does. Not that you're a stalker or anything.*

The only fly in my ointment is Ravi: being something of a mathemagician, he's going to be in the area, too. As I make my way through the corridors, against the flow of hungry students, my Grunt Detectors™ pick up an anomaly in the relentless throngs that are slowing me down. There's a break in the crowds and Paul Green and Lewis Mills walk like two Neanderthal Moseses through the Red Sea of Students. My EM goes into Preservation mode, stooping my shoulders and bending my head down, while sneaking glances from under my brow, hoping not to be seen. All this effort prevents the Glaringly Obvious Question from travelling up the necessary neurones and entering my brain.

IM: *Allow me: *Affects Shaggy voice* "Zoinks! Where's Jason Humphries?"*

A crack to the back of my head answers my question. As I stumble and tumble through uniforms and schoolbags, I can hear his nicotine-stained laugh. But it's OK, it's a drive-by – from my vantage point at the foot of the stairs, I see him smack palms with his Pack of

Grunts and they barge their way against the tide.

A hand grabs me and pulls me up – it's Ravi.

"One day…" he mutters, with a murderous glint as he watches the vanishing forms of Humphries, Mills and Green. And then we both start laughing.

"Yeah," I splutter. "One day we'll really show them!" It's a way of relieving the frustration from knowing that, when it comes to Geeks and Grunts, *we're* utterly powerless.

IM: *And girls! Don't forget girls!*

"What're you doing here?" Ravi asks.

IM: *Bom-bom-BOM-bom…*

"Uh…" The words are queued up, but they don't want to come. A little cough sorts that out. "I'm going to talk to Sarah. Sort things out."

"Oh. Right." Ravi nods, looking serious. "I'll see you later, then. Good luck." And with that, he's swallowed up by the mob. I chuck a look up the stairs, but there's no sign of Sarah. I don't want to just stand here at the bottom, so I duck round the corner and hover in a doorway, trying to look nonchalant and not like a terrified Geek who's just about to take an Uzi to his dreams in the belief that he's Doing The Right Thing.

IM: **Louder* Bom-bom-BOM-bom…!*

Sarah's voice drifts down the stairs, like liquid silver. I can pick it out from the echoes of chatter, heels and scuffs that roll around the walls, pretty much as if they didn't exist. Normally, I'd feel a weird combination of excitement and calm but, right now, my heart feels as if it's about to leap out of my chest. I'm sweating like a Wookiee in a sauna, which probably accounts for the desert-like conditions in my mouth.

IM: *Plays tune on THX surround-sound cinema levels* Bom-bom-BOM-bom...!

Her voice rings closer and closer, her laughter tinkling like wind chimes and I'm pretty sure I can even tell the clack of her shoes from everyone else's.

IM: Doo-di-doooo... Doo-di-doooo...

As my brain maniacally looks for a good opening line, my EM tries to etch something like a friendly expression into my sweat-leaking face.

IM: Doo-di-doooo...

I see her feet first. As the rest of her comes into view, my heart lurches, banging against my sternum like there's a miniature Jason Humphries using it as a punchbag. I take a step out of the doorway, rubbing my slick palms against my trousers.

IM: DAH-DUM!

And then I stop, frozen, as the true horror of the situation hits me. As her head rocks back to release another quicksilver laugh, her companion is revealed: Chris Jackson, AKA The Best-looking Boy In The

School™. I slam myself back into the doorway and, as I do so, I'm sure I hear the words "party" and "tonight" and "going" come from Chris's Photoshopped mouth.

IM: *Silence*

Chris Jackson? She's going to the party with *him*? I watch them walk along the corridor, laughing and talking. There's no way that I'm going to apologize in front of him. And then, despite my Batman-fuelled resolve to Do The Right Thing, there's a flash of jealousy across my cheeks and I'm suddenly watching Chris on a zoom lens, looking for signs that he might be making a move on her.

IM: *She did turn him down, once.*

And maybe they're "just friends". But, in a weird way, that would be even worse – he can do what I can't. I watch them round the corner and then turn in the opposite direction. Having failed my mission, I can't face my friends right now. It's time for another hungry lunch hour in the library.

Ordinarily, discussing tectonics in Geography would have my undivided attention; I like stuff like that. But today, my brain is experiencing an unfamiliar sensation: I'm angry.

What's even weirder is that I'm angry at Sarah. I know I have no right, but seeing her laughing with Chris Jackson has opened the cage and I can't seem to coax my anger back in. I don't really know what I'm expecting from her but, at the moment, a petulant part of me wants her to be as cut up about us not being an item as I am. OK, it wasn't the Romance of the Century…

IM: *Let's be honest: it wasn't even the Romance of the Hour.*

…but it was a big deal for me and you don't see me laughing around the corridors like nothing ever happened.

IM: *But nothing ever did, Sulk Boy.*

Unfortunately, that's the dead end where my angry thoughts keep finishing up. I'm in "if only" territory: if only I'd been honest from the start, if only I had the balls to be up-front about liking her, if only I hadn't blubbed in front of her.

And then the two conflicting things going on in my head start a WWF fight: The Mission To Become Her Friend versus The Fact That I Still Like Her.

IM: *My money's on the second one.*

The bell pulls me out of my self-pitying vortex and I quickly pack up my stuff. I need to think about what's going on, but right now I'm going to see my dad.

IM: *And* not *going to what will probably be the*

best party ever.

Matt and the gang are waiting for me at the school gates, pre-party panic written all over their faces.

"Guys!" I pant, trotting up to them. "I'm not walking back with you – my mum's picking me up."

"Dude!" Conveys *Fear, disappointment and excitement all at once* "We'll let you know how we get on with the lay-deez!" Beggsy makes the shape of a giant, invisible egg timer in front of him.

"Have a good time, Archie," Matt says seriously, like it's the last time we're going to see each other. And, in some ways, it might be – if the guys manage to hook up with Real-life Girls, it could change Everything.

IM: *But let's be honest about this, shall we?*

"Yeah, have a great time," Ravi echoes. And then something changes in his eyes – they flick over my shoulder and register alarm. Same goes for the others; Matt and Beggsy suddenly go quiet and start looking anywhere but straight ahead. My Grunt Detectors™ go online and my EM assumes the required hunched position, bravely keeping my back to the oncoming threat.

"Hey, guys." Sarah's voice sends all my systems haywire, I don't know what to do. "Hey, Archie." An awkward smile plays on her perfect lips.

"Hey." It's all I can manage without delivering a

pavement-pizza. The fact that I get a separate "hey" from everyone else tells me that she sees me as an outsider, that I'm not part of the gang.

IM: *Bom-bom-BOM-bom…?*

"Gotta go," I mumble at the ground and start to walk away, shame at my inability to talk to her scalding my face.

"Archie…" Sarah calls after me, but a demanding parp from Mum's car gives me the exit I need and I pretend I haven't heard her. As I hurry over, the driver's side window rolls down and it's Tony at the wheel, with Mum sitting beside him. My EM opens up a Smile File™, which appears to be corrupted.

"Yo!" Tony bellows. "Let's go!"

IM: *Nothing like feeling wanted, is there?*

I climb in the back and we pull away, leaving school, my mates and Sarah behind. Along with a large slice of my dignity.

"You all right, love?" Mum asks, eyeing me in the rear-view mirror.

"Yeah, I'm good." If Tony wasn't here, I might ask her how you're supposed to be friends with a girl when you still really like her.

IM: *I think you "get over yourself". Thank me later.*

But even if I wanted to say something, I couldn't. With all the social awareness of a walrus, Tony turns up the radio and starts singing along. The fact that he doesn't seem to know the words or the tune isn't a problem, apparently.

We travel, serenaded by Tony, all the way to the train station, Mum flicking me concerned looks in the mirror and me desperately racking my brains to come up with a last-minute excuse as to why I can't go to York and have to go to a party tonight instead.

IM: *Are there comas that can only be cured by dance music?*

"You sure you're OK, Archie?" Mum asks again, giving me a probing look as we walk along the platform.

"For crying out loud, woman!" Tony laughs, like he's actually got a clue about anything. "Leave the boy alone! He's fine!" I love it when adults speak for you, like you don't actually know how to. And I love it that he believes he knows me better than Mum. I love it so much that I can almost feel my fingers round his throat.

IM: *Attempts Force Choke* *Fails*

"Yeah. Just a bit tired." "Just a bit tired" is one of those phrases you use when you want to let your mum know you've got something on your mind, but you don't want to say it out loud. Mum receives the encryption and gives me a hug. As we reach the platform, Tony dives into the newsagent's and reappears a few moments later with a magazine.

"Something for the journey," he nods, like he's handing over a family heirloom.

IM: *What the…?*

It's a copy of this month's *White Dwarf*; the miniature painter's bible.

IM: *He's trying. Try back.*

"Thanks, Tony," I reply, meaning it and feeling a bit guilty for having wished the Force Choke on him.

"Hey, buddy!" he beams back. And does the thing I never thought he would do, but have thought about – and dreaded: he opens his arms for a hug.

IM: *Oh GOD!*

With nothing for it, I go in. It just feels weird. With a Mum Hug™, you get softness, the chance to revisit your childhood and a feeling that everything's going to be OK. Dad Hugs™ give you some sort of inner strength, but Mum's Boyfriend Hugs™ don't give you anything like that, just a reminder that deodorant was invented for a reason. My body tenses up, my teeth almost shatter with the pressure my jaw suddenly exerts on them and the hairs on my scalp feel like they're getting ready to launch themselves into space.

Mercifully, it doesn't last long and Tony makes me feel even worse about myself by pushing a wad of notes into my hand, "just to keep you going".

IM: *You could be using these to buy imaginary drinks*

at the imaginary bar at Kirsty Ford's real party!

The tannoy crackles an announcement that my train is approaching and Mum flinches, like someone's just plugged her in to the mains.

"Send me a text when you get there," she smiles, running a hand through my hair and hugging me again – one of those "I don't want you to go" hugs. Mine says much the same.

The train squeals to a halt and people start getting off. Mum gives me another squeeze and then I climb on and find my seat. I can see her through the window, watching me to check if I'm all right. Tony suddenly remembers that he's supposed to be part of something like a family and puts his arm round her. The train pulls away with a grudging lurch and Mum and Tony scroll sideways into the past.

FOUR

It takes me about thirty minutes to get used to the idea that I'm travelling on my own. After that, I stop looking goggle-eyed out of the window or eyeing the rest of the carriage suspiciously and spend the next sixty just reading my magazine. No one attempts to hijack the train and the countryside doesn't blacken and get more Mordor-like the further away from home I get.

As the train slows to pick up another complement of passengers, I check out the name of the station. York's still a long way away. The boiling disappointment in my stomach gave way to weary resignation long ago and I've resigned myself to my fate – a weekend in the Land of the Vikings with my father and his new wife – the woman who could wipe the smile off the Joker's face with just one of her crappy jokes. When I should be building bridges with Sarah at Kirsty Ford's party, I'll probably be building bridges out of Lego with my new step-siblings. Life sucks.

Loud voices from the far end of the carriage bring my Grunt Detector™ back online. After doing a quick sweep, the threat is identified as a group of four guys, crew-cut hair, ironed jeans, spotless short-sleeve shirts and

Caterpillar boots that could be fresh out of the box. The backpacks, docking-station and what looks suspiciously like some cans of beer in carrier bags confirm my fears: it can only mean one thing. Squaddies. They also seem unable to communicate in anything other than shouts.

IM: *Stormtroopers on their day off.*

As the rest of the passengers quickly look away or sink into their newspapers, I scan the terrain. Luckily, the seat next to me has a reserved ticket on it. *Un*luckily, the squaddies commandeer the four table-seats across the aisle from me.

IM: **Obi-Wan voice* "I'm not the Geek you're looking for." *Rolls fingers**

My EM kicks in and I try to hide behind my magazine.

IM: *Because there's no way a paper wall's going to stop those guys!*

Within seconds I realize I might as well have a sign saying "Geek in Residence. Taunt at Will" taped to my seat. I'm reading *White Dwarf*. Not only that, the cover's of Boris Vallejo's *Amazon*. Think Megan Fox in a metal bikini riding a horse and you've got the general idea. Vallejo's the reason most Geeks get into fantasy art – and it's not for an appreciation of his brushwork.

IM: *Although it's led to a few masterstrokes of your own…*

Just to make sure that everyone gets to join in the party, Grunt Platoon kindly turns up the volume on their MP3 player. Thankfully, their conversation doesn't suffer; they just shout louder so that we can all hear, in bone-scraping detail, the minutiae of their lives. I didn't realize that "picking up" girls was so easy.

IM: *Depends how heavy they are, surely?*

I go back to *White Dwarf* and try to pay attention to an article on painting Snow Elves. But my Fear Department™ isn't having any of it. While I'm aware of lots of words and pictures with lots of shades of blue in them, I'm sat, frozen, not really taking anything in.

"Shouldn't be reading that sort of thing at your age!"

My EM struggles to keep the blanch of fear from my cheeks and the film of sweat from my brow. I turn to face the Grunt Warlord who has just bellowed as conspiratorially as you can at operatic levels.

"Sorry?"

IM: *Please, God! Just one more day! I'll be good, I promise!*

"What you're reading." Oh, my God. He thinks I'm reading porn. On a train.

IM: *And has just announced it to the rest of the carriage!*

"Oh. Ha. No." I stammer. "It's nothing like that. It's more of a—"

"Lessavalook." Before I have time to respond, *White Dwarf* is manhandled across the aisle. The Amazon is greeted with dark chuckles and hungry eyes. I want to die.

IM: *But quickly. Nothing involving my name, rank and number.*

Once Vallejo's masterpiece has been critically appraised, the Grunt Warlord flips through the pages, confusion registering across the six-pack on his face.

"What's all this stuff?"

IM: *Denydenydeny! These men are trained killers!*

"Oh. I don't know. I just picked it up at the station. I liked the cover."

More dark chuckles.

IM: *Good work, soldier. Time to get in behind enemy lines. *Puts on stormtrooper helmet and attempts to blend in**

"Like that sort of thing, do you?" I'm not sure whether "that sort of thing" refers to Megan in her plate-metal bra or the pages of beautifully painted miniatures. I decide to hedge my bets.

"Yeah, sort of."

IM: *Excellent! Vague enough that you can agree with whatever his next statement is.*

Grunt Warlord's next statement is to hoik up the sleeve of his right arm. It threatens to rip over the sheer volume of muscle that even his skin seems to have problems containing, but eventually slides up to reveal an equally massive shoulder.

"What d'you reckon to that, then?"

I'm faced with a large tattoo of a skull with a sword entering the top of the cranium and coming out of the upper palate. Flames lick out of the eye sockets and act as a background to the whole image. My opinion on it is irrelevant; I'm hardly going to tell him that I think it's lame.

But actually, I don't. Although it's not quite the picture I'd choose to adorn my weedy physique with, it does have a certain arcane charm. My EM does the job for me, responding with wide eyes and an open mouth, like I'm a five-year-old who's just met Superman.

"Wow! That's cool!" And then I go for the ploy that's guaranteed to get men of this sort onside: "Did it hurt?"

Cue manly chuckles, a shake of the head and fond patting of tattoo.

"Nah, mate. Not too much."

IM: *Which means it would leave you unconscious through agony.*

Two of the other Grunts join in and show me their etchings. Grunt Lieutenant sports some Chinese characters, which he informs me mean "Sweet and Sour Chicken", so that if he's too drunk to order a takeaway from his local, he can just roll up his sleeve. I only *think* he's joking. Major Grunt is wearing an off-the-shoulder number, meaning he has to unbutton his shirt to show me the dragon that curls across his chest. I briefly consider drawing a face or something on my arm, just so I can join in.

IM: *Who'd've thought that fantasy art would be the bridge between Grunts and Geeks?*

Private Grunt, however, doesn't have his badge of honour and ducks comments about his manliness, saying that he "doesn't know what to get yet".

Over the next forty-five minutes I am the sole student at a public lecture on how to get a tattoo. Topics include: Your Pain Threshold, Choosing Your Design, Choosing Your Tattooist and How Much Girls Like a Man with a Tattoo. By the time the train starts to slow down for the next station, I am emotionally exhausted. I also want a wee.

"'S'cuse me for a moment, guys. I've just got to…" I point awkwardly at the toilet, stationed at the end of the carriage.

"More than two shakes and you're playing with it!" barks Grunt Warlord, as I leave the carriage. With this pearl of wisdom ringing in my ears (and the ears of everyone within a five-mile radius), I sway my way into the toilet.

Confession Time. I suffer from something that me

and my mates have christened PPS or Public Piss Syndrome. In short, it means that your bladder won't deliver the goods if there's anyone else around. We generally agree that this condition only strikes when you can see or sense the intruder. A crowded urinal is the equivalent of building a dam in your bladder: not a chance. However, Grunt Warlord's parting shot has added another dimension to this particular problem: since everyone heard him yelling about more than two shakes, I'm now pretty sure that everyone is waiting to see just how long I take. If I don't get a move on, everyone who saw me come into the toilet will now think I'm some oversexed pervert, unable to keep his hands off himself for more than an hour at a time.

IM: *And your point is…?*

As much as I push or try and relax, PPS has shown its dry, droplet-free hand. Not so much as a dribble. In desperation, I close my eyes and start muttering to myself.

"Comeoncomeoncomeoncomeoncomeon…"

And then I suddenly realize that this might sound even worse from outside the door.

IM: *The man who put the pee in "pantomime"…*

Just as I resign myself to the idea that by the time I get to York I'll have drowned in my own urine, the train lurches to a halt and I hear the sounds of people gathering their belongings and getting on and off.

With this bit of auditory camouflage to hide behind, my bladder finally relents and releases its liquid hostage. I groan in relief and then realize that this sounds even worse than before.

As I nudge my way back into the carriage with the rest of the sardines, I'm anticipating a round of jeers and applause from the Grunt Platoon. Instead, they're focused on my seat, wearing looks that wouldn't seem out of place on wolves. There's a girl sitting in the seat next to mine.

This girl isn't like Sarah at all. But she *is* pretty. And older than me – but I'm not sure by how much. She's wearing a long white shirt, a short black skirt, cowboy boots and a coolly distressed denim jacket. As Beggsy might say: this girl's got 'chood. And long, brown hair. Lots of it. In fact, there's so much of the stuff that you could be forgiven for mistaking her for a Wookiee from behind. It doesn't just hang from her head like regular hair, it's sort of piled on in slightly disorganized layers. With the square-framed glasses setting off her face, she looks like a rock 'n' roll librarian. I love librarians. And judging by their attempts to engage her in conversation, so does Grunt Platoon.

"Go on – have a feel! It won't bite you!" Luckily, Grunt Warlord is talking about the skull on his arm, which is undulating with every flex. Hair Girl just scowls and fixes her sights on the seat in front.

"Don't you like tattoos, then?" Sweet and Sour Chicken has joined the fray and the dragon is just about to enter. Private Grunt, while smiling with all the charm of an alligator, is obviously damning his indecision in the art department. Noting my arrival, Grunt Warlord calls for reinforcements.

"You like tattoos, don't you? You think they're cool!" I can hear the beer and army training in his voice as he drags me into his siege.

IM: *Uh-oh! Sniper fire! Retreat! Fall back!*

I'm now caught in the middle, torn between incurring the muscular wrath of the Platoon and revealing the yellow streak that is tattooed across my heart.

IM: *RETREEEAAATTT!*

But a vital piece of wiring in my head seems to have fused; I don't fall back.

IM: **Frantically searches for repair manual**

I mentally roll a D20 against my Initiative and prepare to take what in my world is perceived as a Considerable Risk.

IM: *Or a "mistake". Of the fatal variety.*

"Ha. Sorry, guys – we were just going to get some sandwiches." Without waiting for a reply, I turn my back on them, so that only Hair Girl can see the pantomime "go with me on this" wink that I give her. "Sorry," I bluff, "I was in the toilet. Shall we find the buffet car?" I give her another wink, just for good measure.

Hair Girl cottons on quickly, but her reply isn't quite what I was expecting. She just scowls and grunts a "Yeah, OK. Come on, then."

IM: *Lois Lane would've been a bit more appreciative.*

I stand aside to let Hair Girl set off in search of the buffet car and, just as I'm about to follow her, I feel a tug on my sleeve. I turn round, fully expecting a killer blow. Instead, Grunt Warlord nods appreciatively in the direction of the departing Chewbaccette.

"Nice one," he grins. "But don't forget to wear your wellies."

I force out a laugh as though I've got a clue what he's talking about and throw a general "catch you later" at the troops.

IM: *Are wellies standard issue when you join The Imperial Empire?*

As I pull myself along the aisle seats behind Hair Girl, I get a sudden endorphin rush as I realize that I got away with it. My face registers the amazement by plastering a goggle-eyed grin on my face.

"You OK?" I ask the back of her head, feeling pretty pleased with myself.

"I could've handled them myself, you know!" Given the look that she flips over her shoulder, I don't doubt it.

IM: **Hissing sound as Manliness Levels deflate back*

to their normal, microscopic state*

We claw and lurch the rest of the way to the buffet car in silence, me feeling more and more like I did something wrong. Batman seems to get nothing but gratitude whenever he saves somebody; how come I'm getting narky looks?

IM: *Girls like it more when you wear your pants over your trousers. Obvious, really.*

As we hit the back of the queue, Hair Girl obviously has a change of heart. Her whole body sags a bit and she turns to face me awkwardly.

"Sorry. Thanks." She doesn't actually sound like she means either word. This isn't going like I planned.

IM: *There was a plan?*

"No worries. Sorry if I did the wrong thing back there."

My attempts to ingratiate draw a blank: Hair Girl responds with a frustrated sigh, a roll of the eyes and suddenly I'm looking at her back again, feeling more than a little out of my depth.

IM: *I don't think she's interested in men of the "ladies first" variety...*

"Look. I'm sorry," she snaps, turning back again. "Those idiots just pissed me off."

"You're hiding it very well..." This is one of Beggsy's and I feel slightly more scared using it than I did when

I was rescuing her, but it has the desired effect: Hair Girl gives me a sideways look, then the ice cracks and she starts to laugh.

"Ha-ha," she snorts wryly. "Point taken. Can I get you a drink or something? Just to say thanks."

IM: *A girl just offered to buy YOU a drink! This is a Great Moment in Geek History! *Faints**

I don't know whether to accept, in case I'm doing the wrong thing, again.

IM: **Flips through the Geek's Guide to Girls* What the…? It's like these pages just don't exist! Did no one think to write this stuff down?!*

"It's cool. I've got sandwiches and stuff in my bag."

"I just thought we might hang here for a bit. Those guys'll get off at the next stop." Her apparent abilities to read the future bring back uncomfortable memories of Sarah reading my aura.

IM: *Uh-oh! Clairvoyant alert!*

"Will they?"

"Yeah. There's an army camp there."

IM: *She has seen it in her crystal ball…*

"Oh. OK. How d'you know?"

IM: *She's a WITCH, you idiot! That's how!*

"I do this journey a lot."

"Right." And for want of anything else to say, I add, "Cool."

"So, can we hang?"

"Fine by me."

"So … d'you want a drink?"

"Uh, yeah… A Coke?" My hand goes to the coinage and notes in my pocket, but Hair Girl raises a withering eyebrow.

"On its way."

While Hair Girl queues, I find a space at the end of the counter and try to mark my territory with the right body language, which seems to be more of a physical whisper. I hold out long enough for Hair Girl to squeeze her way back, bearing drinks and crisps. Just as she's handing me my Coke, there's a burst of heavy breathing from my trousers.

"What the hell is that?" Hair Girl laughs in a horrified kind of way.

IM: *You don't want to know. Trust me. It's even worse than what you're probably imagining…*

"That" is my Darth Vader ringtone. Smiling and shrugging and muttering some weak apologies, I pull it out and check the screen. It's Mum.

IM: *Darth Vader ringtone and a call from Mum. You don't look like a Geek at all. No, really.*

"Hiya." I try and keep the desperate irritation out of my voice.

"Hi, love. How's the journey going? Just thought

I'd check in."

IM: *Throw yourself from the train, Archie! Do it now!*

"Yeah, it's fine." I cover the mouthpiece and mouth a "Sorry" at Hair Girl and feel a little guilty about it.

"It sounds busy. Where are you?"

"Uh… In the buffet car."

"Didn't I pack enough food? I thought I put loads in there."

"No, no – it's fine. I'm just getting a drink."

IM: *Arsenic would be good right now. With ice.*

"I put drinks in your bag. Didn't you find them?"

"Yeah, yeah… I did… I just…"

IM: **Prays for a tunnel**

"Don't go spending all your money on the train – the food's very expensive…"

"Yeah, I know! I'm not! I'm just getting a drink!"

IM: *Blow down the phone! Fake some static! It worked for Chekov in Star Trek Five!*

"And have you had your ticket checked?"

"Yes!" Exasperation finally pushes its way out of my mouth.

"Just checking, love!"

"Sorry."

"Well, I'll let you go. Give me a ring when you get there, OK?"

"OK."

"All right, then." And then to cap off an already embarrassing conversation, she says "Love you!" in a sing-song kind of way. If I was on my own, I'd say it back, no worries. But I'm not and I'm trying to create a good impression.

"OK."

There's a split-second's worth of pause, but it lets me know that she's registered the fact that I haven't said it back. I feel guilty again.

"Off you go, then. Bye."

"Bye."

Hair Girl grins at me knowingly.

"Your mum?"

I give a rueful, heavy-lidded nod that hopefully masks the fact that I feel like a traitor.

"OK, let's do a rewind: I'm Clare."

"Archie."

"Hi, Archie. Pleased to meet you." We pop our cans and open up the crisps and fall into conversation with an ease I wasn't prepared for. "So, where are you going, Archie?"

"York."

"Nice one. What's in York?"

"My dad." For some reason, I then give her the lowdown on my family break-up. Maybe it's because I don't know her, but telling Clare the ins and outs of my life doesn't feel awkward. In fact, it's kind of liberating. But suddenly I'm aware that this whole conversation is about me, so I turn the tables.

"Yeah. So, that's my life. What about you?"

"Going home to see my parents for the weekend. Boarding school."

"Oh, right. Cool."

"Not really. It's a bit lame." Clare's turning out to be one of the most forthright people I've ever met, everything she says is peppered with sarcasm and delivered in a voice that suggests that even talking is a bit too much hassle. But I like it; it's kind of funny. And the more I talk to her, the prettier she gets – but not in a sexy way, just in a pretty way.

After finding out that boarding school's "a bit lame", that her parents "are boring" and her little sister is "an angel", it looks like we'll be seeing each other regularly: she takes this journey every other weekend, too. After a while, the conversational net tightens a bit and we get down to the nitty gritty.

"So, how old are you, Archie?"

"Fourteen."

"Just a *ba*-by," she teases.

"Why? How old are you, then?" I don't mean it as a challenge that betrays my insecurity – it just sort of comes out that way.

"Have a guess."

IM: *Tread carefully, young Padawan.*

She's obviously older than me, but I can't judge by how much. If Beggsy were here, he'd be checking out her rack and trying to judge it off that. He's developed a theory that the size of a girl's rack is somehow related to her age. If that was true, Clare here would be about five thousand years old. She's fairly blessed. She'd even give Kirsty Ford a run for her money.

IM: *I've seen smaller hot-air balloons.*

"My eyes are up here, Archie."

I freeze.

IM: **Hides**

I've been caught checking out her rack! My face suddenly feels hotter than the surface of the sun, while a cold, cold feeling travels up the back of my neck.

IM: *There are three ways out of this! One of them's the window!*

"God … no … I wasn't…"

"Yes, you were."

IM: *What? Have they got EYES in them as well?!*

The trouble is, once I've noticed the size of her attributes, I then find it very difficult not to notice them. Even now I'm looking at her face, my peripheral vision is sending me further data. I screw my eyes up tightly, hoping that everything will disappear, but knowing it won't.

"Sorry. I'm really sorry. I just…" I open one eye, half expecting a slap across the face.

"You're not the first," she says, giving me a "but don't do it again" look.

"OK. It won't happen again." And I mean it. I will never, EVER check out a girl's rack EVER again. I feel ashamed, embarrassed and like I've let myself down. Never again. It's a silent, solemn vow. Another mission to add to the other one.

IM: *And equally improbable.* *Sings* *Bom-bom-BOM-bom…*

There's an awkward silence, thankfully drowned out by the tannoy telling us that we'll shortly be arriving at the next station.

"I'd guess you were about eighteen," I venture meekly.

"Smooth," she nods knowingly, the twin elephants in the carriage apparently forgotten. "But you're not my type. Sixteen."

"I'm not trying to chat you up!" I protest. "I honestly thought you were about eighteen!"

"Well, that's sweet," she says, with a hint of approval.

"Sweet" is one of those words that can break a guy's spirit. It's a word that should only be used on little kids. When you hear the word "sweet", you know that you had your chance and you blew it. However, and this is a big one, I really don't mind it, coming from this girl.

IM: *Runs background scan to check for possible threats and viruses that might be affecting normal programming*

The fact is that even though Clare's pretty, easy to talk to and has a balcony you could do Shakespeare from, I just don't fancy her. I run the scan one more time and the results come back the same: she's not your type.

IM: *Eh? But she's a GIRL and she's ALIVE! What's going on?*

This information has a weird effect on me: I feel relieved. I don't have to pretend to be anything other than I am. I can be me.

IM: *A boob-gazing Geek who does heavy-breathing out of his trousers.*

It doesn't matter if she knows I'm a Geek, that I read comics and I paint miniature elves; it just doesn't matter. A burden lifts and I come back to the conversation with something that smells a bit like confidence. It's not a familiar odour, but it smells good.

"So. What about your love life? Got a boyfriend?"

"Woo! Aren't we forward all of a sudden? Nah. There's this guy I like, but…" The train squeals to a halt and people start getting on and off. "Let's get back to our seats before someone nicks them. We should be safe now."

Strangely, I've never felt more safe in a girl's company and I find myself wishing I fancied her. We make it back to our seats to find Grunt Platoon has left along with my *White Dwarf* and fall into a comfortable conversation. It feels like there are no topics off-limits. I tell her all about Sarah – but, weirdly, my mouth comes up with an edited version. Sure, I tell her about meeting her, getting her in on Dungeons & Dragons, the Games Night and Jason Humphries, going to her house, her reading my aura, but, somehow, I skirt round the point where I told her I was in love with her and she told me that she didn't see me that way. Instead, I paint a picture of a nice guy who gets told that she wants us to be "just friends". And as I do it, I know why: I'm clutching at any available straw, anything that means I don't have to just apologize and give up.

IM: *Or behave like an adult.*

"I mean, what am I supposed to do?" I ask the back of the chair in front of me, perhaps with a little too much animation.

"Well… It depends what she means by it."

IM: *?*

"But … what else can it mean? Y'know … apart from 'let's just be friends'?" Despite my protests and the fact that Clare doesn't know the Full Story, a little Flame of Hope flickers unsteadily into life. There might be

95

another way out of this. I'm a desperate man.

IM: *You know where the toilet is…*

Clare settles back into her seat, like when old people tell war stories. "It *probably* means that there's someone else on the scene; that's the most likely scenario. She just doesn't want to hurt your feelings…"

IM: *Flame sputters. Dies. Leaving only embers*

"…bu-ut, it could also mean something else."

IM: *Blows desperately on the Embers of Hope*

"Like what?" Why does this have to be so complicated?

"Well, if *I* was saying it, it could also mean that I want to know just how *much* you're interested."

IM: *We have Fire!*

"What … like a test?"

"Yeah. Like a test."

My eyes search the back of the seat in front, as though the Secret of Life is written on it. The more I hear from Clare, the more I'm starting to believe my own version of events. She *might* not have meant what she said and *maybe* I didn't come across as badly as I thought I did at the time. Maybe, what with the adrenalin and everything, I don't remember it exactly as it happened.

IM: *And maybe you're lying to yourself. No question mark required.*

"OK," I frown, ignoring the pesky voice of reason in

my head. "But why not just say it's a test?"

"And where's the fun in that?" Clare laughs.

"But how do I know what she means?" I'm in. I've bought my own lie. And it didn't seem to cost that much.

IM: *Just your soul. But I'm sure you can pick one up second-hand. Might've belonged to a hamster or something.*

"Time to man up, snowflake!" Clare replies, enjoying all this a bit too much. "You play her at her own game!"

"How?"

Clare rolls her eyes and sighs. "Look, there's this guy I like – Oliver. He lives in the town near my school and I know he likes me, too. But he hasn't asked me out yet."

"OK…" I still don't get it.

"So, I need to hurry him up a bit."

"How?"

"By ignoring him." She says this like it's the most obvious thing in the world.

I instantly feel sorry for Oliver, whoever he is.

"The point is that I want to see just how much he likes me. It's a test. *I* know I'm going to go out with him, but he doesn't need to know that. Not yet."

IM: *Hmmm. The Universal Translator seems to be malfunctioning…*

"If you want something, you've got to be prepared to work for it."

"OK…" Great. In one world I'm a Level 5 Mage,

capable of communicating with beings from the Elemental Plane. In this one, I can't even understand girls. "Man," I mutter, "I wish you were at *my* school; then you could be my interpreter."

"Hey! I've got a great idea!" There's a wildly carefree look in her eyes. "We could have a Train Relationship!"

"A what?"

"You know, we could be like Train Boyfriend and Girlfriend – see each other every time we're on the train. Like a relationship, but without all the other stuff. Get your parents to book the same seat each time; it'll make the journey a lot more fun."

IM: *And you might learn something about girls!*

"OK! You're on!"

"Excellent – *boy*friend!" She says the last word in a big, fake American accent. I respond in kind.

"Cool – *girl*friend!"

All too soon, the train reaches her stop and Clare has to go, but not before we swap numbers and check our tickets: we'll be travelling back together. She leaves with an exaggerated "Bye, darling!" and is replaced with an old man who falls asleep for the rest of the journey.

I don't care: I've made a friend who's a girl. But isn't a girlfriend. But is. But isn't.

IM: *Anyone else have a bad feeling about this?*

FIVE

It's nearly nine o'clock when I arrive at York; it's dark and the station is echoing with the sound of feet, chatter, tannoys and trains. My train slides to a halt and I push the button to open the door: Dad, Jane, Lucas, Steven and Izzy are assembled on the platform, wearing big, cheesy smiles.

IM: *It looks like a toothpaste commercial.*

Jane, predictably, is the first to break rank. She lunges at me out of the family frieze and snatches me into a hug that wouldn't be out of place in a wrestling ring. It crushes my nose against her shoulder and while I'm fighting to keep my eyeballs in their sockets, I am given a stark reminder – like I'd forgotten – that this woman is not, and never could be, my mum. I briefly wonder how my mum's coping without me.

IM: *She needn't worry; her apron strings are like bungee ropes.*

My mum smells like I think every mum ought to. It's a fresh smell, a homely smell; the smell of fresh bedsheets and hand cream. Jane smells of cloth. It's a medieval musk.

Not content with nearly crushing the life out of me,

99

she then grabs my shoulders and thrusts me backwards so that she can go through the charade of looking me up and down. Like living with my mum is somehow going to incur damage that only she can spot. My EM responds in kind, painting on a smile that would fool an art expert.

"Darling! It's so good to see you! Look: Lu-cas and Ste-ven and Iz-zy have been allowed to stay up late to come and meet you!" She breaks their names down into syllables, just in case I've forgotten the correct pronunciation. "Come on, kids! Archie's here! Let's give him a hug!" Lu-cas and Ste-ven and Izz-y obediently march forward, arms outstretched, and tentatively squash my legs.

IM: *It's like being mugged by a tribe of Ewoks.*

However, Jane is smiling through her immeasurably thick glasses in a doe-eyed daze, her eyes magnified by the lenses to create something quite scary. She cuts an imposing figure, anyway: she's tall and broad, rather like a bespectacled door. And she's got this thing where she can't say "yes" properly. She speaks in such a posh voice, it comes out as "ears".

Dad steps forward and wraps his arms round me. While he feels the same – solid and strong – he smells different. It's like he used to smell of forever and now he smells of part-time.

"Hello, son."

IM: *Wipes a tear from eye*

"Dad." It's all I can manage; the hug has opened up a whole can of anger. Yeah, I've missed him and, yeah, it's great to see him, but I ought to be at a party right now. Instead, I'm shivering in a train station, surrounded by people I don't really care about. And it's all his fault.

"Right. Let's get you home." Dad coughs manfully into Business mode.

IM: *Your home. Not mine. Mine's the one near the party where everyone's having a great time.*

Dad scoops up my bag and we walk through the station which is, Jane tells me, the only curved station in the whole of the United Kingdom.

Not content with that insight, she then asks us all why "the train didn't sit on the tracks". Apparently it's because it "had a tender behind".

IM: *And so it begins.*

It's the first joke of the weekend – and I use the term loosely. Right now, Tony's farts seem like the better option.

IM: *At least you don't have to pretend to find them funny.*

Eventually we make it to the car. As Guest of Honour, I get to sit in the front with Dad, much to the disappointment of the three kids, who insist on letting us know just how much *they* wanted to sit there. All the way to their front door.

IM: *That's a return ticket in your pocket, isn't it? It's not too late to ... y'know... The party might still be going on...*

We arrive at the house, which is tall and thin, like all the other houses in York seem to be. Luckily Izzy's fallen asleep and Lucas and Steven are hurried off to bed as soon as we get through the door. I stand in the hallway, not quite sure what to do with myself and soaking up the overpowering smell of cloth. The Jane Smell.

"Come on in, son. Have a look round. I'll make you a cup of tea." I follow Dad into the kitchen where he sets about boiling the kettle and tells me about various bits of work that still need to be done on the house. "You hungry? Want a sandwich?"

"No, thanks. I'm fine." The Cumulonimbus of Crankiness over my head prohibits me from accepting peace offerings. Even if Dad's unaware that it is one. It's all I've got left to communicate the fact that I'm severely Not Happy.

IM: *Wow. THAT'LL teach him.*

"I'll do you one, anyway." I think forcing food on me is his way of showing that he cares. Too late. If he really cared, he'd've moved somewhere more convenient for me to have a Social Life.

As Dad sets about creating a Man Sandwich (no butter, no salad, no mayo: just ham), there's an R2-D2 squeal from my pocket. It's a text. For a moment, I mournfully assume it's Mum, but Mum doesn't tend to send me multimedia messages – she wouldn't know how. It's from Beggsy. And it's a photo of the party.

Ravi's in the foreground in a darkish room. And, for a Geek, he's looking pretty cool in his "I Speak Klingon" T-shirt. Hopefully the rest of the crowd will interpret this as irony, not one of his ambitions in life. He's pulling his "oo-er" face and pointing across his chest to something behind him, obviously trying not to be too conspicuous. Because the room's so dark, I can't see what he's pointing at properly; there are arms and faces and silhouettes. But one of the silhouettes has got red hair and, caught unwittingly in the flash of the camera, red irises. It's Matt, holding a drink and locked in intense conversation – although there isn't really any other sort with Matt. And the silhouette next to him is undeniably of the female variety.

IM: *But a paradox of this magnitude could rip a hole in the space/time continuum!*

Matt's talking to a girl… And I'm not there. I'm here, staring at the frill-free Man Sandwich that's just been plonked in front of me.

"You OK, son? You're a bit quiet."

"Yeah. Sorry. I'm just a bit tired," I lie. "Long journey."

The great thing about lying to another male is

that they believe you, implicitly. There's no further questioning, no reading-between-the-lines; as far as Dad's concerned, I'm tired from a long journey. The sandwich means I don't have to talk for a bit, which suits me fine. But I shouldn't be eating it – my mouth should be savouring the delights of Party Food, not chomping up mealy brown bread and bits of ham.

After my enforced snack, Jane joins us and suggests a tour of the house. It's got all the usual stuff: a lounge, bathroom, et cetera and there's no denying it's a nice pad, it's just *wrong*, somehow. It doesn't feel like I've got any place in it. Sure, there're a couple of my school photos hanging around, but that's the only evidence to suggest I'm anything to do with whoever lives here. And there's the occasional relic from the house that we lived in when Mum and Dad were Together, but even they look wrong, like they've suddenly had their histories taken away.

I tell you what else is weird: I'm sure I remember Dad hating wallpaper. But *this* house is covered in wall-to-wall wallpaper. A quick inspection throws up some weird sort of vine plants with little birds sitting in them. I don't like it. And I don't like the patterned carpet that doesn't quite cover the bare floorboards on the stairs and landing. It's all a bit like being inside a giant doll's house. I smell a clothy hand in this.

Even weirder is being shown up the first flight of

stairs to Dad and Jane's bedroom. Especially with the "Ta-daaahh!" that Jane gives it.

"So, what do you think?"

IM: *I think you have sex with my father here.*

"Yeah. Really cool," I say – probably a bit too quickly, trying to push that particular image back into the abyss where it belongs.

"Look, we've even got an ensuite," beams Dad, opening a door and pointing at a shower cubicle.

IM: *Sexsexsexsexsex.*

"Nice one." I just want to get out of here.

IM: *We all know what a bathroom's for when there's more than one person using it...*

"And your clever father built these wardrobes," announces Jane, opening some hidden doors to reveal – "Ta-daaahhh!" – some wardrobes.

IM: *Probably in there, too.*

I wish I could turn these thoughts off, but my HeadTV™ seems only to be receiving the Forbidden Channel. I need to get out. Thankfully, Dad's got an ace up his sleeve.

"Shall we show him his room?" he says to Jane, eyes a-twinkle.

"Do you think we should?" she returns, in mock-trepidation.

IM: *Shout "Oh, yes, you should!" and wet yourself.*

That should do it.

"You show him," says Dad.

"Ears, I'd love to!"

IM: *Heeerrre comes a Bonding Moment!*

I follow Jane's formidable backside past the kids' bedrooms and up another set of stairs. There's a small landing at the top, with three doors leading off it. Jane points me at the door straight ahead and motions for me to go in. I take a couple of deep breaths and do a quick rehearsal in my head of the awe that my EM will have to portray.

IM: *'Tis amazeballs! 'Tis most awesome! 'Tis... Oh. Hang on...*

For a moment I forget my Party Woes; it's not the room that's cool – a room's a room when it isn't your own. It's got a bed and it's decorated in fairly neutral colours. And it's definitely not the stereo that's cool – no one plays CDs any more. No, what's cool is the painting desk installed by the window. It's got small shelves already lined with pristine, unopened paint pots, upright wooden tubes holding virgin brushes, more shelvage for displaying models, an articulated lamp for painting those bits that need extra lighting and drawers to keep the rest of the essentials in.

IM: *Coooooolll!*

"Your father's a clever man," Jane says, without a hint

of amateur dramatics. As if on cue, Dad appears in the doorway.

"What d'you think, son? It was all Jane's idea."

IM: *Moment spoilt.*

It's funny how, when there's a new partner on the block, any ideas that might be really, truly epic never seem to come from the parent. It's like they've apparently forgotten everything they know about you and have to be reminded of the basics by the new face who doesn't know you at all.

"Take a look in the drawer. The top one," Dad nods at the desk.

I open it to find a couple of blister packs containing three goblins and three wizards. Nice stuff. In the one below, there's some rag for wiping brushes, a modelling knife and some plastics glue. Even a bathroom tile for mixing paint on. The whole shebang.

"Wow," I manage, my EM painting a fresco of gratitude on to my face. "Thanks, guys."

"No problem," Dad smiles and comes in for a hug. "Welcome to your new home."

But it's not. It's the house where him and Jane live.

IM: *And have sex.*

I chew down my ingratitude and Jane steps in for a clothy hug.

"The kids chose the models," she beams, "but we

had a dreadful time stopping them from breaking open the paints. Perhaps you could give them some lessons?"

I'm fully aware that this is an attempt to integrate me into some semblance of fully fledged Family Membership but, once again, I swallow my instinctive "no" and nod in the affirmative.

"Sure."

"Right," nods Dad, obviously pleased with the way things are going. "It's late and we're going to show you round York tomorrow... So I think it's best if we all turn in."

"Ears," Jane echoes and exits with a cheery, "Good night, Archie. Lovely to see you."

"Thanks, Dad," I offer, once she's gone.

"No problem, son. No problem at all. Right. Bathroom's free and the toilet's at the bottom of the stairs. I'll leave you to it. Night."

"Night."

The door closes and I sit on the edge of the bed, suddenly wishing it was the one at home. My proper home.

IM: *Where your mum and Tony live. And have... I'll stop now.*

Without Dad and Jane hovering over me, I finally send Mum a text:

Arrived. See you Sunday. Love you. xxx

Within seconds, R2 squeals a reply:

Have a great time! Luvya. X

It comes back so quickly that she must've been poised by her mobile, just waiting for me to send her a message. It might only be a text, but it's a real comfort; an invisible thread that links me to my Other Life. I decide to cast another line and send Beggsy a text:

How's the party? Are you still a virgin?

It makes me chuckle as I type it and I fully expect some tongue-in-cheek outrage within the next few seconds. Probably all in capitals and with lots of exclamation marks. But the next few seconds turn into the next few minutes and my inbox remains untroubled. Something acid seethes in my chest – my mates have already forgotten me. While they're at a party, probably having The Best Time Ever, I'm sat in an unfamiliar room in an unfamiliar house, staring at my blank phone screen. Life sucks.

With a guttural sigh of frustration, I stand, looking at the painting desk. It's got everything. Resisting the temptation to pop a pack and start on a wizard, I open the door below the drawers. There's a new edition

Dungeons & Dragons set, still in its wrapper. I open it, bypass the *Players' Handbook* and the *Monster Manual* and pull out the *Dungeon Master's Guide*: new cover art means new rules.

I think I'll have a read before bed – it'll take my mind off everything.

Part of being a good Dungeon Master is knowing the rules inside out. Once I'm done with the DM Guide, I'll hit the *Players' Handbook* and the *Monster Manual*. The great thing about Dungeons & Dragons is that you can choose which rules to bend or completely ignore. But you've got to know the rules before you break 'em.

I need a poo.

No, this isn't over-excitement at a new set of rules, it's probably that ham sandwich having its wicked way with my digestive system. Like that scene in *Star Wars* when Luke Skywalker's in his X-wing Fighter going to go and fire a proton torpedo at the Death Star's thermal exhaust port, I hear my dad's disembodied voice, *à la* Obi-Wan Kenobi telling Luke to trust his feelings:

"…the toilet's at the bottom of the stairs … at the bottom of the stairs … at the bottom of the stairs…"

Well, my proton torpedo has definitely found its way into the tube and all I need to do is make the trench run. Everyone should be asleep.

As quietly as I can, I hit the stairs. While Luke had

to dodge fire from TIE fighters and the Death Star's ion cannons, I'm having to negotiate creaky stairs. I know which particular gauntlet I'd rather be running right now. But each step I take seems to be heralded with a symphony of squeaks and groans. I might as well just stand and shout, "I'm going for a Number Two!" at the top of my voice. Instead, I try putting my feet as close to the wall as possible, working on the theory that these parts of the stair will be less worn than the middle and, therefore, make less noise.

Step.

Nothing.

Step.

Nothing.

Step.

Nothing.

My theory seems to pay off and, after what seems like an hour, I'm stood outside the kids' bedrooms. I can hear the gentle rise and fall of their breathing; they're asleep. But my stomach reminds me that there are more pressing matters to be dealt with than listening to kids dreaming.

IM: *The Force is strong in this one!*

Oh, yes it is, and I'm going to have to get a move on. I stick to my theory and creep tentatively along the edge of the landing, testing each step with a toe before

I commit to the rest of my foot.

Toe.

Nothing.

Heel.

Nothing.

Toe.

IM: *It's going to be a loooonnng night...*

Nothing.

Heel.

Nothing.

Toe.

And then I hear it. It takes a second for me to translate what I'm listening to. For a moment, I think one of the kids is in the early stages of a bad dream; there's a whisper of huffing that starts gently, but grows in urgency and frequency.

IM: *Werewolf?*

The huffing reaches a plateau, like a train that's reached top speed. A second sound is then introduced into this midnight serenade – a low, barely audible, intermittent growling sound.

IM: *Werewolf!*

And then a third sound that tips the table for me: the sound of slow, rhythmic creaking that gets faster and faster, then slows, before picking up speed again. More huffs. More growls. And urgent snatches of the word "ears" being repeated over and over.

IM: *Posh werewolf?*

As the penny drops, my body is suddenly slick with an ice-cold film of sweat. My heart starts to race and I can feel all the blood draining from my face.

IM: *Ohmygod. They're doing it. Dad and Jane are ACTUALLY DOING IT!*

They're doing it! They really are! And they're doing it scant feet from where I'm standing.

IM: *Ohmygodohmygodohmygod!*

Luke Skywalker never faced anything like this. And now I've had that thought, I've got an unspeakable picture in my head of my Dad wearing a Darth Vader helmet and Jane with her hair in one of those weird styles that Queen Amidala had. I want to die.

IM: *But not as much as you want to go to the toilet.*

A twinge from my stomach snaps me out of the *Star Wars*-themed skin flick that's playing in my Cinema of the Forbidden™. It's time to take drastic action; I've got to get away. Taking the most enormous strides possible, I make it to the toilet, ease the door open, silently slide the bolt so it's locked and assume the position.

IM: *Oh, thank you, Jesus.*

OK. Torpedo in tube: check. Target sited: check. Open bay doors…

IM: *We appear to have a malfunction.*

The malfunction is that I'm frightened of being heard. As much as I want to release my payload, the bay doors just won't budge. If I'm caught, literally, with my trousers down, the game'll be up: not only will everyone know what I'm up to, but Dad and Jane will also know that I've heard them Doing It. I try again.

IM: *Use the Force, Archie!*

I use as much of the Force as my body will allow, but my only reward is a staggered squeak and little spots of light blinking on and off in front of my eyes. Not wishing to risk any louder trumpet solos, I hang my head, panting from my efforts.

IM: *Relax. You've got to relax.*

I try. I really do. But the bay doors just won't budge. No amount of closing my eyes or thinking nice thoughts is going to persuade those suckers to open. I sit there, like a stuffed chicken; I've just created a new version of PPS … I've given birth to a monster.

IM: *If only.*

I go in for a final pass, but my stomach decides it's going to keep its hostage until more favourable terms are negotiated. Resigned to failure and damning my Geeky self-conscious streak in absolute silence, I stand and pull my trousers up. Feeling bloated and tired, I now realize I've got another problem: I've got to get back upstairs.

IM: *But have they "finished"?*

From here, I can't hear anything. I've been in the toilet a good ten minutes at least – but is that long enough? How long does this go on for? If my own, solitary efforts are anything to go by, it should've been over while I'd been stood on the landing. But this sounded like there was a lot more effort being put into it.

I give it about five minutes before daring to stick my head out of the door and listen. The darkness on the landing seems like a living thing, broken only by the moonlight that streams through the window by the bathroom. I breathe through my mouth to give my ears a chance and listen hard.

A snore. It's my dad. I take a deep breath and retrace my silent steps. The only problem is that I'm walking for two. Employing all my stealth, I make it past the snores and the kids' bedrooms and creep like a pregnant Gollum back up the stairs to my room. As I get into bed, I can't help but check to see if there are any messages from Beggsy – preferably something about Sarah slapping Chris Jackson in the face. But there's nothing.

I can't be bothered to go back to the rules; they'll do for tomorrow. But I can be bothered with a few pages of the *Dark Knight*.

Batman's faced with a new gang, The Mutants, who're trying to take over Gotham City. He starts out by picking them off one by one, scaring the hell out of them; he's like a vampire or an angel of darkness. But when he takes on the Mutant Leader, he meets his match and gets well and truly pasted.

I'm just getting to the bit where Carrie Kelly turns up to save him, looking all hot in her Robin outfit, when R2 squeals from my bedside table. With a lurch of expectant fear, I scrabble for my phone. This feeling doubles as I see it's from Beggsy. And it's a photo.

I guess the guys are only trying to bring me in on the unfettered joy they must be feeling right now, but it really isn't helping. Especially when the photo in question shows two of my best mates with their arms round Kirsty Ford.

IM: *Photoshopped. Gotta be.*

But it's not. There they are: Beggsy wearing the same sort of expression that you see on those photos of people who've won the lottery and are spraying champagne around and Ravi doing something a bit James Bondy, raising an eyebrow suggestively. And there's Kirsty Ford, practically bursting out of her top and doing her legendary pout. She is so hot.

I stare at the photo, serenaded by the gurgling in my stomach and damning my party-free existence. Without doubt, I have missed The Most Important Night of My Life.

SIX

"Arrrr-chieeee!"

This ear-shattering squeal is almost instantaneously followed by an impact on my abdomen that threatens to resolve the hostage situation immediately. My EM and IM go straight to DEFCON 1.

IM: *Alert! Alert! We are under attack! Launch everything!*

Luckily, my EM decides to open my eyes to see just what we're dealing with and I find myself presented with the face of a four-year-old girl, grinning at me madly. It's Izzy.

IM: *Stand down! Crisis averted! Revert to Black Alert!*

As all systems return to their standard alert status, my EM forces a smile through my fatigue.

"Morning, Izzy."

Izzy giggles and starts rolling around on the bed or, more specifically, on my bloated stomach.

IM: *She has no idea how much danger she's in right now.*

My morning mangling is interrupted by another sonic screech, albeit a more matronly one.

"Morning, Archie! Oh, Izzy! Do get off him, darling!

He's not a trampoline!"

Jane is stood in the doorway, holding a cup of tea. Huddled close to her legs are Steven and Lucas. Steven's holding a plate of toast. And they're all looking at me. I suddenly become incredibly conscious of my unclothed torso and pull the covers up as inconspicuously as I can.

"There you go, Lucas," trills Jane, handing him the cup of tea. "Give it to Archie! And the toast, Steven!"

Rather like two of the Three Wise Men, Lucas and his brother slowly approach my manger. Steven makes it without too much bother, but Lucas can't help slopping tea over the brim with virtually every step he takes.

"Thanks, guys."

"Steven made the toast all by himself!" chirps Jane.

Steven glows proudly and waits expectantly. I look down at the plate to be confronted with what can only be described as burnt offerings.

IM: *Yep. All by himself.*

"Mmm!" I enthuse, through shattering teeth, gaining an excited smile from the chef. A sip of tea helps to remove the taste of coal from my mouth.

"Nice tea. Thanks." But Lucas doesn't respond; he simply returns to the doorway.

IM: I sense a ripple in the Force…

"Arrr-chiee! Can we play? When are you getting up?"

"Give Archie a chance, Izzy! Let him get dressed and then I'm sure he'd love to play with you."

IM: *Huff huff. Ears ears.*

Steven gives a "Yay!" as he's herded out of the door and Izzy joins in. Only Lucas remains silent.

It seems I have no choice but to get out of bed. I'm just about to put on my clothes from yesterday when I hear a telepathic nagging from Mum, telling me to make sure I put on clean clothes every day. Inside my rucksack are a couple of pairs of jeans and a couple of T-shirts. I pull them out, getting wafts of whatever washing powder Mum uses and I do something I've never done before: I sniff my clothes.

IM: *Pervert.*

They smell of home.

I'm almost tempted to try another trench run, but with everyone awake, I make do with a quick wee in the Toilet of Empty Promises. I hit the next set of stairs and walk into the front room. Izzy instantly stops watching whatever's on the telly and runs over to grab my legs.

IM: *A well-timed fart could solve this one…*

"OK, everyone…" Dad gets up from the sofa and lapses into a voice that I remember from my childhood and feel a strange sense of ownership over. "…today, I thought we'd show Archie round York and go somewhere

I know you've all been wanting to go. Where do you think that might be?"

IM: *An enema clinic?*

"Well…" grins Dad, obviously hearing some drum roll that the rest of us can't. "Today, we thought it might be fun to go to … the Jorvik Viking Centre!" Cue whoops and yays from anyone under four feet high. Steven gives me a high five, quickly followed by Izzy; Lucas maintains his position on the floor, but raises his eyebrows in a "that's cool" kind of way.

Jane celebrates with the first joke of the day: "I say, I say, I say… How do Vikings send secret messages?" She doesn't even wait to be asked how. "They use Norse Code!"

IM: **Sounds of life-support machine being switched off**

As we drive through the streets of the Land of the Vikings, I take another look at the photos Beggsy sent me. As I imagine the guys sitting in a café, sipping cappuccinos with their new-found circle of friends, Kirsty Ford probably getting Klingon lessons off Ravi, and Sarah and Chris Jackson probably holding hands, my mood takes a nosedive. And to cap it off, something happens to Dad in the car.

My memories of the occasional trips out when Mum and Dad were Together, were of Mum chatting away cheerfully and Dad just driving. He wouldn't say much, just drive. But as soon as we're underway, it's like Dad suddenly takes over Jane's position as the Entertainment Officer. It starts out with a few questions to the kids, along the lines of "What are you looking forward to the most?" And whatever they answer back, it's suddenly his favourite thing. But times a thousand. And using words and phrases that died out with Tamagotchi and Dragon Ball Z, like "Yeah! That'll be totally 'off the chain'!" and "The Vikings were 'the bomb'."

IM: *Most righteous!*

Even the kids seem a little confused; it's like someone's flicked a switch and put Dad in Party mode. I wouldn't be surprised to find out that he's wearing an ear piece and Jane's feeding him the lines – they don't sound right coming out of his mouth, like if Gandalf's voice was suddenly replaced with Jar Jar Binks's.

IM: *Meesa a servant of the sacred fire! Yousa shall not pass!*

Izzy and Steven sort of roll with it, but Lucas doesn't. I can see him in the rear-view mirror, frowning a little and sometimes doing a little shake of his head.

Dad must have an awareness of this because he

suddenly asks him if he thinks they'll let him try on one of the horned helmets. And laughs a bit too loudly.

"They didn't have horns on," Lucas replies, sounding a little exasperated. For once, I sympathize.

"Really? I thought they did. In all the films I've seen, the Vikings have got horns on their helmets." But Dad's delivery is all wrong – it's like he's talking to a four-year-old.

"But the films have got it wrong."

"Have they? Are you sure?"

IM: *OK, he just sounds like an idiot, now.*

"Yes."

IM: *And Lucas obviously thinks the same.*

"OK. Let's make a bet: if you're right, *I'll* give *you* a pound. If you're wrong, *you* give *me* a pound. We'll find out when we get to the Viking Centre." Dad chucks me a huge, pantomime wink that makes me grit my teeth.

"Oooh! I wonder who'll be the '*Loki*' one?" Jane gushes. Nobody gets it.

IM: *She's here all week, ladies and gentlemen!*

Even once we've arrived, Dad doesn't let up, and continues to play out the charade with Lucas about pretending he can't quite remember if the helmets had horns or not. But like, in a really big way. I know he's my dad, but I'm starting to feel really sorry for Lucas. It's like Dad's trying to be something he's not and just making himself look like…

IM: …*a Tosser?*

Oh my God. My dad's turning into a Tosser. It's got all the hallmarks of how Tony used to behave when we first moved in together – everything was mega-exciting and like it was part of some massive deal. One of the main qualifications to becoming a step-parent seems to be a massive loss of perspective and a sudden and inexplicably enthusiastic interest in whatever your inherited son or daughter likes doing. Which'd be fine if there was genuine interest to back it up, not some empty pantomime.

IM: *Maybe this is what happens when you get stepkids.*

But if I follow that one, there's the possibility that Tony wasn't a Tosser before I met him.

IM: *You Tosserized him!*

I shudder at the thought, watching my once-familiar dad acting like a complete stranger. Even waiting in line to buy tickets doesn't seem to calm him down.

Queueing done and tickets bought, we strap ourselves into the "time capsule" and "prepare to travel back in time" to the world of the Vikings.

OK, so this isn't Disneyland. The Viking villagers are very obviously dummies and the "animatronics" involved wouldn't be out of place in a Christmas window display.

But what they have got is authenticity. By the bucketload. In fact, the most authentic things are the smells. As we glide by the fish market, our noses are assaulted by the odour with all the ferocity of a Viking raiding party. A commentary babbles away in the background, but it's drowned out by the "Eeeews" and "Gross!" from the kids and the occasional "off the chain!" from my father. After checking out a Viking street, we hit a Viking house and our noses take another Viking battering.

IM: *Smells familiar, doesn't it...?*

I know this smell. But where do I know it from?

IM: *Jane.*

Oh. My. God. Jane smells like a Viking house.

IM: *Maybe she* is *a Viking! She's certainly got the build for it...*

We travel on through the year 975, encountering a wood-turner, gossiping women, fighting dogs and various other aromas. But nothing, not even the smell of the Viking cesspit, which I look at longingly, can remove the smell of the Viking house from the memory cells in my nose. Jane is a Viking.

IM: *And if she isn't, then she smells like one.*

The ride only lasts about ten minutes, then we wander into the museum and start looking at the display cabinets. Dad spots a helmet and makes for it.

IM: *Brace yourself…*

"Oh *no*! That's so cool!" His amateur dramatics are loud enough to catch the attention of a bunch of other tourists, who look at him warily. I take a couple of steps back from it all, just to make sure no one thinks we're actually related. Lucas, not having that problem, joins him.

"Well, you got me there, mate!" Dad declares, shaking his head unconvincingly. "Here's your pound."

As he puts his hand in his pocket, he tries to cast me a surreptitious wink, bringing me in on the game. But Lucas spots it and something changes. A look crosses his face.

"You knew," he says, accusingly, as much as to me as to Dad. "You knew."

"No!" Dad splutters, offering out the pound. "I didn't. I thought they had horns! You won the bet!" Lucas just looks at him for a moment, then turns and walks away to join his brother and sister. I watch Dad standing there looking stupid and guilty. I ought to go and say something to him, but Jane steps in, rallying the troops with a morale-boosting gag. And, yes, I'm being sarcastic.

IM: *Pulls gun from holster*

We leave the Viking Centre and spend the next fifteen, silent minutes, wandering around various narrow streets, trying to find a good old, traditional Yorkshire coffee shop. Just as we find one, I spot something on the other side of the street, calling me like a siren.

It's a Games Workshop.

IM: *It's not quite The Hovel, but it'll do!*

"Hey, Dad – can I go in there for a minute?" I ask, desperate to put some distance between me and this forced family outing for a bit.

"Yeah, sure. D'you want some money?"

"No, I'm fine. Tony gave me some." I see the words impact on him like little Bombs of Treachery™ as soon as they leave my mouth.

IM: *We have a malfunction in the Edit Suite: rogue words are escaping. Normal service will be resumed as soon as possible.*

"OK." Dad seems to shrink a little. I want to say sorry, but I don't. He smiles sadly. "What do you want to eat?"

I ask for a toasted sandwich and a Coke and then cross the road and disappear inside, revelling in my own company for a short while.

As I take a turn round the display stands, soaking in all the blister packs and looking at the beautifully sculpted miniatures they house, my brain does action replays of Dad's Greatest Goofs: the over-enthusiasm, the hopeless attempts at Groovy Talk and the Giant Viking Wink. I shake my head and sigh; I know what Dad's doing. He's trying to get on-side with the kids. And while he might have won over Izzy and Steven, Lucas is making him work for it – maybe out of loyalty to his dad or something. But the harder my dad works for it, the more of a Tosser he looks and the more of a Tosser he looks, the harder Lucas is going to make him work. It's a vicious circle. But why did he have to try and drag *me* into it?

IM: *What the…? Rational, considerate thought? We can't have this! *Searches for photos of boobs**

As much as I'm hacked off at my "so cool!" father, I know I can do something to help. And, in spite of the part of me that thinks I should just let him get on with it and cock it all up by himself, there's another part of me that knows what it's like to have something blow up in your face when you think you're doing the right thing. Grudgingly, I give in to it. For one night and one night only, I shall come to the rescue.

IM: *With all the panache of a hobbit on a donkey.*

What Dad and the kids need is a common goal: a sense of unity. They need to come together to fight something that threatens them all. They need…

IM: **Drum roll* *Waits patiently for life-changing revelation**

…a game of Dungeons & Dragons.

IM: *And YOU need a spell in Arkham Asylum. WHAT? A game of Dungeons & Dragons? Are you NUTS?*

If ever there was a game that lets you find out about your teammates, that's it. Plus, it'd give me a chance to have a little fun of my own… I can allow certain people to win and certain other people to be not so successful… It plays out in my Head Cinema™ in glorious Technicolor.

The scene: a subterranean tunnel somewhere in York. Five adventurers make their way stealthily through the darkness, with only a flaming torch for light. Rats scurry about their feet. The camera pulls back to reveal that they are being watched through a crystal ball, belonging to the dire figure of… The Dungeon Master!

Izzy: Eeeew! This place smells of cloth!

The others gag in agreement. Only Jane, a thief, seems unaware of the rank odour.

Dad: Look! Up ahead! A door!

Lucas: Wow, Archie's dad – you're awesome!

Dad: Just call me "The Bomb".

The door is strong and wooden and locked. Not even Dad's heroic attempts can budge it.

Steven: Mum! You're a thief! You can pick the lock!

Jane: Oh! Ears! Of course I can! Coming through!

Jane, her glasses flashing in the torchlight, steps

forward and pulls out the tools of her trade. A few seconds later, there is a "click" and the door opens a fraction.

Dad: So cool, darling! Pretty soon we'll be out of here!

Jane: I say, I say, I say...

Beginning a joke, she steps forward but, unfortunately (cackle, cackle), steps on to a rigged flagstone; darts fly out of hidden recesses in the tunnel wall, inflicting damage on the party. Once the shrieks of pain have died down, Steven asserts himself.

Steven: Perhaps you should use your thief skills and check the room for traps, before we go in, Mum.

Jane: Oh, ears! Good idea!

Jane stands in the doorway, using her special abilities to discern whether there are any more threats to the adventurers.

Jane: All clear!

She steps into the room, walking through a tripwire. A hatch in the ceiling above her head opens and douses her in hundreds of scorpions. She staggers to the wall, putting out an arm to steady herself. Unfortunately, she presses a hidden switch that opens a disguised sarcophagus. An undead Viking warrior lurches out, waving his battleaxe.

Lucas: It's true! They do have horns! Why didn't I listen to you, Archie's dad?

Dad: Stand back, Lucas! I'll dispense with this awesome creature! You can just bask in my Bombness!

Lucas: Let's all live in peace and harmony, with Archie as my wise older brother!

Jane spots a large treasure chest and, using her lock-pick, opens it. Unfortunately, it is home to a werewolf, which leaps out, huffing and growling.

Lucas: Mum! You're the worst thief ever! You're ruining this for everyone! If only Archie were here, he'd know what to do!

Back in the Dungeon Master's throne room, the DM toys idly with his Dice of Fate and chuckles.

DM: Oh, I am here, Lucas. In fact, I am closer than you think. And your faith will be rewarded. But right now, I need a poo.

It's true. The over crowding in my stomach is getting serious. Quickly, I pick a character for everyone and waddle to the counter to pay. While me and the Not Big Marv exchange some small talk, my inner hostages send out an appeal to the outside world, albeit a silent one.

IM: *Ye gods! That would drop a charging rhino!*

I leave quickly, pretty sure I can hear the paint peeling off the walls as I do so.

Just as I hit the pavement, R2 squeals from my pocket, making a passing group of girls jump and giggle. One of them breaks from the herd and steps towards me.

"What was that?"

It's got to be said that there don't appear to be any

unattractive girls in York. The only way to describe the four girls in front of me is: *sexy*. These girls are sexy. First off, there's the skin: it's not quite orange, more beigey – but in that dusty way that tells you a spray gun was involved. Then there's the clothes. Don't get me wrong: I like to think I've got a certain amount of depth to my soul and a level of romanticism that's slightly out of place in the twenty-first century, but present any fourteen-year-old boy with four girls in Uggs, skin-tight black leggings and those strappy T-shirts that are cut just a bit too low for comfort and you'll get the same result.

IM: *My, these trousers aren't as loose as they used to be...*

I think I'm even developing a thing for hair that's tied back in a ponytail. Right on cue, my EM abandons any sense of responsibility and sends every red blood cell in my body to my cheeks.

IM: *Remember, Archie: these girls don't know you're a Geek...*

My IM's right. I don't have to be afraid. No one here knows me for what I truly am... Maybe this "away from home" thing has its perks. Here, I don't have to be Archie the Geek. Here, I can be Arkki, Norse God of ... Lurve... I mentally roll a D10 against my Charisma.

IM: *Watch out, ladies. I'm packin' a horn or two...*

"That noise? What was that noise?"

131

This anonymity thing is like plugging into a reservoir of confidence. My EM is suddenly full of pelvis; I slouch a little and put my weight on one leg, letting my hips shift to one side. Even my eyelids relax with a gunslinger's cool.

IM: *Who do you think you are – Justin Bieber?*

"Just my phone."

"Your phern?" It's that Yorkshire accent.

IM: *Sounds a bit … dirty.*

I like it.

"Yeah."

"What phern you got?" This must be part of some ancient Nordic mating custom. I pull out my phern and lightly toss it into the air. My EM, obviously unused to such demands on it, responds by apparently removing all the bones from my fingers and my phern clatters to the ground. The girls laugh.

IM: *This isn't going so well, Justin. Why don't you try grabbing your crotch? That's bound to work.*

I try and recover some ground and go to pick up my phern. Unfortunately, the Gods of Chance are on a cloud somewhere, rolling dice of their own. Somebody must've rolled a six because, as I bend down, the hostages in my stomach see a chink of daylight, a possible escape route. And they decide to call for help. Loudly.

IM: *Scrabbles for Elven Cloak of Invisibility* *Finds nothing* *Dies of shame*

My EM doesn't know what to do, so it just pulls the plug. Fearing a possible jailbreak and with no other options on the plate, I freeze, bent double, with one arm outstretched and a probable trail of green smoke pluming from my backside.

IM: *Maybe they're deaf...?*

The hysteria that follows says otherwise. The girls turn and walk away, their footsteps beating out much the same rhythm as my racing heart. And, just as they think they're out of sight, the word "Geek" is carried back to me by the treacherous northern winds.

IM: *This is tragic. Seriously.*

"Archie! Over here!" Jane's waving and staging her own mini-opera outside Ye Olde Coffee Shoppe, just so that everyone in the city is aware that I'm completely incapable of being on my own for extended periods of time. I cross the road, hating myself for my mere, fart-firing, poo-retaining existence.

"And who were those 'young ladies'?" she smiles conspiratorially, waggling her eyebrows up and down.

IM: *I have a clear shot. Just tell me when.*

"Wanted to know the time," I mutter.

"They're very friendly up here. Must be a northern thing."

Must be. But Geeks are Geeks, wherever you are. Remembering R2 in my pocket, I check my phern again. It's Beggsy, but, thankfully, no photo this time:

Dude! BIG party news! Speak Monday!

Great. There's no time to call him now. I'm just going to have to wait to find out what went down last night. Why Beggsy can't be straight with me, I've no idea, but it's like some form of long-distance torture.

Sarah and Chris. It's got to be Sarah and Chris.

"Archie ... are you all right? Is everything OK?" My stepmother's voice drops from its usual stadium levels to something like normal volume. If I were braver, this would be the perfect moment to unburden myself – emotionally, at least – and 'fess up that I've been hacked off about the party. It would be the sensible thing to do; have the row or conversation or whatever and then everyone gets to start over. But I don't want to; I don't want to give Jane – or Dad, for that matter – any glimpses into my private life. It's called "private" for a reason.

IM: *The "life" bit's debatable, though. Private existence?*

My EM quickly salvages a smile from the murky depths.

"Yeah, I'm fine! Why?"

"You just haven't seemed your usual, chatty self. I wondered if there was something on your mind, that's all."

IM: *Last chance, kid...*

"No ... I ... ah ... I've got a bit of stomach ache. Probably the food on the train."

IM: **Double-handed facepalm**

"Oh!" Jane looks horrified. "Ghastly muck! I'll make you some sandwiches for the journey back."

"Thanks."

I've got to get a grip. My sour mood is obviously being picked up on and, apart from ruining my limited time with Dad, it could also lead to further questioning. I sit at the table, resolving to cheer the hell up and offer Dad a helping hand. I shall clear my mind of all things Sarah and Chris and focus on the here and now. Tonight shall be a Games Night.

By the time we get back home, via York Minster and Whip-Ma-Whop-Ma-Gate (small street, big name), and with a solid wall of silence built between Lucas and Dad, it's early evening and I feel like I've just won the Olympic Gold for Cross-country Smiling. While the occasional rumble from my stomach predicts an oncoming storm, the only motion passed is that there's going to be fish and chips for tea, which is greeted by Jane with such an appreciative groan that I think I've just seen her Sex Face™. It's not something I want to remember.

IM: *Stores image to be replayed at inconvenient moment*

With Lucas, Steven and Izzy watching TV, I hit my room and pop the blister packs I bought in town. There's a fighter, a wizard, a cleric and a skulking thief. With time against me, I opt for a black-out – spraying the miniatures with Chaos Black and, as soon as they're dry, give them some base colours. There's not much more I can do to them, other than tinting up their weapons and armour; they're fairly basic, but I can always add the details at a later date.

IM: *It's all in the details.*

The sound of the front door and Dad bellowing up the stairs about fish and chips finally brings the curtain down on my Quiet Time and I head down to join the assembly in the lounge, resolving to undertake my mission to get Dad and Lucas onside with each other.

IM: *It's that time again! *Coughs* Bom-bom-BOM-bom…*

OK, so Yorkshire fish and chips are pretty good, but they seem to stop just below my Adam's apple – I'm running out of space. And the way Jane's going on about it, you'd think nobody'd ever had it before. The first few bites are each accompanied by her Sex Face™, just to ram the point home. Dad's not much better: he offers up a few throaty groans interspersed with satisfied chuckles. It's like listening to the soundtrack of one of those films that I shouldn't have seen but might've done, depending on who's asking.

I think it's time to make my play.

IM: *Bom-bom-BOM-bom...*

"Guys," I offer up, mainly to the kids, "I was wondering... I've got this new version of Dungeons and Dragons upstairs and I haven't tested it yet... Would you be up for a game after tea?"

Lucas looks at me a bit suspiciously, but Steven and Izzy are in. Dad flicks me a look that's a mixture of pride, approval and gratitude. Jane's probably the most excited of all of them.

"Ooh, yes!" she gushes. "Can I be a dragon?"

IM: *I hate to tell you this, but...*

"It's not quite like that," I smile painfully. "I'll go and get the game and set up."

I go to my room and have a sudden realization: in all my efforts to help my dad build bridges and having accidentally skunk-sprayed a bunch of girls outside Games Workshop, I've overlooked the blindingly obvious – if you're going to play a Game, you need monsters! For experienced adventurers, such as me and my mates, this wouldn't be a problem: you simply pretend, you use your imagination. But I don't think the under-tens will be satisfied with this suggestion and I haven't got time to paint the three goblins in the drawer.

I head back down to the lounge with my rule books and announce the problem.

"I didn't get any monsters." I say stupidly.

"Oh no!" Jane declaims. "Is it important? Do we need them?" If I was Emperor Palpatine, this would be a blue-lightning moment.

IM: *With possible full stormtrooper assault.*

"Yes," I mutter through my glowing cheeks. "We kind of do."

"Oh dear."

"Have you kids got any plastic monsters or anything like that?" I don't think Dad fully understands the problem; to play a game of Dungeons & Dragons, you need proper miniatures, conduits for the imagination – not a bunch of half-chewed plastic farm animals. You wouldn't ask Gandalf to fend off the Balrog with a magician's wand – it's the same principle.

"I know!" Steven announces, like someone's just put two hundred and forty volts through him. "My Lego men!"

IM: *Bom-bom-BOM-bom…*

Two seconds later, he's back with a plastic tub

brimming with Lego men. And two seconds after that, I'm frantically rooting through them with him to see if there's anything that'll pass for a monster. Surprisingly, Lego have got a few things up their plastic sleeve and it only takes a couple of minutes to find three skeletons, a couple of zombies, some *Star Wars* aliens, some *Harry Potter* wizards and an assortment of *Lord of the Rings* monsters that pass muster. There're even some swords and daggers to play with. It's not ideal, but it's better than nothing.

It's only as I put up my Dungeon Master's screen that I suddenly realize I might feel a bit embarrassed about this. Dungeons & Dragons is a world that, until now, I've only ever shared with my mates. It's for Geeks to lose themselves in, to forget for a while that we are weak and weedy and to spread our imaginary wings and fly. In playing the Game here, I'm opening up a side of my life to two people who have no real interest and whose imaginary wings were clipped a long time ago. It suddenly feels very, very weird. And I suddenly feel very, very exposed. Just as I would if Mum found out that the real reason I keep those Next catalogues under my bed isn't due to my fevered interest in fashion.

"Can we play now?" Izzy's boredom threshold sends the fish and chip papers to the bin and everyone sits round the table expectantly.

IM: *Doo-di-doooo… Do-di-doooo…*

"OK, Archie – what do we do?" Jane's voice is verging on hysteria. I briefly imagine bringing her down with a tranquilizer gun.

Ordinarily, I'd start with some background to the adventure, hint at some clues, drop in a red herring or two and add a sprinkling of atmosphere. But judging by the already wavering attention of the two younger kids, I'm going to have to thin this dungeon soup right down. I quickly tell them they have to find a crystal and kill lots of monsters, before telling them who they are: Dad's the fighter, Steven's the wizard, Izzy's an elf, Lucas is a cleric and Jane is a thief. Unnervingly, only Jane is giving this her full attention, her glasses reflecting the light, making her look like some grinning owl. Lucas looks like he'd rather be anywhere else but here, steadily ignoring Dad's uphill attempts to engage him in any sort of conversation.

I know Dad's coming across as an epic fail but, if I'm honest, Lucas is really starting to piss me off.

IM: *Probably because he reminds you of how you used to be with Tony.*

"OK," I sigh, without making it sound too much like I'd rather be slicing the soles of my feet with a potato peeler and dancing in seawater, "You've wandered through a forest until you see a door set in the rocks in front of you. What do you want to do?"

Jane squeals and claps her hands, throwing the question out in an excited whisper.

"What shall we do?"

"Open it?" Lucas sounds surprised at his mother's inability to spot the blindingly obvious.

"Good idea!" she declares. "We want to open it!"

IM: *Mwa-ha-ha-haaa! Everything is proceeding as planned…*

"OK. How do we open the door?" Jane asks breathlessly.

"You have to work out who's the best person to do it," I explain. "You don't know if it's locked or anything. It might even be rigged with a trap." I don't know how much more obvious I can make it, short of saying: "You're the thief. Open it."

"Is it?"

"What?"

"Rigged with a trap? Or locked?"

"I can't tell you that," I say, trying to keep the grating frustration out of my voice.

"So how do we know?"

"You're the thief. Open it."

IM: *It happened.*

"But *I* want to open it!" Izzy really needs to shut up.

"But Mummy's the thief, darling, and there might be traps."

"Can I do some magic on it?" At least Steven's showing some initiative.

"You could, but you don't have an Open Door spell."

"Why not?"

"You just haven't, that's all." I'm trying not to sound unkind, but I'm sure I can feel my veins tightening with the stress of it all.

"What am I?"

IM: *Oh, it's awake!*

"You're a warrior, Dad. A fighter."

"Why don't I just kick it down or chop it up or something like that?"

"No, darling! There might be traps!"

"Are there, Archie?"

"I can't tell you," I repeat, wearing one of those grins that show both sets of teeth.

"Oh."

"I know! Why don't *I* open the door? I'm a thief!"

IM: *You said it.*

"Great!" I gasp, as the fog lifts from everyone's eyes. "Check your character sheet and roll the D20 against your Intelligence score."

"The what?"

"Sorry – the twenty-sided die."

"Which one's that?" This is starting to feel like I'm giving a lecture on subatomic physics in an old

142

people's home.

"The blue one."

"OK. Twelve. What does that mean?"

Behind my screen, I roll a die, but don't even bother to look at the score.

"It means you've managed to open the door, but you didn't spot that the lock was rigged."

IM: *Throws rule book out of the window*

"What does that mean?"

"Oh dear." I roll and ignore another die. "It means that you've sprung a trap. Metal darts fly out of the wall, taking two Hit Points off everyone."

IM: *So chew on that!*

"Oh." Jane looks genuinely disappointed. Having established my position as the Alpha Male, I carry on.

"The door creaks open." At this point, Izzy and Steven make creaking noises. I can't tell you how much I hate it. "A horrible smell wafts out of the tunnel in front of you."

"What does it smell like?" Izzy wants to know.

"Do you remember that smell in the Viking Centre – the one in the Vikings' house? Well, it smells like that."

Izzy holds her nose and Steven makes a gagging noise. I don't look at Jane.

"What do you want to do?"

"I want to go in!" says Steven. I think he's starting to get it.

"You all have to roll against your Initiative to see who goes first."

"*I* want to go first!" No prizes for guessing who said that.

"But, darling," Jane smoothes, "we have to roll the dice. Archie said so and he's in charge."

"I don't want to roll the dice!"

"But, Izzy, you have to."

"No, it's fine," I sigh. "She can go in first. But if everyone else rolls, then we'll know who's where, kind of thing."

IM: *Doo-di-doooo...*

The order of play works out as: Izzy, Steven, Lucas, Jane and Dad. Dad's not too chuffed with being last, but I tell him that it's the best place for a fighter, he can protect their backs. It shuts him up.

"You're walking through the dungeon, when you spy an old treasure chest in front of you." I put a Lego brick on the table, my heart sinking. "What do you want to do?"

"Open it!" cheers Jane. I decide to forget the whole dice-rolling thing and tell her she's opened it.

"A skeleton warrior jumps out." Compounding my position as The World's Greatest Fool™, I put down a Lego skeleton, holding a plastic sword.

"*I* want treasure!" Izzy pouts, sounding as far from an elf as you can possibly get.

IM: *DAH-dum!*

"We have to fight the skeleton, darling. Look – isn't he scary?"

"*I* want treasure!" And with that, Izzy starts crying.

"*Some*body's tired," Jane coos. "*Some*body needs to go to bed."

This is supposed to be the bit where Dad and Lucas get to team up; Lucas can use his clerical powers to paralyze the undead creature and Dad can then hack it to bits. But Izzy doesn't seem to want my plan to work.

"No! No! I'm not tired! I'm not!" But with every protestation, she gets more and more teary until, with an apology that I'm sure she doesn't mean, Jane scoops Izzy off to bed. Me, Dad and the two boys sit, looking at each other.

"Can we keep playing?" Steven asks, warming my Geeky little soul.

"I think so," Dad says. And then there's a funny look in his eye like he's just had An Idea.

"OK," I say, wondering what's going on. "The skeleton comes towards you, waving its sword…"

Suddenly Dad detonates to the right of me. "…And we go and kill it!" he shouts. "Come on, men!" And then he's grabbing everyone's miniatures and pushing them up against their Lego adversary. My jaw drops even further when he starts making sword noises and killing sounds.

Lucas echoes my sentiment, but in a far more direct manner.

"Why do you have to be so *weird* all the time?" he blasts. His eyes mist up with tears and his jaw sets as he stands. "Why can't you just be *normal*?" And then there's a stifled noise from his throat and he bolts for the door and up the stairs.

Me, Dad and Steven look at each other again.

"Oops," Dad says eventually. "Looks like I blew it there."

"You going to go after him?" There's more challenge in the question than I intend, but I'm still reeling from Dad's ability to mess things up.

IM: *Like father, like son…*

"Don't know. He might just need time to cool off…"

But he doesn't. I know he doesn't, because I've heard Lucas's song before – I've sung it myself. And when you walk/run away from a situation like that and you shut yourself in your room, the truth is that, no matter how angry you are, all you really want is for someone to come and make it better. Right now, that's what Dad should be doing. But, looking at my dad, I can see that he's scared. He might be bigger than me and tougher than me and all the things that are supposed to make him a father, but he's out of his depth and he knows it.

"*Dad!*" This time, I give way to the exasperation I'm feeling, but then I realize Steven's still here and cut it short. The kid doesn't need to know what a Tosser his stepfather's being – and Dad doesn't need another member of his new family to turn against him. But Dad's determined to dig his way to the earth's core.

"Steven," he mutters, "I think it's time you went up as well."

"But it's not my bedtime!" Steven looks aghast.

"Go on. Up you go." There's a hardness in Dad's voice that means the conversation's over and, with a film of tears glittering in his eyes, Steven leaves the room. A silence fills the void between me and Dad. It gets uncomfortable, so I stand up and try and get myself together; it's time I said something.

"Dad…" I begin gently, "What…?" My hand makes a motion like I'm weighing the air.

IM: *It's pretty heavy.*

"What's going on?" I manage finally.

"Teething problems, I guess." But I'm sure he knows it's more than that, from the way he's staring at his wine glass.

"But, Dad – that's *twice* you've blown it with him. Twice. Big style."

Dad looks up sharply, his fingers splayed out in a sort

of claw on the rim of his glass.

"I'm sure it looks pretty easy from where you're standing, son. But let me tell you, it isn't. It's hard."

"I know..."

"No, you don't. You'll never know until you've had a child of your own and you're trying to be a dad to someone else's." Beneath his steel, Dad suddenly looks old and tired, but it's his words that burn me. I'm tired of being where other people want me to be and tired of being what other people want me to be and it all comes out in four, granite-hard syllables.

"I *do* know, Dad," I shoot back.

Dad looks me straight in the eyes and sits back, like he's waiting for something; our horns lock across the living room.

"And what do you know, Archie?"

"I know what it's like to have a stepfather and I know what it's like to *be* a stepkid." I can feel my lips tremble angrily round each word as it crosses the chasm between us. And they hit home. Dad blinks, flinches and seems to shrink, before sagging slightly.

"Yeah. You do." I can hear the white flag of surrender in his weariness. And then Jane marches in through the door.

"Is the game over?" she asks brightly.

IM: *She's all about timing, that one.*

148

"I think everyone got a bit tired," I blurt, my EM punching up a second-hand smile. "I think I'm going to go up as well."

"Looks like it's just you and me, then, dear!" Jane announces to my wilting father as she tops up her wine.

"Night, Archie," he smiles sadly. "Thanks for tonight. It was a good try." His words carry a double meaning: father-and-son code.

"Night, Dad," I reply. "Maybe we'll have another go, another time."

I feel sad as I go up the stairs. At least when Dad lived near me, I could go and see him without everyone else in tow. The only real moments we've had alone are the moments we've come close to having a row – and it's not even about anything that's really to do with me. Treacherously, I want the night to pass as quickly as possible.

I want to go home.

SEVEN

After yesterday's drama, there seems to be a bit of a fog in the house, but no one's talking about it. For most of the morning I'm holed up in the Lair Mark Two, giving Steven a masterclass in miniature painting. And actually, he's not bad and picks up the basic concepts of washing and highlighting pretty quickly.

IM: *Welcome to the Geekhood, Brother Steven. Study hard and you too can achieve a lonely life, devoid of female company and any other form of social interaction...*

After winding up the painting class and packing my bags, I call Beggsy but it goes straight through to answerphone, so I head downstairs to find out what's going on. Jane's in the kitchen, rummaging noisily in the fridge.

"I've made you some desert food for the train, Archie."

"Sorry?"

"Desert food." There's something pretending to be a punchline straining at the bars; I can see it on her face. And there's no option but to follow it through.

IM: *Facial clamps on standby; we'll have that smile up and running in about an hour...*

"Desert food? I ... uh ... I don't..."

"You'll never starve in the desert, because of the sand which is there!"

IM: *Tries to produce Force-lightning* *Fails*

There's a sickening silence, where Jane looks me expectantly in the eyes, obviously anticipating some reaction or other – but I honestly haven't got a clue what she's talking about.

"The *sand which* is there..." she repeats slowly, raising her eyebrows as far as they'll go.

IM: *Sandwiches, for God's sake! It sounds like sandwiches!*

"Ah!" I exclaim. "*Sand* which is. Yes. I get it. Sandwiches."

But I can't even muster a laugh; instead I just nod a bit too much. Jane, however, seems oblivious and goes back to the fridge, trilling a happy tune to herself. Luckily, Dad appears and mans the kettle. But their combined presence is too much for me and I duck out as tactfully as I can, wearing as pleasant a smile as possible to head off any questions in advance.

And there's something I've got to do. I have a mission to fulfil.

IM: *Sighs* Here we go... Bom-bom-BOM-bom...

I lumber up the stairs, feeling the weight of last night's fish and chips pushing against my stomach. Lucas's bedroom is at the end of the landing and I walk up and knock on the door gently. When there's no answer, I slowly turn the doorknob and step inside. In the morning sun that's streaming through the window, I see him sat on his bed; a tight-lipped scowl with sulky eyes.

"Hey, mate. How're you doing?"

Lucas just shrugs.

"D'you want to talk? About my weird dad?" I throw in the last sentence, hoping to get a laugh or, at the very least, a smile. But I just get another shrug.

IM: *Bom-bom-BOM-bom…*

I slide down the wall by the door, until I'm sitting on the carpet, my arms resting on my knees.

IM: *Now would be a bad time to cut the cheese.*

I clench up and look around the room, thinking of something to say. It's cool, as nine-year-olds' bedrooms go; a few Minecraft posters, some DVDs, a couple of NERF swords and a bunch of toys in a plastic box. I rack my brain trying to think of an opening line – something profound, something meaningful, something that will appeal to him.

"God, adults can be such dorks, can't they?" The words leap out of my mouth before I've even had time to exercise any quality control.

"He's worse when you're here," he shoots back.

Wow. Wasn't expecting that one. Somehow, I'm part of this. Mentally, I try and root through my Bag of

Experience™ to find something to build a bridge between us, but the Gods of Circumstance have other ideas.

"Archie!" Dad bellows up the stairs. "Time to go! Shake a leg, buddy!"

Conversation over. Taking my cue, I get awkwardly to my feet and leave Lucas alone, without the time to offer him anything to cling to. Part of me knows that it's not me that should be talking to him but, after Dad's comedy wink at the Viking Centre, I think I'm on the "Not To Be Trusted" List as well. But with time against me, this is a mission that I'll have to come back to.

IM: *Bom?*

Fast-forward the journey to the station and I'm standing beside my train carriage, facing my dad, my stepbrothers, my stepsister and Jane. Jane rushes in for a clothy, rib-cracking, wrestling-hold of a hug and Izzy and Steven follow her lead. Lucas opts for an abrupt handshake. Last on the hugs list is Dad. It's only when he speaks and I hear that his voice is a bit thick that I realize he's close to tears. My throat burns in response: a silent whale song that acknowledges how much I'll miss him.

"Safe journey, son." Dad smiles awkwardly. "Send us a text when you're back."

Man, I feel guilty. It hasn't been a great weekend for either of us and I've only added to it all by wandering around with a Face Like A Farmer's Arse On A Frosty Morning ©Beggsy for most of it. I know I've tried to help, but I'm also aware that I've behaved like a bit of a sulky jerk.

IM: *Post-Jerk Stress Disorder. A common complaint among many teenage guys.*

But, despite the fact that there's barely anyone else on the train and I can hide behind the seat in front of me, I can't afford the luxury of tears. Dad and the rest appear at the window next to where I'm sitting and wait. I sit hard on my emotions and smile a cracked smile through the glass. Dad picks up on it and, just as the train lurches to go, he steps forward, puts a hand on the window and mouths "I love you".

IM: *It's like that scene out of* Star Trek *where Spock dies. *Makes Vulcan salute**

My throat feels like the centre of a sandstorm and my eyes are hot and blurry, but I hold on and mouth the same back. I thought I could hack this, but now I'm not so sure; I didn't think it would be this hard. Just as the train leaves the station, I briefly see Dad's shoulders hunch and Jane sweeps an arm round him and then they're gone.

I feel alone. Dad's got Jane, Mum's got Tony... Who have I got?

IM: *Chris and Sarah. At a party.*

I need something to take my mind off things, so I blink furiously and root through my bag, until I find my copy of *The Dark Knight Returns*. I don't think I see the first couple of pages properly because I'm still blinking back boiling tears, but the Caped Crusader soon has me in his jagged embrace, as he gets into another fight with the Mutant leader. But this time, he doesn't try and fight him on his own terms. He does it with brutal, surgical precision, bringing him down in a mudhole in Gotham, humiliating him in front of his troops. Everyone wants a piece of him, even the police, but he sticks to what he knows is right.

IM: *Are we paying attention, everyone?*

I wish I was a haunted multi-millionaire with rippling biceps and anger-management issues.

"Hey there, *BOY*friend!" A false American accent returns me to my usual, unimposing height and my muscular shoulders quickly deflate back to their real-life, invisible status. It's Clare, all glasses and chest. I do not check out her rack. At all.

"Hey, *GIRL*friend," I return. "What's up?"

"*Well!*" she replies, storing her bag on the shelf above and settling into her seat. "I was thinking about us this weekend…"

IM: *"Us"? "US"? Ohmygod! She said "US"!*

Already there's a familiar feeling in my trousers;

it's like the thing's got ears.

"...and how you like that Sarah girl and how I like Oliver..."

IM: *False alarm. Stand down.*

"...and I had an idea..."

"'K..." I try, but fail, to keep the note of suspicion out of my voice.

"Don't worry, it's nothing bad," she coos, before adding, with a very bright twinkle in her eye, "Well, nothing *too* bad..."

"'K..." Same as before.

"Sarah and Oliver don't know what they're missing, right?"

This is a debatable point. I think Sarah may have a vague idea about just what she's missing: an insecure Geek who spends his spare time inhabiting fantasy worlds and discussing the finer points of *Star Wars*. If Oliver doesn't know what he's missing, he might want to think about getting hold of some textbooks on the female anatomy.

IM: *Not that you're looking.*

"What if," she begins, "what if they were suddenly to feel a bit unsure about the way we feel about them?"

"Rii-iight." Same again, just a different word.

"So what if *we* were suddenly both unavailable?"

I've always thought I was pretty intelligent, but I can't see where this is going.

"What d'you mean 'unavailable'?"

"Supposing you had a girlfriend and I had a boyfriend? Wouldn't that make them *jealous*?" Clare says the last word like it tastes of chocolate.

"But how do we do that? I mean, I'm sure you could get a boyfriend any time you like, but girls don't exactly queue up outside my house. And wouldn't it be a bit lame to go out with someone just to make somebody else jealous?"

IM: *Well said!*

Clare rolls her rock 'n' roll librarian eyes, shakes her head and deflates with a groan.

"*Listen,*" she scowls, obviously frustrated. "You're not hearing me. You and me – we pretend to go out with each other; a 'fauxmance'. Get it?"

There's a bit in *King Kong* where the filmmaker guy leads his clueless crew through some fog without telling them where they're going. But as soon as they step off the boat, they realize they're on Skull Island. I've just disembarked.

IM: *This is a Girl Plan.*

I've just been given an invite to a How Girls Think Party and it's in full swing. Even with a gun pointed at my head, I wouldn't have thought of this. It's brilliant. No one gets hurt, no one else has to know and no one can prove it's not true.

IM: *The treacherous song of the Siren! *Puts fingers in ears**

"But what if it doesn't work?"

"Then you're no worse off than you are now, are you? If they don't go out with us, you could always play the heartbroken hero. That'd do it."

"It's genius," I murmur. "Genius. A fauxmance. What do we do?"

"Thought you'd like it," Clare grins. "OK. Here's the plan…"

The plan is so simple, it's breathtaking. We Facebook each other, like we're going out. Sarah hasn't dropped me from her friends list yet, so she'll see the posts and so will Oliver. On top of that, our friends will hear about it and there'll be a buzz about the fact that we're "dating".

IM: *What's that up ahead? The Rocks of Despair!*

I mentally roll a D10 against my Honesty. With a minus two modifier for Inexperience. And fail. I'm in. A hundred per cent. No questions asked.

"But you can't tell anyone, OK? Not a soul."

"Not even my mates?" I don't know if I can keep a secret this big from the gang.

"*E*specially not your mates. The fewer people that know, the less chance there is of somebody blowing it for you. 'K?"

"K."

"So, *boy*friend," she laughs, "what music do you like? What's on Archie's iPod?"

I name a few bands and get a groan in response. "*Misery* music!" she mutters, pulling out her iPod and sticking an earphone in my ear. "Check this out." Sticking the other earphone in hers, she hits play and suddenly I'm listening to Lady Gaga's latest album. Not what I'd normally do on a Sunday. What's even weirder is that, as we go through the tunes and have a little bit of a chat over the top of them, I actually start to enjoy it.

IM: *This is Not Good.*

If my mates were here, my IM'd be right. But they're not and I'm sat with Clare, a pretty rock 'n' roll librarian, who I don't fancy, who might be about to save my love life and who's telling me about some festival that's going on near her school in a couple of weeks and how Oliver's going and how she wants to go, and I'm actually enjoying Girl Music. Sure, I feel a bit guilty about it, but not enough to make her turn it off.

IM: *Like you could, Geek Boy.*

Eventually, we reach her station and with a "Later, *boy*friend!" she's gone.

I can't wait to go on Facebook tonight.

159

Mum picks me up from the station, giving me a hug that doesn't threaten to rupture my major organs and doesn't smell like a Viking's armpit; it is just right. We hop into the car, my stomach gently starting to protest again.

"So, how was York?" Mum asks, as we drive through town.

"Yeah; it was fine."

"And what about your dad's new house?"

"Yeah; it was OK."

"Did you have a good time?"

"Yeah; not bad."

I catch Mum doing one of those staggered blinks that says these aren't the replies she was looking for, but she doesn't say anything. The problem I seem to be having is that I feel any information I give is going to be privately weighed up for potential threats, like I'm suddenly involved in a Which Parent Do You Love The Most? competition. I could lay it on the line and moan on about Jane and Lucas and the smell of cloth, but then I'd feel like I'm betraying Dad. And if I say that it was great seeing Dad, then I'm going to feel like I'm being disloyal to Mum. Suddenly everything I say could be taken the wrong way, so my EM pulls the power on the Mouth Department and we travel the rest of the journey in silence.

"Archie," Mum says, as we get out of the car. I can hear a question waiting to be asked.

"Yeah?"

For a moment, Mum just looks at me like she's going to say something important. Instead, she gives me one of those Mona Lisa smiles that Yoda does: all-knowing and wise, but tempered by the weight of the universe. She draws me in for another quick hug.

"You know I'm only being interested, don't you?" she says over my shoulder.

"Yeah. Sorry. I had a really nice weekend," I lie. "Really good."

"Good – I'm glad. Come on, then. In we go," she says, like everything's OK. "Go and freshen up; dinner'll be on the table in half an hour. It's your favourite, roast lamb."

"What – real lamb?" For all I know, it could be one of Tony's soya-bean creations in a woolly jumper.

"Yes – real lamb."

IM: *And all is as it should be.*

I drag my bloated self up the two flights of stairs to my Lair, dump my bag on the bed and send Dad a quick text:

Arrived. See you soon. Love Archie x

With that out of the way, I fire up the laptop and hit Facebook to see if my new "girlfriend" is there.

IM: *There's still time to back out!*

There's a friend request, with a message attached:

Hey, boyfriend! Confirm me and we can start posting! But can you change your profile pic? No offence, but you look a bit young for me and we've got to make this believable! Girlfriend xxx

For a second, my ego is affronted – I *want* to look old enough, I *want* her to fall in love with me and I *want* it to be utterly believable that she would. And then I remember that I'm a fourteen-year-old Geek who looks young for his age with a pronounced absence of hair follicles on his upper lip. Grudgingly, I trawl the net, looking for images that might put me in a better light. Eventually, I hit on an old favourite: Han Solo. It's that classic pose where he's under the Millennium Falcon, blasting at stormtroopers. I upload the photo to my profile and confirm Clare's request. And wait.

While I'm waiting, I check out Beggsy's Timeline to see if there are any clues about his "big party news". There's nothing. Just as I'm considering messaging Ravi or ringing Matt, my Facebook Timeline announces one new story:

Hey, Gorgeous. Thanks for a fantastic weekend. You sure know how to show a girl a good time! Can't wait to see you again. Xxx

IM: *No backing out now.*

Clare's profile pic is just right; obviously taken at a party where she got dressed up and there's enough of her rack showing to make it suggestive without being overtly sexy. Not that I'm looking.

IM: *Your go. If we're really going through with this...*

OK. I re-read Clare's message. She knows what she's doing: insinuating that *something* has happened, but without saying what it is. I need to reply in kind but, never having had a girlfriend, not even a pretend one, I'm a bit stuck for words. Should I appear romantic or like some red-blooded rogue?

IM: *Pretend it's Sarah. I mean, if you REALLY want to mess things up.*

Genius! If I pretend it's her, I can show her the kind of guy that I would like to be if I was her boyfriend.

IM: *Romantic, it is. But with manly undertones. Dig deep.*

It takes me eight deleted attempts before I'm finally happy with what I write:

I would rather spend one lifetime with you than live forever in this world, alone.

It's inspired by *The Lord of the Rings*, natch – with a dash of Archie thrown in, to give it that personal touch.

I hit post.

In a little under thirty seconds, my Facebook beeps at me; somebody wants to chat. It's Clare:

Back up, Archie! We're not getting married! Delete it and try again!

IM: *Hmmm. Just what do girls want their ideal man to be?*

It's a good question but, while I'm sure I'll find the answer when I hit adulthood, it's a bit beyond me now. As I delete the offending love note, I remember my dad giving me some advice about just being yourself a little while ago but, in the Real World of Lying Convincingly, that seems ridiculous.

IM: *Think Han Solo! What would the cynical Corellian smuggler have to say?*

And then it comes:

Hey – you're not so bad yourself.

No kiss; it's complimentary in a don't-really-care kind of way. I'm sure I read somewhere that girls like that sort of thing.

IM: *And where would that be –* White Dwarf?

My page scrolls down suddenly, announcing that

164

Clare is "In a Relationship". With me. There's even a big, pink heart alongside the text, just in case anyone's in any doubt as to what it means.

IM: *Mission: Improbable is GO! Bom-bom-BOM-bom...*

I stare at the screen stupidly for a moment. There's something bizarre about seeing my name next to a cartoon heart. But instead of it feeling like a triumph, it feels weirdly empty, like I've betrayed a bit of myself – the part of me that always throws a secret look into florist windows, wishing that I had somebody to send some flowers to. The part of me that wants romance to be true, even though everybody else says it's not cool. The part of me that would throw my cape in a puddle just to keep Sarah's feet dry has been let down, like a big, pink, heart-shaped helium balloon.

IM: *Oh, grow a pair, Romeo! This is your mission – get on with it!*

A relationship request comes down the wire, and with a surprised sigh, I confirm it and go to the update page. There's a drop-down, marked "Relationship Status", which gives me more options than I thought were possible. I don't even know what an "Open Relationship" is, but I don't think I'm in one and, much as I'd like to pick the "It's Complicated" option, I highlight "In a Relationship" and click save. My lie is now in the public domain.

My weary resignation is quickly replaced by fear: I don't know anything about this Oliver guy. What if he's some muscle-bound killer type with a thing for hurting Geeks?

IM: *Note to self: must conduct more experiments with gamma radiation.*

I check through Clare's friends and find the only Oliver there. He's good-looking. And, yes, he looks like he could grow a moustache way quicker than me. I curse my facial baldness. A squeal from R2 wakes me from my Hormone Envy:

gd 2 c u soz if I ws grmpy spk sn lv dad x

Reading Dad's horrendous text-talk and his muted apology seems to provoke a physical reaction in me.

IM: *Irritable Vowel Syndrome.*

For a moment, I'm in one of the *Alien* films; something's trying to get out of my stomach and, with the usual exit out of order, it's trying to make a break for it through my navel.

IM: *The Time Has Come…*

Running when you're nearly doubled over with abdominal cramps is pretty tricky, but I make it. I bolt the door and, for a split second, all my senses revel in the fact that I'm in *my* bathroom, in *my* house, looking at *my* toilet.

IM: *Self-destruct sequence initiated… Prepare to abandon ship…*

What happens next will remain between me and the bathroom. Suffice to say that a medieval exorcism would have looked less dramatic. Job done, I stand on the landing, marvelling at how weightless I feel.

And then something else happens: I realize that I am *starving*. Facebook's going to have to wait – the smell of roast lamb is suddenly overpowering and I charge downstairs to the kitchen.

A few minutes later, I'm filling the newly made canyon in my stomach. Even Tony seems to forget his diet, although there's less of the mighty Sarlacc about him with the roast potatoes and he's a lot less liberal with the salt. It could almost be the perfect family meal, if it wasn't for his repeated attempts to kill any canaries that might be in the vicinity.

About halfway through, there's a burst of heavy breathing from my trouser pocket. I pull it out: it's Beggsy ringing.

"Archie," Mum says, with a pained expression on her face, "can it wait until after dinner?"

"But it's Beggsy…"

"Please?"

"But, Mum…"

Darth's breathing apparatus cuts out, as Beggsy gets bored of waiting and hangs up.

"You can ring him later," Mum soothes. "Let's just see if we can enjoy a nice meal together."

With Beggsy gone, I don't seem to have a choice in the matter, but I practically inhale the rest of dinner, so that I can call him back. Much to Mum's weary frustration.

I race up the stairs to my Lair, clutching my phone. But just as I find Beggsy's number, I notice a small, brown package on my bed.

IM: *Could it be…?*

Yes, it could! I scrabble at the padded envelope, popping the bubble wrap as I go. Inside are two, brand-new elvish ear-tips.

IM: **Shouts* ELENDIL!*

Nothing else matters: I've *got* to try them on! I hit the bathroom and slide them over my ears. While the mirror isn't tuned into exactly the same station as what's playing in my head, they're not bad; maybe if I did something with my hair, I might achieve the willowy, mysterious look that I imagined. I head back to my Lair, feeling a bit like Orlando Bloom.

IM: *It's more Dobby than Legolas, let's be honest…*

An apologetic knock at the door signals Mum's

arrival, so I quickly kill the laptop.

"Everything all right, love?" A cup of tea is plonked on my painting desk and Mum sits on my bed. And then she starts laughing. "You found your package, then?"

"Yeah," I grin back, self-consciously. "Ears." I think of Jane as I say it. Not willingly, though.

"They look great," Mum giggles. "Did you ring Beggsy?"

"Uh … no. Kind of got distracted."

"So I see," Mum chuckles again, looking at my ears once more. "So, come on," she grins mischievously. "Are you going to tell me about your weekend, or not?"

There really is no end to my mother's nosiness, but I know it's not malicious; like she said, she's just being interested. But it looks like Beggsy is going to have to wait; no one escapes Mum's Spanish Inquisition. With a grudging laugh, I sip my tea.

"OK. What do you want to know?" My EM powers up a scowling smile, letting her know she's won and she wriggles on the end of the bed, making herself comfortable. But I'll only give her the edited highlights – she doesn't need to know about Jane the Pain or Dad and Lucas or the almost-row we had. Just the good stuff.

"What's the house like?" she smiles.

IM: *It's good to be home.*

169

EIGHT

Monday begins at 6.30am, with a feeling like molten wax on my stomach. As I realize what this sensation means, my brain mercilessly gives me a quick action replay of fragments of the dream that gave rise to the situation.

IM: *OhmyGOD! *Shudders* Nooo!*

This isn't the reaction I usually get after a dream of this variety. Usually there'll be a faint grin of satisfaction as I chalk up another Dreamworld Conquest™. But dreams of this variety usually don't feature my stepmother. In a horned helmet. And a metal bikini.

IM: *Gaaah! It must be Satanic possession or something! Call an exorcist!*

I just can't believe it. But the evidence is there on my stomach. It's like I've ignored a certain organ for too long and it's decided to have its revenge. All over my pyjamas.

IM: *But ... Jane! That's just a whole box of wrong!*

After a couple of minutes I accept that no amount of staring at the cold, hardening proof is going to make it go away.

IM: *You've got ten minutes to dispose of the bodies. All 300 million of them.*

As I dress, I weigh up my options: sneaking my PJs into the washing machine is a no-no – Mum'd spot them a mile off. And I used the old routine of scrubbing them by hand and pleading a toothbrushing disaster last week. In the end, for want of a better idea, I stuff them under my mattress, to be sorted at a later date.

Heading down to the bathroom, I bump into Mum on the landing.

"Morning, love," she smiles. "You're up early!"

IM: *You have no idea...*

"Uh ... yeah. S'pose I am." It's not the best answer in the world, but it's not even seven o'clock yet. Besides, my evil brain seems to have worn itself out creating images of my stepmother during the night. This thought hangs over me as I brush my teeth and all through breakfast. What's wrong with me? How could I even have a dream like that? I even feel awkward giving Mum my customary kiss goodbye as I set off for school.

I remain so lost in thought that I almost walk past Beggsy and the gang, who are waiting for me on the corner of Hamilton Road. As soon as I see them, my heart lurches and I brace myself to hear the news about Chris and Sarah. My EM powers up a smile and goes into Trying Not To Look Too Desperate mode.

"Hey, guys! Come on, then – fill me in: what happened?"

"Dude! *Dude!*" Beggsy bubbles, bouncing from foot to foot.

Ravi interrupts him with a deep chuckle. "Wait til you hear this, Archie – it's awesome!"

"It's *beyond* awesome!" Beggsy punctuates this with an actual jump. "It's *epic!*"

"Yeah? What is it? Did you get off with someone at Kirsty Ford's party?"

Ordinarily, this would prompt a series of snorts and looks that suggest I've lost my mind: Geeks don't get off with girls at parties, unless it's part of a game scenario developed by a Dungeon Master and the girl in question happens to be a sorceress with Mind Control Lipstick. This did happen once, but we were young and stupid. And there was no girl – it was all pretend.

IM: *Not a lot's changed.*

But, today, my throwaway gag gives way to a ripple of sly smiles and sideways looks. At Matt.

"What?" I goggle. "No WAY!" My amazement is turbo-boosted with a tidal wave of relief: it's not the Chris and Sarah news I was anticipating.

"Way," Ravi grins.

All eyes are on my red-headed friend and, boy, does he hate it. Matt's pretty awkward at the best of times but, right now, it looks like he's been stuffed; his arms are locked by his sides and his legs are so stiff there's a distinct possibility that his knees will pop out through the back. The only signs that he's alive are this weird, rocking thing he does on his feet and his fingers flexing and closing in jagged, nervous movements.

"I didn't get *off* with her," Matt scowls. "We just talked, that's all!"

IM: *By Geek standards, that pretty much counts as marriage.*

"And thanks for the vote of confidence," he adds sharply. "Mate.'"

Matt's done it; he's broken through the invisible but ultra-thick barrier that separates Geeks and Girls and Made Contact. And for it to be *Matt*, the Geekiest of us all...

"Who was it? What happened?"

Matt just scowls again and scans the pavement for answers.

"It was *Cait*-lyn, dude!" Beggsy beams, with wide-eyed wonder. "And she *talked back* to him!"

IM: *Rewinds audio* *Replays* Yep: he said "Caitlyn"...

"*CAIT-lyn?*" The name bursts out of my treacherous mouth, like a disbelieving cannonball.

"What d'you mean, 'CAIT-lyn'?" Matt squints, with a comeback no doubt armed and ready.

"Nothing – I'm just ... surprised! Way to go!" I laugh,

slapping him on the shoulder. He just sort of stands there and takes it, expressing neither happiness nor irritation. Or anything, really.

But what bothers me about CAIT-lyn is that she's the girl who called me "immature". Now on the Geek Scale of Insults, that's small potatoes, as they say in the movies. Really small ones; I've been called far worse and by far more threatening people. But what niggles me about that particular insult is that it was...

IM: ...*and still is...*

...a bit too accurate for comfort. But the next thought I have, is an even bigger one: Caitlyn is Sarah's best friend. Her "BFF". And that means that I'm already a step closer to Sarah, without even having tried. Anything I say about Clare will get straight to where it's supposed to. And I might even be able to get some information back.

IM: *Bom-bom-BOM-bom...*

The other guys are all staring at Matt with big, stupid grins on their faces, but the envy flying silently around has almost got its own flavour – to all intents and purposes, he is a Geek with a Girlfriend. I've got to admit that I'm feeling a little jealous, too, but Matt deserves his Moment of Glory.

"And what about you two losers?" I throw at Ravi and Beggsy. "You had your arms round *Kirsty Ford!*" This subject merits some discussion. If we were sat round the lunch table, it'd be as long and as detailed as the Council of Elrond.

"She's actually really nice," Ravi muses. "Obvious reasons aside."

"She liked The *Begg*ster…" Beggsy announces in some weird American accent.

"The who?" I laugh.

"The *Begg*ster. All the ladies wanted a piece of The *Begg*ster."

IM: *This could get annoying…*

"And who did The Beggster get off with?" It's a sneaky bit of bubble-bursting between two mates.

"The *Begg*ster worked the room," he nods, pulling his Cool Face. "The *Begg*ster has options."

"Yeah," Matt cuts in evenly, "And the options are that The Beggster can either stop talking like that or The Beggster gets a punch in the face." Matt's bubble-bursting technique is a bit less subtle than mine.

"But this is how The *Begg*ster talks."

"The only character who's earned the right to talk in the third person is the Incredible Hulk," Ravi states, seeing the opportunity for a bit of Geeky debate. "What powers has The Beggster got?"

"The *Begg*ster has the Powers of *Lurve*," The Beggster replies in his American accent.

"And how do they manifest?" Ravi wants to know. "Eye-rays? Flying ability? What?"

The conversation continues all the way to school: The Beggster announcing his sexy superpowers and the rest of us taking the mickey. But as we get closer to the gates and the crowds start to thicken, a few faces call out to him: "Yo, Beggster!" or just "Beggster!" The Beggster responds with a casual wink and a wave. And then Ravi's name is called out. And even Matt's, but he doesn't respond.

"What did you guys *do* at that party?" Not going to it looks to have been one of the worst things that's ever happened to me. My mates are slowly moving, by some form of social osmosis, into the Ranks of the Normal. And I'm not. The way things are going, I'll end up friendless as well as being girlfriendless – I'll be The Last Geek.

"We just showed up," Ravi shrugs. "We showed up and we talked to people."

"They showed up with The *Begg*ster!" Cue jeering and rolling eyes from the rest of us.

"And haven't *you* got some big news, Archie?" Matt suddenly smarms with a sly smile.

IM: *Looks for Fauxmance Script* *Finds nothing*

My EM responds by gouging out a smile that threatens to split my head in half.

"Have I?"

"Who's Clare?" Ravi baritones.

IM: *You arrive at a fork in the road. One path is signposted "Truth" and the other is signposted "Treacherous Lies". What do you want to do?*

This is one part of Clare's brilliant plan that I hadn't factored in: lying to your best mates. Dimly, I can hear Clare's instructions in the back of my head: "The fewer people that know, the less chance there is of somebody blowing it for you..."

Unfortunately, it makes horrible, treacherous sense; the fewer people who know the truth, the less likelihood there is of it being exposed as a lie. But, between Geeks, this is a Big Lie. And if I go through with it, I'll also be elevated to the position of a Geek with a Girlfriend. Without actually having one.

IM: *Yet. *Whistles innocently**

"Ha! Oh, yeah – you've been on Facebook, then?" I don't think I sound that convincing.

"Ye-eah!" Ravi booms like I'm an idiot.

IM: *No comment.*

"So ... who is she, then, dude?" Despite Beggsy's apparent manic delight, I can see what's going on under the surface. Geeks fear Change like Frodo feared the Nazgûl and its shadow is a long one; I can already tell that he and Ravi are envisaging the end of our gaming group, friendships crumbling and the destruction of civilization as they know it. Which only serves to make me feel even worse. But, I've committed.

IM: *Bom-bom-BOM-bom...*

"Uh... Just some girl I met on the train to see my dad..." This isn't as easy as I thought; I should have come up with a back story.

IM: *But this isn't a game, Archie...*

"*Just some girl?*" Ravi repeats, before turning to the rest of the guys. "You should check out her profile pic – she's hot!"

"Dude!" Beggsy squeals at a pitch that probably causes every dog in the vicinity's eardrums to explode. "Have you ... you know...?"

"What?"

"You *know*... Have you done anything?" Thankfully, he drops his voice to a more reasonable level, as we pass through the school gates.

"*What?* No!" I really wasn't expecting this; two of my friends have turned into detail-hungry journalists for the Geek Times. And I'm sure Matt's biding his time. "She's ... it's not like that!"

Desperate to shut them up, my EM turns my guilt into apparent outrage. But Beggsy's fascination with the female form knows no bounds.

"Dude! Have you ... you know ... charted her 'twin moons' ?"

"Jesus!" I explode. "What's the matter with you? She's just a girl!"

Luckily, the bell prevents this going any further and the group splits. Me and Matt go one way, Beggsy and Ravi the other, still chattering excitably in different keys, like a vocal version of Laurel and Hardy.

"Sarah was at the party," Matt says.

"Oh yeah?" I reply, trying to hide the fear threatening to bloom under my skin. "Did she have a good time?"

IM: *Translation: did she get off with Chris?*

"She hung out with a few people. Chatted to Chris. We chatted a bit."

"OK. Cool."

"And then she went home with Caitlyn."

I can only hope that the relief I'm experiencing isn't transmitted by my face. My EM goes along with the charade, painting it with Nonchalant Flesh and giving it a wash of Devil-may-care Tan.

"So, d'you think you'll be cool with Sarah now? I mean, you've got a girlfriend and everything…" There's a tint of Desperation Green in Matt's voice – the sooner I'm friends with Sarah, the sooner everyone can hang out without there being any awkwardness. And, for an awkward guy, Matt hates awkwardness.

"I guess." I smile lamely, before walking ahead.

IM: *Sits back to enjoy the show* Popcorn, anyone?

By the time the bell goes for lunchtime, word has spread like wildfire around our year: Archie the Geek has got a Girlfriend. If I really had, I'm sure I would be striding down the corridors like the Hulk going to an arm-wrestling contest. But the fact that it's all one big charade just makes me feel depressed. I want to jump into my TARDIS, travel back in time and not agree to this madness.

All my energies are routed to trying to make sense of the situation I'm in, cutting off vital power to my Grunt Detectors™. I don't notice that the stream of students breaks and passes round an Immovable Object up ahead – my own, personal dam, Jason Humphries.

Even without his usual entourage of Grunts, Humphries is an imposing figure. But, without my Detectors online and my apparent fascination with counting shoes as I walk, I hit him before I'm even aware of it. His chest is like a brick wall.

"So. The Geek's got a girlfriend."

IM: *It's Matt! He's got one! It's a case of mistaken identity!*

My EM short circuits due to a fear overload and all I can do is stand and try not to make more eye contact than you would with a hungry lion.

"Like Geeks, does she?" This manboy can imbue every word he speaks with some sort of physical threat and he doesn't even have to move.

IM: *...and I leave my models to Beggsy, who I know will paint them better than I ever could...*

"Yeah ... I think so," I stammer. Even the words are too frightened to come out of my mouth.

"You won't be having anything to do with Sarah, then. Will you." I can hear the absence of a question mark in the last sentence. Details like punctuation are unnecessary when you're tougher than the universe.

While my body appears to have forgotten most of the fundamentals of living, like breathing, my mind is spinning like a vortex. The fact that Humphries has taken the time to have this little chat with me tells me something that I don't think he wants me to know: in some respect, I am still a threat to his orbit around Sarah. This piece of information is filed away under "Dreams Yet to be Fully Crushed" and I give Humphries the reply he's looking for.

"She doesn't talk to me anyway."

Humphries leans in close to me, and places a blunt finger in the centre of my chest. My heart stops beating entirely, in case it's uncomfortable for him.

"Good. Keep it that way." And then he tries to walk through me. Details like the Laws of Physics are also unnecessary when you have biceps the size of Bane's. Considerately, I manage to fall out of his way.

IM: *It's Victim Etiquette.*

Picking myself up, I watch him go and then just stand, shaking for a moment. All Geeks know the feeling I'm having – it's depression, rage, fear and self-loathing all at once. The fact that someone can make you feel so insignificant doesn't mean they have to. I rewind the whole conversation a million times in about a minute, blasting Humphries into oblivion each time. Once I'm convinced that my legs will support me, I walk to meet the guys in the canteen, my Grunt Detectors™ cranking at full tilt.

Matt, Ravi and Beggsy are already seated at a table.

"Dude!" Beggsy looks ready to launch into another round of questions.

"What?" I reply wearily. "If it's about Clare, forget it."

"Aw, come on!" Ravi cajoles me. "You're the guy who 'knows how to show a girl a good time'. We just want a few crumbs from your table, O Wise One." He starts doing some representation of worship, lifting his hands up and down like he's flapping a bedsheet. Of course it spreads like a mexican wave round the table.

This is getting way out of hand. My Geek friends think I know what I'm doing. I've got to find a way to head this off at the pass.

"OK," I sigh. "I met a girl on a train, we got on, found out we liked a few of the same things and that was kind of it." I'm hoping my vagueness somehow translates as Man of the Worldness.

IM: *Well, these guys don't know any different, do they?*

"And what about this 'good time' you showed her? How 'good' was it?" Even Ravi's resonant reserve has disintegrated, revealing his inner pervert.

IM: *AKA fourteen-year-old male.*

I opt for vague again, but this time with a hint of mystery.

"Well … I guess you've either got it or you haven't." And then I back this up with a quick diversion sign, "Eh, *Beggster*?"

"The *Beggster* is working on it. The *Beggster* does not rush these things."

"OK. So that's that – let's talk about this QuestFest." It's less of a topic change and more of a subject-swerve. Complete with skidmarks.

IM: *Draw your own conclusions.*

"*Breast* Fest," Beggsy quips, sounding like a debauched parrot. I decide to try and keep the conversation going in any direction, just as long as it's away from my fictional love life.

"Hey – I got my ears!"

"Dude! I got my beard!"

"How does it look?"

"Awesome! How 'bout you?"

"Elftastic, mate!"

"Dwarfmungus!"

IM: *This could only be a Geek conversation...*

"This could get orcward..." Matt deadpans, to a chorus of groans.

"And what about the weapons? Did you get anywhere with them?" I can feel the burden of Clare's Girl Plan lifting from my shoulders as we get involved in some good, old-fashioned Geek Speak™.

"Yeah," Ravi says bitterly. "We checked out all the sites – they're really expensive. And you can't use wooden swords or plastic ones, because they've got to be 'game safe'."

"And what makes them game safe?"

"Dude..." Even Beggsy sounds downcast. "The deal is that they've got some sort of rigid core and then they're covered in foam-latex, so you can't hurt anybody."

There's a lapse in conversation as four Geeks scour their brains for a solution. And suddenly, I've got one.

"NERF!" The word explodes out of my mouth, even surprising me.

"Bless you." Matt could work as a stand-up comic on Vulcan, his delivery's so dry.

"NERF swords!" My Head Cinema™ plays me a

quick scan of Lucas's bedroom. "They're foam, but they're rigid!"

"But they've got to look real," Ravi frowns. "The ones on the LARP sites look really good."

"But we're Geeks! And what do Geeks do best…?"

"We paint them. That's what we do." I love the way Matt's so quick, but so matter-of-fact about it.

"Dude! That's it! I might be able to borrow a spray-gun from Big Marv!" Beggsy's fingers pump an invisible trigger in his excitement.

"Awesome!" I grin. "We could swing by the toyshop on our way home and pick up some swords?"

This time, Matt's not so fast or cutting in his delivery. In fact, a couple of minutes pass while me, Ravi and Beggsy rifle through our pockets for any cash before he says anything.

"I can't tonight."

"How come?"

"I'm … walking Caitlyn home."

Beggsy does an actual double take, while me and Ravi just look up from our pathetic piles of change. Judging by the twinkle in Beggsy's eyes, there's a comment about to be unleashed. Judging by the hunted look in Matt's, it's better if it's not. Ravi cuts in before I can.

"I haven't got much on me anyway. What about tomorrow?"

"Yeah," I reply. "Good for me."

"And what about *you*, Mister 'I'm Walking a Girl Home'? Does that fit into your schedule?" Beggsy never knows when to let things go and I'm expecting Matt to bite back. But he doesn't. Instead, he pulls out one of his books and flips through it.

"Get your people to talk to my people and we'll see what we can do." Although it's a gag, there's a hint of challenge in Matt's eyes; I hope Beggsy sees it, too. But just as they're loading their conversational duelling pistols, Sarah walks into the canteen with Caitlyn and they both head to the salad bar. My onboard computer displays the likely outcome: Caitlyn will see Matt and come and join us, which means that Sarah will, too. Time to make myself scarce.

"Gotta go, guys."

IM: *What about the whole Bom-bom-BOM-bom thing?*

"Where are you off to?" Ravi bassoons.

"Library," I blurt. "Research. Art." No Geek will ever question another Geek's dedication to schoolwork.

I should stay and see my mission through. There's a moment's indecision, before I hurriedly grab my bag and head for the exit. I should, but I can't. Not yet; it all feels wrong, somehow. And, anyway, shouldn't she be searching me out or weeping my name into her sleeve in the Great

Unknown of the Girls' Toilets or something? I need to think. I don't want to get caught out like I was with the guys. I need to know exactly what I'm going to say.

IM: *Next stop: library. One to beam up.*

I spend the rest of the day damning myself for my cowardice. I also spend the rest of the day damning myself for getting involved in Clare's fauxmance in the first place – when we were on the train it didn't sound like it would be this complicated.

IM: *You could tell the truth. Weird concept, I know…*

I could, but then I'd be letting Clare down. Plus she's on my Facebook page and if I suddenly backed out, what would happen then? I might get to discover just how much fury a woman scorned actually has.

IM: *And your trips to York could get pretty uncomfortable.*

This is such a mess.

The final bell goes and I leave the world of univariate polynomials behind, lost in my thoughts as I'm carried down the corridor by the flow of feet and pheromones. Ravi and Beggsy are waiting for me at the gates, but there isn't much said on the way home; we're all noting Matt's absence, but for different reasons. I'm just glad he's not here to hassle me over running out of the canteen – Ravi and Beggsy aren't up to that level of confrontation.

$$\xrightarrow{\hspace{2cm}}$$

Walking down the drive to my front door, I see that Mum's car is gone, but Tony's Beemer is parked up. This is the situation I used to try and avoid: me and Tony, alone in the house. But these days, my Tosser Detectors™ are little more than background noise.

As the door clicks behind me, I call out my customary "Helloo!" and make my way to the kitchen for a can of Coke. The can is millimetres from my mouth, spitting flecks of sugary goodness over my top lip, when I hear the sound of a toilet flushing. This is followed by the thunder of hooves on the stairs and my sort-of-stepfather clumps into the room.

"Arch." There's something in his eyes that says It's Serious. Whatever it is.

My EM cranks up the voltage, but can only manage a tight smile. It's been a long day.

"Hey, Tony."

"We need to talk." He lumbers away to his study in a way that tells me I'm supposed to follow. By the time I get to the Inner Sanctum, Tony's sat on his leather swivel chair.

"Close the door," he nods.

IM: *OK. This is weird.*

Tony fixes me with a look, while he works out how he's going to say what's on his mind. The thing is, he's not my dad and he knows it and the way he can't quite meet my eyes for more than a few seconds at a time tells me that he's entering uncharted space.

IM: *No known coordinates beyond this point! All personnel are recommended to return to their stations and await further instruction!*

So, instead of saying anything, Tony dips into his trouser pocket and pulls out a small box, which he throws to me. The last time he did this, there was an engagement ring for my mum in it. This time, it's...

IM: *OhmyGod! OHMYGOD! OMG! OMFG!*

...a packet of condoms. My EM, unused to such high demands on its reserves, goes straight into Hibernation mode, leaving me standing, frozen, like I've just gazed into the eyes of Medusa. While clutching a packet of johnnies.

IM: *Not real. Not happening. Not possible.*

"Know what they are?" Tony asks, like I've just arrived on the planet.

"Uh-huh," I manage through the rigor mortis in my face.

"And you know what they're for?"

IM: *Kill yourself, Archie. Do it now.*

"Yeah." The word flies out of my mouth so fast that it practically burns up on re-entry into the conversation.

"And you know how to put one on?"

IM: *If he asks for a demonstration, go through the window on your right.*

"I've never…" The words are whispers now. I've got no volume left; horror has turned me down.

"There are instructions."

"OK."

Tony sits back in his chair, crossing his arms and legs, but still unable to maintain eye contact, which, right now, is the only thing stopping me from spontaneously combusting and leaving nothing more than a pair of smoking trainers behind.

"I know about Clare," he adds, as if this explains everything.

IM: *WHAT?*

"What?"

"Saw your post on Facebook, Arch."

My black alert is suddenly upgraded to red. My early attempts to get on with Tony have come back to bite me in a way I never thought possible. I wish Facebook had never been invented, let alone accepting Tony's friend request to keep the family peace.

Tony takes my goggle-eyed, open-mouthed silence as some sort of permission to continue.

"She's sixteen, Arch. You know what that means, mate. And you're fourteen. And I know what it's like when you're fourteen. And I know that things happen." Even the fact that every red corpuscle in my body appears to have vanished can't stop him now. "I can't tell you how to live your life, Arch, but I can help you stay safe. Wear your wellies, mate. It'll stop you catching anything and it'll stop there being any Little Archies, if you know what I'm saying." And then, in perfect Tony style, he caps it off with just that bit of extra information that I really didn't need or want to know. "They're not just for kids. Adults use them, too. I do, with your mum."

If my life was a film, this would be the bit where the special-effects team would have rigged up some sort of hose along one side of my neck, so that I could projectile vomit across the room, spattering Tony's chest with something green and slimy, before I run screaming out of the room and off the nearest cliff.

"I'm glad we can chat like this," Tony nods sagely, before getting up and patting me on the shoulder. "Man stuff. I won't say a word to your mum."

IM: *Collapses weeping*

I suppose I could be living a badly scripted sitcom, because it's at this point that Mum turns up, coming in through the front door, laden with carrier bags.

"Hello?" she calls. "Archie? Anyone home?"

Pocketing the condoms, I quickly compose myself and meet Mum in the hallway.

"Fancy a cup of tea?" she asks.

"I've got a Coke open."

IM: *Anything to wash away the taste of Durex.*

IM: *That didn't come out right, did it…?*

Much as I'd love to run upstairs and hide my contraceptive contraband, I help Mum carry the shopping into the kitchen and try and act like it's just another day. Sitting in the kitchen with her, going on about how *her* day was acts as a nice and normal distraction from the fact that, right now, my life has become like some crazy fairground ride that I can't get off. My mates think I'm something I'm not, my stepfather thinks I'm *doing* something I'm not and the one thing I *am* doing – lying – I wish I wasn't.

IM: *Maybe you need to relax. Where's the Next catalogue?*

"You all right, Archie?" Mum's scanners are obviously picking up a disturbance in the Force and I feel a lurch in my stomach as The Truth thinks it might be time to come out. But I bite it down, make my excuses, and head on up to my Lair, Tony's condoms burning a hole in my pocket.

I change into a pair of johnny-free jeans, quickly trawl through my homework, then hit Facebook. There's nothing much going on and, to my relief, there's nothing from Clare. Almost without realizing it, I find myself on Sarah's page, looking through her photos. She is The Most Beautiful Girl In The World™. There are photos of her in her Goth gear and photos of her wearing just ordinary clothes; each style just seems to heighten a different aspect of her beauty: the Goth make-up makes her look elegant, sexy and somehow vulnerable, while make-up-free photos make her look as shiny and innocent as an apple on a tree. It's the Goth that makes my heart race and my breath shallow, but it's the apple that makes me crumble inside. Could I ever really be friends with a girl who can do that to me?

IM: *I hate to say it, but she hasn't done anything to you. ANYthing!*

There's a knock at the door, so I jump to my homepage.

"Dinner's ready," Mum announces, putting some washing on the end of my bed. I head downstairs and try not to make eye contact with Tony through some sort of birdseed that I'm told is "couscous". I manfully choke it down.

Back upstairs, with nothing happening on Facebook, I decide to take some solace in *The Dark Knight Returns*.

I never realized that Batman and Superman didn't get on, but they don't. This book sells Superman as a hired killer; he zips around the world, sorting out wars for the Government and, in return, they leave him alone. He's like the deadliest weapon any country could ever have and all he's got to do is play by the rules.

IM: *Therefore, Superman is a Geek. Just with muscles. And superpowers. And... Oh, forget it.*

But Batman doesn't play by the rules at all and that's why the Government doesn't like him and that's why they want Superman to bring him in. I love the artwork and the way it's been painted; it's all a bit blurry and bleeding into the page, but you get a real sense of the mood in each panel.

It's just as I'm putting the book down and deciding that I ought to get ready for bed that I notice the pile of washing on the end of it. There, on top of some jeans and T-shirts and towels, are my pyjamas.

IM: *Yep. Yours. They've got your name in and everything.*

My pyjamas.

IM: *And your DNA...*

My pyjamas, once saturated with the result of a depraved dream, are now washed, dried and ironed. This means that, while I was at school, Mum came into my room.

Mum enters the Lair, humming happily to herself. She stops in the middle of the room and sighs, marvelling at how wonderful her son is. Then, happy just to be his mother, she goes to the dirty laundry basket and pulls out yesterday's clothes. As she strips the bed, she notices something sticking out from under Archie's mattress, like it's poking a tongue out at her. "What can it be?" she wonders and reaches in and pulls out her beloved child's pyjama bottoms. And sees the Huge Wet Patch...

IM: *Possibly not so wet at that point. Just sayin'.*

...identifies the patch as the mass grave of recently jettisoned genetic material...

IM: *Possibly pretty cold by that point as well.*

...and spends the rest of her life in therapy. After she's put it in the wash.

I throw my head, unfortunately still attached to my treacherous body, into my pillow and groan as loudly as I can.

This escapade has made me realize three things:

1) If any mother anywhere deserved a bunch of flowers from her son, it's mine.

2) There are no secret places in my bedroom. Therefore...

3) The condoms have to go.

IM: *Bom-bom-BOM-bom...*

NINE

Waking up without an entire civilization stuck to my pyjamas is a good way to start a Tuesday. More important is the fact that Jane and her metal bikini haven't been guest-starring in my dreams. But today, I have another Important Mission to fulfil: today is Operation Condom (Get Rid Of). After getting dressed and folding my pyjamas and putting them on the end of my bed to send a signal to Mum that I'm back in control of my body, I quickly check Facebook. There's a post from Clare:

Missed u last night. Shame you don't live closer... X

IM: *Computer voice* Pro-cess-ing, pro-cess-ing...

OK, I think I get this one; she's letting that guy, Oliver, know that he's got a chance. I obviously don't live nearby, which means that we won't be seeing each other all the time, which means that the novelty might wear off, which means that he ought to make his play. I'm learning to think like a Girl. If I'm going to buy into this fauxmance, then I've got to do it one hundred per cent; everybody already thinks I've got a girlfriend, so I might as well see it through.

Although there's a nasty taste in my mouth, I commit to the mission and bang out a reply:

See you soon.

No kiss. I'm the cool one in this relationship.

IM: *It's definitely fake, in that case.*

Without waiting to see if I've said the wrong thing, I kill the computer, have breakfast and hit the road for school, a packet of condoms pressing into my thigh. Thanks to the spring in my step, I arrive at the corner of Hamilton Road just as the guys are gathering. Briefly, I wonder what the collective noun for a gathering of Geeks is.

IM: *An awkwardness? A convention? A self-consciousness?*

Fortunately, me and Matt are let off the hook; there are more important things to talk about as we make our way to school, such as how we're going to paint our swords. Beggsy reckons that the best way would be to mix up a combination of black and metal as the base, drybrush metal over that and then drybrush again, using metal mixed with white. I like his style, but I'm distracted by my rubber burden and observe the conversation, instead of throwing myself into it.

As school comes into view at the end of the road,

I get that prickly feeling that Peter Parker gets whenever something's about to go wrong. It hasn't even started and I'm already wishing this day was over.

It's hard to concentrate in an English lesson, when you've got a packet of Ferret Socks ©Beggsy burning into your thigh. As a result, I fail to experience the surprise semaphored by Mrs Hughes on discovering that William Wordsworth's poem "Upon Westminster Bridge" was actually about a bridge, not a girl; I'm too busy thinking about how I'm going to get rid of the contraceptives in my pocket. I could just drop them where I'm sitting and hope that nobody notices but, knowing my luck, Mrs Hughes will spot them after I've left and remember where I was sitting.

I spend break hovering near bins with one hand in my pocket, but Beggsy and Ravi are sticking to me like glue, obviously still under the impression that I'm going to suddenly run away with Clare. This is probably reinforced by Matt's decision to hunt out Caitlyn instead of hanging with us, like he normally does. I get no further inspiration in Geography and a mad part of me flirts with the idea of handing them out to my mates, but it would be like when the Ewoks discover speeder bikes in *Return of the Jedi*: a lot of hyperactive shrieking that would no doubt attract the unwanted attention of the local stormtroopers. By lunchtime, I'm fairly resigned to the idea that I'm going to fake a Close Encounter of the Turd Kind, but I need to choose my moment.

IM: *Perhaps the old "Can I go to the toilet?" routine in Biology, this afternoon?*

It's perfect. There shouldn't be anyone around and I can cast my unholy burden into the abyss. With this plan in mind, I head to the canteen to catch up with the guys. By the time I hit the table, the others are already in full swing.

"Yeah, but they've got to have hoods, dude! Hoods are standard issue!" For a brief, sweat-slicked second, my ears interpret Beggsy's squeaking as something to do with condoms.

"Hey, guys. What's up?"

My mates suddenly go quiet and start throwing each other looks, like they're rolling twenty-sided dice with their eyes. They've obviously been building up to this bit.

"We wondered," Ravi says slowly, "whether your mum would help us with the cloaks…"

IM: *Annnd … relax!*

Mum's costume-making abilities are legendary. Each Halloween for the past nine years she's made me a costume. Luckily, me and the guys didn't know each other the year she decided to dress me up as the Gruffalo. Although they have seen the photos.

"I can try…" I nod vaguely. "But it's a big ask to come up with four cloaks by Friday…"

There's another silence.

"What?" Silences are irritating, unless they're instigated by me.

"Six cloaks," Ravi shockwaves. "We might need six…"

"How come?"

"We thought we might invite the girls."

IM: *Sounds of piano being dropped on head*

"What?"

IM: *Either you're going mad or they just said "invite the girls".*

"You want to invite the girls? Sarah and Caitlyn?" Like we know any others.

"Dude, why not? I told Sarah about it at the party and she thought it sounded cool."

There are a few why nots pinballing around my head at the moment. The idea of Sarah seeing her would-be-Romeo dressed up like some pointy-eared reject from Santa's grotto has got to be pretty high on the list. And it suddenly makes the whole idea of LARPing seem really stupid – the idea of prancing around in the woods wielding a foam instrument of death and pretending to be one of the Eldar has got to be a Geek-only experience. It's one thing to invite a girl to a tabletop game, where there are domestic anchors to reality all around you, but this is madness. I'd be revealing an aspect of my personality that, quite frankly, I'd rather not; it'd be like coming out of the Geeky closet.

IM: *The one with a direct link to Narnia…*

But while these thoughts are doing a Wall of Death around the inside of my cranium, another one hits the throttle: I can't say anything about liking Sarah or I'll have to 'fess up to the fauxmance.

IM: *1) Take gun. 2) Aim at foot. 3) Pull trigger.*

I'm going to have to appeal to the guys' Geekier natures. My EM scrunches up the expression of disbelief on my face into a more thoughtful look.

"Yeah, but, guys," I say. *"Girls?* I mean … *really?* They won't do it properly…" I sense a flutter of uncertainty round the table, so continue with my so-far-watertight argument. "They'll just mess it up! Matt, I can understand you wanting to spend some time with your girlfriend, but…"

"She's not my girlfriend."

"What? But you spoke to her?"

IM: *The Prosecution rests its case.*

"She's not my girlfriend, Archie. All we did was talk."

"But you like her, don't you?" This is unfair

questioning and I know it. Geeks don't put each other on the spot like this – not in public, anyway. Any public admission of liking someone reveals that you have hopes and dreams beyond your Geeky existence. It's like a sort of inverse arrogance.

"Yes," Matt scowls. "I like her. So?"

"Well, d'you really want her to see you looking like you even know what cosplay *is*? D'you really want her to know you're a Geek?"

"But I am," he replies logically and without any anger. "And I'm not going to hide it just because I like someone. Besides, she's a bit of a Geek."

"In what way?" This is turning into a cross-examination, but I can't seem to stop myself; there's too much riding on it. Matt does a slow, single blink before breathing in deeply and answering with a sigh – he's getting annoyed.

"She thinks *Lord of the Rings* is the best book ever written."

IM: *As good as a DNA test: she's a Geek.*

Ravi, obviously working for the Defence, backs up Matt's testimony.

"It's true, Archie. She even knew the Fangorn Forest/Macbeth thing…"

IM: *Objection, Your Honour!*

Wow. That fact is a hallowed one, and one that only

a few of us know. My Brain Barrister is about to try and tenuously argue the case that that's Nerd Knowledge, rather than Geekspertise, when it comes up with another ploy. One that'll get me off the hook. Relaxing back into my seat and nodding as though I've seen the light, I throw it at the jury.

"Well, OK…" I begin. "If that's what you want. But they'll never come."

My closing statement thumps on to the table. Matt and Ravi exchange looks; they know I'm right. There's no way on Middle-earth that you could ever persuade two girls to come camping for the weekend, dressed up as fantasy characters.

IM: *Not unless you pay for it.*

But the Defence puts a surprise witness in the stand. Just as I'm sure that I'm going to get the verdict I want, a squeaky, hyperactive voice rings loud and clear across the unofficial courtroom.

"Don't worry about that, dude! Leave it to The *Begg*ster!"

IM: *OB-jection!*

But the approving chuckles from my friends mean that I'm overruled before I can even say anything.

My fate rests on Beggsy's unknowing shoulders.

Up in the Biology lab, testing a leaf for the presence of starch gives me a short break from thinking about my problems but, three-quarters of the way through the lesson, a fizz of fear reminds me that now might be time to try and ditch the Love Gloves ©Beggsy. My EM boots up to project a look of hassled desperation as I approach Mrs Knowles's desk while everyone else is up to their elbows in iodine.

IM: *And you're up to your neck in excreta.*

Part one of Operation Condom goes fine; ordinarily, Mrs Knowles is one of those teachers that subscribes to the "you should have gone at lunchtime" or "you'll have to wait" philosophy. But, if you're a Geek, do your homework on time and are actually interested in what you're learning, then you're more likely to get away with it.

The nearest toilets are up two flights of stairs, on the same floor that Sarah has Chemistry. As I walk by her class, I can't help but flick a look through the glass of the door to see if she's there. She is and a cloud of glitter erupts in my chest at the sight of her. My Head Cinema™ plays a quick trailer where Sarah looks up, sees me, melts into a smile and we fall in love. Both of us.

IM: *Meanwhile, back on earth…*

It takes a real physical effort to walk past the door and, as I do, a sorry sigh escapes. But Operation

Condom is nearing completion and I walk down the corridor to the toilets, fingering the packet in my pocket. The cardboard one.

It's possibly the glitter in my chest affecting my sensors or it's the fact that I don't usually roam the school during lesson-time, but my Grunt Detectors™ aren't powered up and as I push open the toilet door, I'm met by the sight of Jason Humphries and his Pack of Grunts™ hurriedly dropping the tail-end of a cigarette out of one of the little windows that opens above the big ones that won't.

IM: *Of course they're in the toilets; where else would they be?*

Legs on Geeks evolved, long ago, for running. CaveGeeks probably had to run from CaveGrunts who made their lives difficult while they were busy inventing the wheel. My twenty-first century legs forget their Prime Directive and lock, along with every other part of my body. I am possibly to stay this way forever; a fresco in a toilet doorway. Needless to say, the Grunts are not happy at my having interrupted their cigarette break.

"It's the Geek," Paul Green announces, like I'm a guest at some posh party. The sound of the urinals auto-rinsing is the perfect overture to my impending doom.

"The Geek," Humphries growls, wearing an alligator smile. "What are you doing here, Geek? Shouldn't you be learning something? Or have you come for a smoke?" This prompts a series of snorts from the other Grunts, who both start to move slowly towards me. I've seen lions doing this on wildlife programmes, only less threateningly.

"No," I squeak, "I was just going…" I point at the cubicles, so that I don't have to commit to a particular bodily function.

"Go on, then," Humphries dares me, in a quiet, "I've killed before" kind of way.

IM: *Scotty! Energize!* *Bashes communicator against rock* *Static*

"Uh… I'm actually OK, now. I don't really need to…"

IM: *Not sure that's entirely accurate at this moment in time…*

"Don't be shy," Humphries soothes, which is much like being soothed by one of the Uruk-hai. "We'll help you out – GRAB HIM!"

The other two Grunts respond in a flash: as Humphries gets an arm round my neck, Paul Green grabs my arms and Lewis Mills has my legs; suddenly I'm in the air being held like a battering ram, staring fearfully at the floor and three pairs of grubby trainers.

IM: *They really ought to tie their laces a bit better. Might fall over.*

Victim Etiquette dictates that the more fuss I make, the worse the experience I'm likely to have, so I try and keep my cries down to a minimum. Any that do pop out, I try and make sound like I'm sort of enjoying the thrill of it all, with a few "whoas" and "heys", like I'm on a roller coaster. Unfortunately, I'm unable to keep the pain out of my yelps when the Grunts do decide to use me as a battering ram and open one of the cubicle doors with my head.

"Come on, lads; in he goes!"

Suddenly I am looking into the thankfully clear water of a toilet bowl. Unlike the Mirror of Galadriel, these waters only tell my future. Wriggling like a fish, I somehow manage to wrestle my arms free of Green's grip and clamp my hands on the toilet seat. Now it's a battle of wills: my arms are locked stiff and no force on this earth is going to bend them. Humphries tries to drag my head tolietwards, while Green joins Mills on my legs, raising them higher and higher until I'm practically doing a handstand on the loo. At this point, my pockets decide to empty themselves: coins clatter on to the tiled floor, a pen bounces off one of my ears and into the water below, and something lands with a loud plap at someone's feet. There's a split second where no one does anything; we just hold this frieze, me upside down, trying to resist getting any closer to the porcelain than I already am.

"Look at that!" Green grunts in something like amazement. "Johnnies! He was carrying johnnies!"

Suddenly I'm upright and up against the cubicle wall, with Humphries's T-bone forearm pressed across my neck and a packet of Extra Safe stuck under my nose. I briefly wonder if they'd be any help right now.

"What you doing with these?" Humphries demands, his cigarette-breath practically a cloud between us.

"Getting rid of them," I croak. "Don't want them!"

The pressure on my throat eases as confusion ripples and rolls across the muscles in Humphries's forehead.

"You having a laugh?"

"No," I gasp. "Have them."

The stunned silence is broken by another round of barking laughs.

"You wouldn't know what to do with them, anyway," Green joins in.

"Dickhead."

"Yeah. Dickhead," Humphries grins, revealing wet little teeth. "Hold him."

Lewis Mills takes over Humphries's position, keeping me up against the cubicle wall.

It's pointless struggling – there're three of them, one of me and we're in a confined space. I pray desperately for someone, *anyone*, to come in and get me out of this, but my powers as a Dungeon Master are less than useless in the Here and Now. Humphries turns his back to me and I hear an ominous ripping sound.

IM: *OhmyGod! He's tearing one of his own arms off so he can hit you with it!*

"Hold him," he says again, turning round. Lewis and Paul tighten their respective grips on me and something bites into my forehead. My vision goes all blurry, but it's not due to any physical damage: Jason Humphries is pulling a condom over my head. Which isn't as easy as it might sound; there's a lot of stretching involved and a couple of failed attempts as my rubber mask snaps back up over my head and into the air. I struggle, moving my head – but not too much. If I wreck their plan, I'm likely to get hurt and my brain quickly works out that wearing a contraceptive as a tight-fitting hat is going to be a lot less painful than getting punched.

Thankfully, my Extra Safe headgear won't go below my nose, so I'm not going to be found later, suffocated to death with a johnny on my head. Once their work is done, the Grunts ease off a bit, to appreciate their handiwork. More laughs and insults follow. My Fear Department obviously has some override function on my EM, because I start laughing along with the Grunts, although my laughter is a lot more high-pitched and manic. Sweat starts to drip into my eyes, but I can't wipe them, so I stand against the cubicle wall, giggling and blinking madly. I can't think of anything else to do.

This obviously wasn't the effect my assailants were looking for because, within a matter of seconds, the only person laughing is me.

IM: *Time to shut up. Now.*

Through my Durex deerstalker, I hear the sound of the bell.

"Think it's funny, dickhead?" the pink blur that is Humphries demands. "Let's see just how funny it is."

As my heart races, the Grunts bundle me out of the cubicle and through the toilet door. Judging by the laughter that echoes off the walls in the corridor, it's pretty funny. But it's not enough for them that what sounds like the whole school is laughing at me – a few sharp shoves push me to the top of the stairs.

IM: *Couldn't they just ask? I'm sure you'd be happy to throw yourself down them and save them the bother.*

I don't know what to do. If I take off my Condom Cowl™, they'll simply destroy me. But the blurry pink of the staircase doesn't look that inviting, either. A hush falls in the corridor. There's a lurch in my chest as Fear kicks in, good and hard. I'd love to report that I await my fate with a Bond-like calm but, underneath my rubber mask, my eyes brim with tears.

As I brace myself for the shove, there's a yell from somewhere behind me. I think it's Mills and the sound of pain, but I keep my position, facing the stairs; whatever's happening, I know my place. Then there's a voice.

"Idiots! You could've really hurt him!"

I know that voice.

IM: *Batman...?*

It's Sarah.

And then I hear Humphries. "Don't be stupid! We was only mucking about!"

And then there's a noise like something's knocked the air out of him and Sarah's mercury voice, now low and hard as steel. I don't catch all of what she says, except "...unless you want everyone to know about..."

There's a bit more scuffling and then a dangerous noise comes up from the crowd. It's not a cheer, but one of those rising vowels that signifies everyone's seen something that could go either way. And then Humphries's voice cuts across it all, from further away now as he shouts the word "dickhead" at me.

IM: *I think you've just been rescued.*

"Archie?"

IM: *You can still throw yourself down the stairs...*

Even through my rubber haze, I can make out the ebony frame of Sarah's hair. From in here, she looks like a fuzzy Cleopatra.

IM: *We all know what you look like.*

"Hey," I manage. Standing in a corridor, half blind, with a condom on my head wasn't the romantic reunion I was hoping for.

"Archie…" It's Sarah again. Her mere presence is like a life ring. "Why don't you take it off?"

"Uh … yeah," I reply stupidly, peeling back my Durex face and blinking at how cold the air seems to be on the upper half of my head. "What happened? Why did they go?"

"Are you OK?"

It might be that I'm standing at the top of the stairs, but I feel like I could fall into her eyes.

"Yeah… But what happened?"

"Let's just say I don't think Jason wants it known that I read his aura." She's holding something back, but I'm too relieved to push it. I hold my hands out in front of me, like I'm about to play the piano; they're trembling.

"Whoa," I manage. "Thanks. Thought I'd had it!"

"Well…" It's one of those sentences that usually has "I ought to go" stapled on the end of it. But it hangs in the air just a little bit too long and there's half a smile attached to it, like she's waiting for something.

IM: *Contact made. Mission is go. Phase One: Launch Charm Missiles! *Presses button**

"Look … I'm sorry, by the way. Just … you know … sorry."

IM: **Presses button repeatedly* We have a malfunction!*

"Archie … it's cool … don't worry about it…"

"No, I really want to apologize. I've wanted to for ages. Just for … you know … being such a dork and everything."

Sarah smiles half a smile and I see a light switch on behind her eyes and I just know everything's going to be OK.

IM: *Bom-bom-BOM-bom…*

"It's *fine*, Archie. Stop worrying about everything."

"Yeah. Well, I am. Sorry. Ha." I don't know why I make that last stupid noise, but the other half of Sarah's smile attaches itself, so I'm glad I do. A surge in the crowds around us indicates that it really is time to go to our next lesson.

"What're you doing later?" she adds, starting to move backwards into the slipstream of schoolbags and illicit mobile phones.

"Me and the guys are going into town."

"See you at the gates? We'll chat then. See ya." She vanishes like a beautiful ghost.

IM: *Phase One completed.*

Grabbing my books and bag from the Biology lab, I head off to Geography, feeling light and floaty, as though I'm made of helium.

As I trot through the thickening porridge of students, I bump into Beggsy.

"Dude!"

"Ah! Sir William of Beggs!" I announce, in my best Big Marv impression.

"No – *dude*! I heard about Sarah beating up Humphries! What happened?"

"Beating up...?" My mouth is suddenly very dry.

"She nearly broke his wrist doing some ninja moves on him! I thought you were there!"

"Ninja...?"

"Yeah! She's like a black belt in karate or something! *Dude!* What *happened*? Somebody said you were wearing a hat or something!"

IM: *Or something.*

Wow. Karate? For some reason it doesn't fit with the idea I have in my head of what Sarah does in her spare time. Reading auras: yes. Smashing blocks with her head: no.

IM: *Or is it that you don't like the idea of being saved by a girl...?*

I elaborate on the Condom Incident, omitting to tell him that they were mine.

"Dickhead," Beggsy chuckles, as though he'd thought of it.

"Yeah." I feel like one.

"But at least you and Sarah are talking again."

"Yeah," I nod. "Maybe I need to go and thank Humphries for his input."

We walk into Geography, hit our respective desks and are soon learning about rivers that don't seem to quite know which direction they are headed in.

As soon as we're done, me and Beggsy go and meet the others, taking a cut through the Science block, just in case of Durex Reprisals. My Grunt Detectors™ scan the crowds, but there's nothing to report.

Matt and Ravi are at the gates, waiting for us.

"Hey, guys," Ravi subsonics, "to the armoury!"

"Just got to hang for Sarah," I throw in, as casually as I can. "She's coming, too."

"They've made up!" Beggsy announces, his voice taking a ride on the Squeaky Train™. "Now we can ask her to the LARP! How cool is that?"

"Way to go, Archie," Ravi smiles, with genuine admiration. The Fingers of Guilt trace along the back of my neck, causing me to shudder involuntarily. I can't really take the credit for the Peace Talks.

"Didn't think you'd do it, to be honest," Matt concedes, and my guilt levels ratchet up another notch. But not enough for me to say anything.

IM: *Vader voice* Never underestimate the might of the Dark Side!

"Incoming!" Ravi booms, looking over my shoulder. I turn, just in time to see a group of girls expel Sarah from their ranks. She waves at them and walks over to us, like she's just one of the gang.

"Yo! Sarah!" Beggsy bellows in a voice that's suddenly down in his boots and he scampers into a matey hug. It's not without some jealousy that I notice how he keeps his arm round her waist as they saunter towards us. Ravi throws a high-five at her and Matt just steps forward; it's as demonstrative as he gets.

"Message for you, Math-*thew*," Sarah semi-sings. "Caitlyn says she'll call you later." Matt gives a curt nod in reply, but the hard edges of his mouth soften. I envy him that moment.

IM: *Initiate Phase Two! *Scrabbles through paperwork* Must be here somewhere…*

"Archie!" A mischievous twinkle plays across Sarah's eyes. "I almost didn't recognize you without your condom on…" You can almost hear the sound of bone breaking as Matt's and Ravi's jaws hit the ground.

"Ha," I grin ruefully, before going through the whole Condom Incident again for Matt and Ravi's benefit. Sarah throws in some narration, describing the finer points of what I looked like and we walk and laugh, like nothing ever happened between us.

IM: *Let's be honest: nothing really did! Could've saved* *yourself a lot of grief if you'd had the guts to do this earlier...*

Slowly, the pavement dictates that we walk in two groups. Matt and Ravi silently defer to my renewed friendship with Sarah and walk up ahead. But Beggsy doesn't seem to get the hint and buzzes around us, between us and in front of us like a chubby hummingbird.

"Nice work with Jason Humphries – you really kicked his ass!" Beggsy should be the poster boy for all things American.

"It needed kicking," Sarah shrugs, tossing me an apologetic smile.

"Never thought he'd be taken down by a girl!" There's a challenging twinkle in his eyes and I'm not sure Sarah sees it; Beggsy's up to something.

"Why not?" Sarah laughs in astonishment. "I haven't seen you chasing him round the school lately!"

"But that's because you've had *train*ing, dude! If I'd had *train*ing, I'd have busted him up good!"

"But that's not what '*train*ing's' for; it's about self-defence."

"Naw..." Beggsy shakes his head disparagingly. "If The *Begg*ster had had training..." He ducks, grinning, already anticipating the playful slap that swishes over his head. "I'd have taken him *down*! Seriously," he continues, dancing in and out of striking range, "you've just got to face it: he probably didn't put up much of a fight, because you're a girl!"

Sarah squints and gives him a sideways look, a wry smile playing on her lips.

"You need to be careful, Mr Beggs. I'm the girl who levelled the guy who even beats you up in your dreams!"

IM: *One-nil to Sarah!*

There's some verbal fencing going on and while Sarah's realized it's a game, I can see that her blood's up; there's an angry flush to her cheeks and her smile is glittering and dangerous. But I need Beggsy to play his hand before I even think about joining in.

IM: *Spoken like a true coward!*

"Yeah, yeah," Beggsy yawns, rolling his eyes. "Blah, blah, blah… When are you going to face it? There are things that we can do that you guys can't!"

IM: *Like waking up with an entire civilization encrusted in your navel? Just saying.*

"Like what?" Whatever bait Beggsy's thrown down, Sarah's taken it.

"Girls can't make machine-gun noises. Fact." There is devilry in his eyes.

"What?"

"Girls can't make machine-gun noises," he repeats evenly. But with a grating squeak as his voice does a bungee-jump down and back up again.

"Why would we *want* to?"

There comes a point in every bit of teasing where one side starts to forget it's a joke. Sarah's forgotten. But Beggsy keeps trotting backwards and forwards, like an evil, boxing hobbit.

"See – you can't!"

"Yes, I can!"

"Go on, then."

Sarah suddenly stops walking and a look of intense concentration scrunches her face. Me and Beggsy freeze, in anticipation of what's going to come out of her mouth. Beggsy's bonkers argument has suddenly become Very Important. There's tension and suspense and everything.

"Pthhbbbthhfffppt." It sounds like a balloon deflating.

IM: *One-all.*

"Hahaaa!" Beggsy squeals, like he's just won something. "See? Told ya! Girls can't make machine-gun noises!"

"Well, *so* what?" Sarah demands. "We don't *need* to!"

Whatever Beggsy's doing, he's got Sarah where he wants her. "Dude!" he chuckles. "You're missing the point: we make machine-gun noises because we play imaginative games and we play imaginative games

219

because we have better imaginations than you. It's simple!"

"You do NOT!" If Sarah doesn't punch him, then her outrage will.

"We do so! Think about it: who invented Role-playing Games? Guys. Who *plays* Role-playing Games? Guys. Girls don't do that stuff because they don't have the imagination."

IM: *Isn't it because they have lives?*

"*I* played a Role-playing Game!" Sarah protests through her indignation. "You were there!"

"Yeah, but you didn't really get *in* to it. You didn't *live* it. You can't – you're a girl!"

IM: *I feel a trap about to spring…*

"My imagination is far better than yours!"

"Prove it."

"How?"

"You know that LARP thing I told you about at the party…"

IM: *Consider it sprung.*

"I said I'd think about it…" Sarah's realized what she's walked into and there's a reluctant smile playing across her lips.

"No imagination!" Beggsy shrugs, trotting backwards towards Matt and Ravi and, just before he turns to join them, his hands grip an invisible submachine gun and he lets off a couple of vocal rounds. Really authentic-sounding ones. "The *Beggster*!" he smiles and then leaves our orbit.

IM: *That was class! Hope you were taking notes.*

"You don't *have* to come," I say, secretly hoping she won't, so I don't look like Count Dorkula in front of her. But then I realize that if she was to come, then it might give me a chance to do some fencing of my own, so I add, "But it *would* be funny if you did."

IM: *Oops! Almost forgot! *Ahem* Bom-bom-BOM-bom…*

"He is *such* a bastard!" Sarah laughs in that way girls do when they've kind of enjoyed being wound up.

"He really is," I chuckle back.

"So, this LARPing thing sounds like a laugh," she says.

"Yeah," I grin. "We're off to pick up the weapons now."

"What about your girlfriend? Is she going to the game?"

My Adam's apple bobs like it's Halloween.

IM: **Calculates* So, if light travels at 299,792,458 metres per second, that means that gossip must travel at … wait for it … warp speed!*

So. It's happened. The news has reached Sarah's ears, just like Clare said it would.

IM: *Bom-bom-BOM-Bom…*

I scan Sarah's face for any trace of what she might be thinking.

Unsuccessfully.

"Nah – it's not her bag."

"That's a shame. So, what's she like?"

IM: *Pulls out script*

As I'm giving Sarah a rough description of what I know about Clare and how she looks, I'm aware of a change in the energy between us. This is going to sound a bit weird, but it's the only way I know how to say it: usually it's quite taut, like a stretched rope but, now, as I'm chatting about my fake girlfriend, it's like the tension goes out of it, as if we're suddenly aware that there was more rope than we realized.

IM: *Do-di-doooo… Do-di-doooo…*

I'm dimly aware of her asking questions about what Clare likes to do and my mouth seems to have had some Cruise Control function installed, firing off lies like a Phaser of Fiction™. But it's the change between us that throws me off-centre for a moment. And then I get it: she's relaxed. And, even more weirdly, so am I.

I guess it's because she's thinking that she's now off my radar; that she doesn't have to worry about my ham-fisted attempts to try and go out with her.

IM: *Not quite the jealous reaction you were hoping for…*

Which is a bit of a downer. But maybe that means I've got to up my game and start talking about Clare like she's actually my girlfriend and I really like her and stuff. I leave it for the moment and come back to the conversation. Which has returned to the LARP.

"What're you going to be?"

"An elf." As I say it, I realize just how stupid it sounds. But Sarah's easy laugh makes it all seem perfectly normal. "And what about you? I mean – if you were going…?"

IM: *Doo-di-doooo…*

"We'll see."

IM: *DAH-dum!*

It's not a yes or a no, which suits me fine, because I'm not sure which one works best for me.

Just as we're walking past the Hovel, Beggsy asks Sarah if she'd like to look at his vampire lords in the window. We do and I feel a flare of jealousy as she reacts with the appropriate awe.

IM: *Reality check! It's only Beggsy!*

We hit the toyshop and eventually locate the NERF swords, and an axe for Beggsy. The swords are sold in packs of two so there's a spare one, which I fleetingly imagine presenting to Lucas as a peace offering. Much to our surprise the weapons are better than we thought they'd be – they're rigid, but the latex is soft enough so that you can whack someone and not hurt them. We know this because we spend about five minutes thumping each other until a shop assistant asks us if we're actually going to buy them or are just here to play. A little shame-faced, we pay up and leave, keeping our armaments hidden in carrier bags – none of us want to be spotted by Grunts while carrying an arsenal made from foam.

It's only me and Mum for dinner; Tony's out, sealing some deal at the snooker club. I like it when it's just the two of us and Mum's endless cups of tea. For some reason, the tea's an important part of Our Time; it used to act as a soother for her after she and Dad split up.

And I like the fact that she's done egg and chips for dinner. It's the food equivalent of a cuppa; a hug on a plate.

"Mum, d'you think you could make some cloaks for me and the guys?" I ask, forking a chip into the yolk. "For the LARP thing?"

"Hmm. I'd need measurements. What sort of thing do you want?"

As we eat, we discuss the types of cloak she can make and settle on something hooded and not too long, like the elven cloaks worn by Frodo and the other hobbits.

IM: *Because you really need to be fashion-conscious when you're dressed as an elf and waving a rubber sword around! *Facepalms**

After dinner, I head on up to the Lair, wondering whether I should put something a bit more obvious on Facebook, something that might light the Fires of Jealousy inside Sarah. But I bottle it, feeling stupid and childish for even thinking it. Instead, I check through my messages. There's one from Dad:

hi son how r u? gr8 2 c u on wknd wish it wz longr! i kno it wzn't gr8 with lucas & thnx 4 trying. things still not gud with him. ne ideas? LOL anyway cu soon. Lu dad xxx

IM: *Numbers! Numbers instead of words! GAH!*

It's hideous. Just hideous. In fact, it's so hideous that part of me wishes he wouldn't bother; I don't know why grown-ups feel they have to jump on the Groovy Train with things like text-talk. Maybe it's some sort of attempt to appear relevant. Whatever it is, it just irritates me.

"**ne ideas?**" Wow. For my dad, that's a biggie. I don't think he's ever asked for my help before. Dad's the kind of guy who just shuts up and gets on with it – he doesn't really do problems. Not his own, anyway; it's the one thing he doesn't share.

The whole Lucas thing ought to be a lot simpler than it is: Dad's being a jerk and so's Lucas. But I can't help feeling that I'm missing something.

I send a message back, telling him I love him and leave it at that.

But there's another buzz of frustration that just won't go away. When Clare explained the Girl Plan to me on the train, it all seemed so simple; I hadn't factored in lying to my mates, being given a packet of Peter Parkas ©Beggsy by my stepfather or a complete lack of reaction from Sarah. In my head, the equation ran:

Lie + Jealousy = Girlfriend

Instead, I just feel like I'm waist-deep in doo-doo.

IM: *And I have a sneaking suspicion that it's your own.*

Time to go for a little Brain Cleaning, in the form of sword painting.

I bust my sword out of its cardboard packaging and give it a once-over. It's pretty cool, but it looks like something you'd find in a *Transformers* movie, not something forged from the shards of Narsil...

I mix up the base coat according to Beggsy's instructions and it already starts to look a little better. While I'm waiting for it to dry, I hit the *Dark Knight*, hoping to find some answers to my problems in the ragged artwork of Frank Miller's seething world.

I've always loved the Joker. From the moment I started reading DC comics, you just knew he was a cut above the other villains – the crazy smile, the clown face and the insane vendetta against Batman. But in the comics and the cartoon series, you never took him that seriously; you knew that Bats was always going to scupper his mad plans. The film with Heath Ledger got closer to what we all wanted the Joker to be: dangerous, deadly and without a motive that you could describe as reasonable. The Joker in this graphic novel is just that. And then there's Batman, who's haunted by the idea that he's responsible for all the people the Joker has killed, because he just hasn't got the guts to do the same to his arch-enemy.

"How many more lies – before I finally do it?" he growls, as the body count racks up.

I haven't got Bruce Wayne's thirst for danger but, like the Caped Crusader, I've got this sneaking suspicion that the only enemy I'm battling is the one that looks back at me from the bathroom mirror every morning. Usually with a toothbrush sticking out of his mouth and flexing his arms to see if there's anything like a bicep on the horizon. Somehow, I've turned into a liar and I don't like it.

TEN

Wednesday arrives, bright and sunny. Apart from the blemish on my Timeline. From Clare.

Hey there, hot stuff! Can't wait to see you on the train next week! Maybe we'll get stuck in a tunnel this time... ;) x

IM: *Aaaarrggghh!*

Oh God. My dad's text has been out-loled with a semicolon winky-face! If there's one thing I can't stand above a lol, it's the sideways use of punctuation to somehow suggest a face or emotion. This is just Plain Wrong. Loling is bad enough, especially in a sentence like Dad's, where there is plainly nothing to lol about. But whoever was lying on their side one day and somehow made a winky-face out of some brackets and a semicolon, should be sent to the Spice Mines of Kessel until they see the error of their ways.

IM: *XD*

Part of the problem with being a Geek is that you have this default setting marked "Compromise" and however much I want to back out, I dejectedly find myself writing back:

Hey there, yourself. Can't wait to see you, too.

The bitter tang in my mouth follows me through breakfast and for most of the walk to meet the guys.

"Hey there, hot stuff!" Beggsy teases, as my Smile Department™ looks through its rapidly dwindling supplies.

"Hey there, yourself."

The ribbing's over pretty quickly and the conversation turns to the swords and how we're painting them and the school gates sort of catch us by surprise. Just as we're debating the finer points of whether we should add Runes of Power, using authentic Tengwar, time slows as I see Sarah running towards us. Apart from the radiant excitement on her face, I can't help noticing every bounce of her chest as she runs, so I turn away, pretending to look at something else, remembering the promise I made to myself on the train.

IM: *Boobs. Boobsboobsboobsboobsboobs. Bouncing, beautiful boobs.*

"Hey!" She arrives, all breathlessness and shiny skin. Whether I like it or not, the image is logged for later appraisal.

Beggsy shamelessly Tiggers over to her and gives her

an easy hug. And I watch enviously. But I've got a girlfriend and I'm not supposed to care.

"Hey, Sarah," Beggsy rasps in some approximation of a sexy voice. "How's your machine gun?" This time he's too slow to dodge the swipe that connects with his shoulder, sending him staggering to his left, with a melodramatic "Ooow!"

"Not as good as my right hook," she says, with more than a little smugness. "But I've had a chat with Caitlyn and we're up for this LARP thing. We'll see who's got no imagination! I'll need that spare sword!"

Beggsy recovers his dignity by clicking both of his fingers and doing some sort of pelvic thrust.

"The *Begg*ster!" he declares proudly.

Caitlyn appears, defusing any sarcasm bombs that Matt's got lined up. She stands beside him, smiling, but not quite able to make full eye contact with him. Matt goes rigid, like he does, and they fall into a conversation that is in complete contrast to their body language. It's like watching a courting dance between two ents.

Sarah saunters over, rubbing Beggsy's shoulder better, and he leans towards her with a sly grin on his face. It all seems so disturbingly *normal* that I just can't get my head round it. Geeks don't do this.

IM: *Perhaps they're de-Geeking...*

"And how are *you*, 'hot stuff'?" There's a wry smile

and a raised eyebrow attached to Sarah's tease, which doesn't make it any easier to bear. Nor does Beggsy's grin. I hate Facebook.

IM: *Wishes for Elven Cloak of Invisibility* *Gets the Jacket of Conspicuousness*

"Ha." It's all I've got as I register the flood of blood to my cheeks.

"It's always the quiet ones you've got to watch…" Sarah smirks in a way that makes me want to take a vow of silence. This whole interacting-with-girls-like-normal-humans thing is going to take some getting used to.

My mind's on anything but double Maths. While everybody else's is applied to Pythagoras, mine soars above all my problems, trying to get something of an overview, before eventually settling on the Lucas Branch. There's something I'm missing. It's what Mum calls a Moustache Problem: everyone else can see it, but you can't, because it's right under your nose.

IM: No wonder you can't see it, then; there's nothing there. Even after four weeks!

My hand unconsciously strays to my smooth-as-a-baby's-bum upper lip, in a mirror of a scene from The Dark Knight Returns, where Bruce shaves his 'tache off before he puts the tights back on again.

"He's worse when you're here." That's what Lucas said. But why? When Dad wasn't living in York, it never seemed to be a problem; I'd go round to where he lived with Jane, play with the kids – even if I was a bit grumpy about it – and then go home again. Sometimes I might go round for tea in the week and it all seemed cool. What's changed since they moved away? Why does my presence mean that Dad's turned into some sort of *über*-jerk?

IM: *Kerching!*

I think I've got it. For once, I might know what the problem is and, as the bell sounds, signifying the end of this numerical torture, I resolve to test my theory and call Dad tonight.

As I wander along the corridor, my Grunt Detectors™ pick up an anomaly in the crowds ahead of me: Paul Green and Lewis Mills. But it's a distraction tactic, just like the raptors perform in *Jurassic Park*: I turn round and am faced with the figure of Jason Humphries.

All I can do is find a wall to put my back against and make sure I don't look anyone in the eyes; it's the position that signals surrender, without having to beg out loud. Humphries closes in on me, his brow rippling and sinews standing out on his neck. Even though I'm already up against a wall, he puts a shovel-sized paw on my shoulder and pushes me.

He leans in close and just looks at me, an expression of disgust warping his stone-carved features.

"Dickhead." His voice is low and dangerous – this is the moment before the storm breaks. But it doesn't. Instead of the battering-ram blow to the body that my body anticipates, I get a blunt finger-jab to the shoulder.

Maybe Sarah's threat to let everyone know he asked her to read his aura is a bigger hazard to him than I'm aware. There's a moment where I think Humphries is trying to set my soul on fire with his eyes, but then he just sneers and walks away.

IM: *I guess that's the argument over.*

A hand on my shoulder sends a Distress Call to my brain as I expect more violence from Mills or Green, but the whispered squeak of Beggsy's concern sets all my systems back to zero.

"Dude!" Conveys *Is worried*. "You OK?"

I sag, relieved to find that I'm still alive.

"Humphries?"

"Yeah," I breathe, pushing myself tentatively off the wall.

"What did he want?" It's a standard Geek question; you check out what somebody else was whacked for, just in case you're due to get whacked yourself.

IM: *There's no honour amongst Geeks.*

"Just letting me know he cares."

We walk in silence for a bit.

"Dude. Awesome that you and Sarah are buds again."

"Yeah," I nod. "It's cool."

There's a bit more silence, but this one has some texture to it.

"And are you good with that?" Beggsy asks, as though he's been building up to it. "You know … just being friends?"

IM: *Memo to Lie Department: you're on overtime.*

"Yeah. I reckon."

"I mean, you've got a girlfriend, so you must be over Sarah, right?"

"Right." It's weird how Beggsy's so concerned about it. But I guess having girls in the gang is new for all of us and he doesn't want things to go belly up.

"Awesome. Catch you at the gates."

It's nice not to dread Art. In fact, I'm looking forward to it. I reach my desk and Sarah and Caitlyn appear about two minutes later. Mrs Cooper wants us to get into pairs to work on something about perception. We're supposed to draw each other, but try and capture the essence of the person we're drawing. It's not meant to be an accurate sketch, which is great because my sketching skills aren't that hot – everything ends up looking a bit cartoony.

IM: *A bit like your life.*

To my delight, Sarah turns in her seat and points a finger at me, then at herself and raises her eyebrows in a facial question mark. I manage to contain my joy enough to raise a thumb and she gathers her stuff and comes over.

"You're going to need a bigger pad," I say.

"Why?"

With a serious face on, I flex one of my microscopic muscles; it's like someone's balanced a baked bean on a piece of string – but it gets the required result: Sarah's silver laughter decorates the air between us.

"You shouldn't put yourself down!"

"Got to get in there before anyone else does!" I smile back, flipping open my sketchbook and squinting at her, like you're supposed to when you're drawing something.

"Be kind," she says, nodding at my hovering pencil. "Especially with my eyes."

"What d'you mean?"

"My right one's a bit bigger than my left."

IM: *Eyes. She's talking about her eyes. Those things in her head, not those things up her jumper.*

"Is it?" I frown, leaning forward and looking hard. And she's right. It's hard to see, because of the trademark black eyeliner she wears, but her right eye *is* a little bigger. As I stare, I become aware of a faint flush spreading across Sarah's cheeks. I think I'm making her

235

self-conscious, so I say, "Nope, can't see it – you're being paranoid."

Sarah raises a wry eyebrow. "Either my make-up's good today or you're just being kind."

"For a cyclops you look pretty good to me…" I'm taking a chance that Guy Humour and Girl Humour are similar things.

There's a moment's silence, before Sarah starts to laugh again. It begins in stuttering bursts, like someone starting a car on a cold morning and then she starts, like, *really* laughing – so much so that Mrs Cooper calls our names across the classroom in her Warning Voice.

"Sorry," Sarah sniffs, wiping her imperfect eyes. "That was just … funny!"

IM: *Time for a change of theme tune, I think. Of course! James Bond! Here we go… Dinga-dingding-a-ding-a-dinga-dingding-a-ding-a…*

We calm down and start sketching, the silence punctuated by little tremors of mirth from Sarah. It's weird to begin with – looking at each other this intently, but it gives me a chance to really explore her face. Slowly I realize that her make-up hides a lot, like the eye thing. But it's her eyes that draw me in and, as I stare at them and she stares back, I detect something else I'd never seen before – they look a bit sad.

Sarah's sensors are obviously online or I'm staring

just a bit too long, because she suddenly breaks the eye contact with a nervous smile. I pretend not to notice, but on my picture, as though she's looking through the loop, I sketch the ankh she's wearing round her neck over one of her eyes. Which, in my portrait of perception, are exactly the same size.

"How're things with Clare?" Sarah asks. For a moment I forget who Clare is – everyone else just refers to her as "your girlfriend", which makes it easy to remember.

IM: *Dinga-dingding-a-ding-a-dinga-dingding…*

"Yeah… Pretty good, I think." I don't think I squirm that much. But I've got to remember what this is all about – I'm trying to make her jealous.

"You think?"

"Well … we haven't talked much because…"

IM: *Scrabbles through Clare's profile* Um … she hasn't got a mouth?

"…she's at boarding school." Telling the truth is so much easier, it really is.

"Oh, I see. That must be hard."

"Not really. It's cool."

"Not sure I could handle it, myself – too much like hard work." We're both sketching now, flicking each other occasional looks and speaking across our sketchbooks.

"I dunno; you don't seem frightened of hard work."

Sarah's eyes widen as she stares at her page and she shakes her head deliberately. "Nooo," she half mutters. "Daddy's girl, Mum used to say. Meaning spoiled. Get what I want, apparently."

IM: *Incoming! This is Important Information!*

This must be a slip up. I've never heard Sarah mention her dad before and, to be fair, I've never asked. As I watch her draw, her jaw clenches slightly. And although I ought to be on my mission to make her jealous, something in me responds.

"Do you still see him?"

Sarah blinks at her drawing before she answers.

"No. One day he just left. Haven't seen him since. But that was a long time ago. Ancient history." There's no sadness in her voice, she's got perfect control of that. But it's in her eyes – her beautiful, asymmetrical eyes.

"Yeah," I nod at my picture. "When my folks split up, I had this weird idea that it was all my fault. Like I'd somehow caused it or that I wasn't … I don't know … I wasn't…"

"Like you weren't worth it? Like you didn't deserve the things everyone else has?"

"Yeah." I look up to see Sarah's still sketching. But it doesn't matter – we're sharing something and it suddenly seems more important than a kiss or holding her hand.

"That's the one. You had that, too?"

"I just thought it was because I wasn't good enough. Like, if I'd been better, they'd never have split up."

I nod, knowing just how she feels. "But you know that's not true, don't you?" I say. "And that idea about not being worth it … it goes."

Sarah looks up, a worn smile hanging by a thread from her face.

"I know," she murmurs. "But sometimes it still … creeps up on you."

IM: *Terra firma, Captain.*

"We've all got room for improvement!" I say. And to diffuse any awkwardness, I flex my bee-sting bicep. "But you're forgetting something – no one can be as good as you at being you! And it doesn't matter what anyone else thinks, as long as you think it!" The urge to say "I think you're perfect," is stupidly strong, but I hold it back. It's not the right time for that sort of thing.

Sarah's eyes tighten and she frowns, like she's reading my face.

IM: *Brain to Aura Department: shut that damn thing down!*

But I don't think she's trying to read my aura. The sadness in her eyes looks like it's reached breaking point, but she blinks it back so quickly that you'd barely see it.

"Thanks," she smiles. There's a moment where we're

just looking at each other again, but she breaks it by suddenly flipping over her pad and showing me her sketch. "What d'you think?"

The picture is definitely me, but without being *me*. For a start, I've got muscles and I'm carrying a Gandalf-style staff, while shooting some sort of magical light out of my other hand. It's done in a manga style that makes me look way cooler than I ever could be. I look like some heroic prophet.

"Wow," I grin. "Wish I had muscles like that!"

"It's all about perception, Archie. Remember?"

IM: *Incoming message, Captain – but it appears to be encrypted...*

I wish I knew more about what girls mean when they say stuff. It would be worth having Clare here just to decipher Sarah's sentence or to tell me that I'm reading too much into nothing.

IM: *Which is more likely?*

"Let's have a look at yours." Sarah nods at my pad, so I hold it up.

It's a lot messier than hers. I think I've been trying to copy the jagged art style in *The Dark Knight Returns* to put across the emotions in the picture. But, by comparison, it looks like it's been drawn by someone with frostbite. Instead of the full-body experience that Sarah's drawn, I've just gone for her face, but I've double-lined it, like there's two faces, one hiding behind the other.

"It's really good," she nods, looking at it intently. "Do I really look that sad?"

"Like you said," I return, "it's all about perception, remember?"

The sun's shining by the time the lesson ends and the guys are already waiting for us, when me, Sarah and Caitlyn make it to the gates. Beggsy's making them laugh with some clowning about and Matt hovers close enough to Caitlyn that he could touch her, but doesn't. Only Ravi seems unaffected by the presence of the girls, just watching and observing with the hint of a smile on his lips.

While it's cool seeing the whole gang together, part of me wants to carry on the conversation with Sarah. It felt like we were really starting to get to know each other, like I was getting a glimpse behind her perfectly made-up mask. But, as we walk through the streets, she seems pretty keen to put some distance between us, walking up ahead with Beggsy. I guess she doesn't want to have that conversation in public, but it's like the drawbridge that was lowered in Art has been swiftly pulled back up again. I've been left in the moat.

Weirdly, Caitlyn seems to notice and drops back along the pavement to walk with me, but all I can think about is trying to keep the connection I've made with Sarah from slipping through my fingers. I need something that brings us all together. Something not too heavy.

IM: *A foam-rubber club?*

Bingo!

"Hey, guys!" I call. "I'm going to need to measure you for the cloaks!"

"Have you got a tape measure?" Ravi booms, turning round.

"No."

"What about rulers, dude?" Beggsy chirrups, from under Sarah's arm. Sarah doesn't say anything – although she smiles at his suggestion.

"I guess that'd work. What are we supposed to measure?"

"Across the shoulders and down the back." It's Caitlyn.

IM: *Scanners indicate presence of a Geek. Identified as the female of the species!*

I flick a look at Matt, who responds with a sage nod, like he measures people up every day.

IM: *Preparing for his future as an undertaker, no doubt.*

"Caitlyn knows these things," he states benignly.

"OK," I defer cheerfully. "Let's do it!" I pull out my ruler. "Who's first?"

"Come on, then," Ravi says, presenting his back to me. "Somebody'd better write this down."

Matt pulls out a schoolbook and stands by, pen at the ready.

Under Caitlyn's instruction, I measure Ravi's shoulders, marking where the ruler ends with my finger, before continuing with the rest of the measurement. It's a bit of a hash up, but Caitlyn says it'll do. She calls out the numbers to Matt, who faithfully writes them down. Then I measure down Ravi's back to his knees in the same way, eliciting a sharp "Steady on!" as I have to press my finger just above his butt. Cue laughter from all involved. Including Sarah. I think I can hear the drawbridge being lowered.

Matt's up next and he does a comedy back-arching thing when I get to the same place and shouts out a "Wahey!" as though I've just pinched his backside. Beggsy follows and then, without thinking, I call for the next victim – and am suddenly looking at Sarah's back.

IM: *Whatever you do, don't faint. It's not that impressive.*

It's all in the details, from the way the feathers of her jet-black hair contrast with the silken ivory that is the back of her neck. As I place the ruler on her shoulders, my senses are overwhelmed by the way she smells. It's pure and delicate, like a snowflake ought to smell.

Her perfectly sized shoulders measured, I'm suddenly aware of where the ruler's going next. Sarah doesn't say anything, so I assume she's cool with it.

IM: *Get yourself together! It's only her ... bum. Her perfectly formed bum. *Slaps own face**

In fact, nobody says anything. I can almost feel the stares of apprehension from my mates boring holes through the back of my head. My palms are suddenly slick with a film of sweat and there's an unwelcome surge of heat in my groin, which I try to ignore and dispel, but to no avail.

IM: *Conjures images of dead kittens* Nope.

I measure to the centre of her back and press a finger there, drunk on the softness of her jersey and the way it disguises the strength of her spine.

IM: *Karate. She does karate.*

I line up the next measurement from my finger, which will take the ruler down to the flawless contours of her skirt-clad buttocks.

"Dude! What are you *doing* down there? You're not mapping for Google Earth!"

I hate Beggsy SO MUCH right now, but I'm in the minority. Everyone else snorts, laughs or chuckles, including Sarah, whose mirth is translated into little jiggles of her backside. I don't think I can handle much more.

IM: *Don't think you could handle any of it.*

I kneel down to keep measuring and try not to stare at what's behind the ruler. It also gives me a chance to relieve the pressure that's steadily growing in my trousers.

"Get on with it!" Ravi jeers, as I fumble and drop the ruler, muttering "sorry" over and over, like some religious incantation. For once in my life, I'm glad I don't have X-ray vision.

IM: *Your utility belt would have to be PACKED with Kleenex. Just sayin'.*

I pick up the ruler and place it on Sarah's behind. With trembling fingers my senses go into overdrive, trying to increase their sensitivity to everything they encounter, while my brain tries to ignore it and quell the steam in my strides.

"What does it say, dude?"

"What?"

"It's in Braille, isn't it?"

"Cut it out Beggsy," Sarah laughs.

A nasty little part of me wishes Beggsy wasn't coming to the LARP. I reach the hem of Sarah's skirt, which floats just above the back of her knees, and call out the final figures.

"You all right down there?" Matt smiles darkly, offering me a hand up. He knows the problem I've got right now, but luckily, the sight of his grinning face is the perfect antidote.

"Shall *I* measure Caitlyn?" he asks. "Might be a bit too much for you…"

The pulsing in my pants slowly fades to a dull ache and I tentatively stand, checking for signs of Wigwam Trousers, before handing the ruler to Matt.

"It's so lovely of your mum to do this," Sarah smiles, as Matt measures his sort-of-girlfriend, and I sense that there's a bit more slack on the drawbridge ropes.

"She likes making stuff," I reply, making a mental note to ask Mum for two more capes.

"She's awesome at it!" Beggsy chipmunks, taking a detour via Darth Vader. "You should check out the photos of the Gruffalo costume she made him!"

IM: *Deny! Deny! Deny!*

For a lightning flash I hate him – that information was for Geek Eyes Only. It's like he's trying to make me look stupid. But, as Sarah dissolves into laughter, I realize he's done me a favour, whether he meant to or not. The rest of the journey home is about how cute/stupid/lame I looked and I roll with it, enjoying the attention. But Beggsy goes a little bit quiet and I'm left with the feeling that I'm missing something.

I walk in through the front door to find Mum on the phone in the hallway.

"Oh, hang on – he's just come in; I'll put him on." She hands me the receiver and before my brain has the chance to wonder who it is, she mouths "Dad" at me. I look at her for a second. While Dad's called the landline a couple of times since he moved away, he tends to favour the joys of grammar-free texting.

IM: *lol.*

Diplomatically, Mum just nods towards the handset and then goes into the kitchen. I can hear the kettle being flicked on.

"Hey, Dad."

"Hey, buddy – how're you doing?"

"Good. You?" The kettle's starting to boil. Talking with your dad when he doesn't live under the same roof feels a bit weird. I know Mum says she's cool with it, but I can't help feeling it's like I've summoned a ghost from her past, even though he's called me.

"Yeah… Look. I wanted to chat to you about a couple of things…"

There's a flurry of panic in my stomach. It sounds like I've done something or upset someone, but I can't think what.

IM: *Jane. You didn't laugh at her jokes. Gotta be.*

"OK."

"Well, for a start, I owe you an apology. I'm sorry about getting all ratty when Lucas got upset. I know you were only trying to help and I didn't mean it to come out like that."

"Dad," I say, "it's cool. You texted me."

"Yeah, but it's better to say these things, sometimes. Texts can get misunderstood."

IM: *esp whn u swp nos 4 letrs…*

"OK. Well, it's cool. But listen, I was going to call you too – I think I know what the problem is with … you know … the thing you texted me about." I don't want to say it out loud, in case Mum hears; I want to keep my parents' private lives separate from each other. But it makes me feel a bit guilty at the same time.

"You mean Lucas?"

"Yeah! I think I know what's eating him."

"Go on."

"OK. Here's the thing. I tried to speak to him in his room about you being 'weird' like he said and he said that you were worse because I was there." I've got to be careful of how I phrase this. I don't want to cause more problems.

"OK…" Dad sounds a bit wary, but I keep going.

"Do you think you act differently when I'm there?"

"I was trying to make Lucas feel as important as you… Was I going overboard?"

248

"Yeah," I say softly. "You were a bit." I can virtually hear Dad's shoulders sagging from here. But at least I can picture him standing in his house, talking to me. Now I've visited the house, he's not just some disembodied voice. It's comforting.

Dad sighs. "You're right, Archie. I was trying to stop him from feeling threatened by you by … I don't know … being 'one of the boys'. You're my son and I love you, but I wanted him to feel like there's no difference – because I do care about him. Even though he's not my son. I was just trying to show him that I'm interested in him, too – even when you're around. But it looks like I went a bit over the top." He sighs again. "Are you OK with me telling you this, Archie?"

"Yeah, course I am. But you ought to have a chat with him. And you ought to just be yourself…" It's something Dad once told me I should do and he laughs at the reference.

"Wise words," he chuckles ruefully. "Thanks, son. Now, I actually phoned to chat to you, not have you solve my problems."

"What's up?"

"Just what I was going to ask you. I know things were a bit funny with Lucas, but you weren't yourself, either. There was something on your mind… So…"

It's my turn to sigh.

"Ye-ah," I groan, through twisted lips. "Sorry... It was just that..." I groan again. "I'd been invited to a party at the weekend and I really wanted to go. And everyone else was going and I just... Sorry."

"Hey – there's no need to apologize! Look, I thought it might be something like that. I've had a chat with your mother and we've agreed that if there's ever a time when you want to do something else instead of come up, then just say. As long as you're happy, I'm happy – *wherever* you are. OK?"

"OK, Dad. Thanks. Sorry."

"No need for sorries, son." There are voices in the background. "Better go, the kids have just got home. I'll text you. Love you, Archie."

"Love you, too," I rasp and the line goes dead.

"Tea?" Mum's suddenly beside me, a steaming cup in either hand. "You all right?"

"Yeah. I'm good," I smile. "I just miss him, sometimes."

Mum puts her hand in my hair and sweeps it off my face.

"I know," she says.

"I got those measurements. For the cloaks," I gabble. "And would you be able to make two more? Caitlyn and Sarah are coming."

"Girls?" she teases, giving me a quizzical look.

"No problem, love. Tony got the old curtains down from the attic, so I'll have a go tonight."

"Thanks, Mum."

After dinner and homework, I get serious on the sword, hitting it up with some hardcore highlights. About halfway through, I find myself staring at my reflection in the bathroom mirror, wearing my elf ears. There's something not right.

IM: *You're fourteen years old and you're wearing Vulcan prosthetics... Anything else?*

On a whim, I sweep my hair back and suddenly the transformation is complete: the ears accentuate the cut of my cheekbones and my exposed forehead adds an intellectual air to my face. I look pretty good.

IM: *On YOUR planet, maybe.*

By bedtime, I'm almost a fully paid-up passenger on the Hope Train: my sword's going to be good, I'm going to look good and things between Sarah and me are pretty good. And I've started the ball rolling with Dad and Lucas. If this was a tabletop scenario, the Dungeon Master would be awarding me bucketfuls of Experience Points right now. All things considered, I should be levelling up, but there's just one thing holding me back: the fauxmance. It's like a weight round my ankles.

ELEVEN

Thursday begins with another post from Clare:

Hey there, sexy. Great to talk last night. There's a smooch waiting for you. All you have to do is come and collect it... x

IM: *Plays funeral march*

The thing is, not only are these messages not for my benefit, but they're ruining my personal life, too. All they do is keep hammering home that I'm lying to my friends and playing a stupid game with the girl I ought to be completely honest with. I briefly consider sending her a private message to tell her that I want out, but my Geeky Code of Manners just won't let me. We don't make demands. It's no wonder there are no Geek Terrorists:

The Goblin's Hovel has been occupied by the Geek Liberation Front and is surrounded by police cars. Crouching behind a vehicle, a police negotiator calls through a megaphone, "What do you want?"

Archie, the rebellious GLF ringleader, shouts back from behind a window, armed with a foam sword: "We politely request to be allowed to say 'no' to

people without feeling like we've let them down!"

There is a flurry of activity behind the police cars as the negotiator talks to the Chief of Police. Urgent voices betray the tension of the situation. After what seems like an eternity, the negotiator raises his megaphone once more. "I'm sorry – we just can't meet those terms!"

"OK. We'll be out in a minute. Sorry to have troubled you."

That's how we roll: backwards, if we're asked to.

IM: *Over broken glass, if required.*

Anything as long as it makes everyone else happy. But I can't even think of a reply; my brain doesn't want to play today. So I just shut the laptop down and get ready for school.

The guys are waiting, as they always are. But there are subtle differences in Matt: he's walking less like a guy who fears being judged with every step he takes and more like someone who doesn't care quite so much.

Beggsy, by comparison, is as hyper as usual, and there are constant looks for approval between his gags and stupid comments. Exposure to girls seems to be messing with him a bit. Only Ravi remains constant – quiet, observant, but dependable, like he's gathering information on how we mere mortals conduct ourselves.

IM: *He's picked the wrong bunch if he's looking for information on Normal Behaviour...*

We arrive at school and the morning passes in a blur of Biology and Geography. At lunchtime I head to the canteen with Beggsy. By the time we get our food, the rest of the gang have already staked their claim on a table. The word "gang" now incorporates Sarah and Caitlyn as Honorary Members: Caitlyn's sat by Matt, who is apparently so interested in whatever she's saying that the rest of the table might as well not exist. Sarah's sat by Ravi, and Beggsy takes the seat the other side of her, before hooting his way through some tale about his last trip to the dentist. Ravi just observes, smiling and nodding, but it's Sarah I'm watching, suddenly aware that every confident laugh and every swish of her jet-black hair is some sort of camouflage. The Most Beautiful Girl In The World™ has problems. Just like the rest of us.

"Hey, Archie," Ravi detonates. "What's up?"

"Nothing much," I shrug, sitting down next to him.

"How's Clare?"

IM: *D'OH!*

The word "Clare" drops on to the table with a clang and there's a slight dip in the atmosphere. Maybe it's just wishful thinking, but I'm sure I sense Sarah's ears pricking up.

"Yeah, she's cool," I smile breezily, as I sit. "Oh! I didn't get a drink! Anyone else want any water?" It's a bit lame, but it gets me out of a corner. By the time I get back, the conversation's taken a new direction.

It's the word "toilet paper" that catches my attention. The LARPers are now discussing what we ought to be taking with us for the weekend and Matt says "toilet paper".

"What for?" I ask distractedly, dishing out the cups.

"What do you think?" Matt fires back. "Not for blowing your nose!"

IM: *And NOT for your research into Next catalogues!*

"But why?"

"Dude! It's a camping trip! There won't be any toilets!" I'm so glad Beggsy is here to offer his expert opinion.

The trouble is, this information adds a frisson of fear to my already overloaded brain.

IM: *No TOILETS?*

I don't know which is worse: a toilet in York where you might be heard or overhear something you shouldn't or the possibility of having to do your business in the Great Outdoors, where you might be discovered at a moment's notice.

IM: *Dressed as an elf.*

Beggsy's introduced the phrase "squat and drop" to the conversation, so it's time to take charge and steer it in another direction. I don't want Sarah's mind filled with images of me either squatting or dropping.

"So – everyone got their costumes ready?"

It has the desired effect. Pretty soon, we're all talking about what we're going to wear.

I spend the rest of the day in a bit of a fug – everything in my life seems to be going pretty well, for once. Apart from that one, big stupid decision I made to get involved in Clare's Plan. I guess this is the point where I wish Dad was around. He always has this way of stepping back from a problem and helping you look at it like you're flying above it. Unfortunately, his son can't quite see above ground level.

As I join the gang at the gates at the end of the day, part of me wishes it could all go back to how it was before I met Sarah. It all seemed a lot simpler then.

I dip in and out of the conversation, which morphs into Matt and Beggsy explaining the rules of combat and magic to the girls. They end up giving an impromptu display with their rulers, while Matt narrates. But as much as everyone else is laughing and as much as my EM goes into overdrive to make the appropriate noises, my heart's just not in it. I feel like I'm going to be exposed as a fraud and a liar at any moment.

By the time we've all said goodbye and I hit home, there's a solar eclipse taking place over my head.

Even the mischievous grin on Mum's face as I go into the kitchen can only raise an apology of a smile in return.

"You all right, love?" she fusses, ruffling my hair and plonking a cup of tea down on the table in front of me. "You look like you've got the weight of the world on your shoulders."

"Yeah... I'm fine," I sigh. "Just ... you know ... just Life." It comes out sulkier than I mean it to, but I think my EM's trying to tender its resignation.

"Maybe this'll cheer you up." Mum buzzes over to the kettle, and picks up a brown-paper parcel. She puts it in front of me and does one of those funny, shivery smiles she does when she's excited.

IM: *Could be a new life.*

Confused for a moment, I just stare at it. And then, next to where the stamps are, I see some faded red ink; just enough to make out the words "...er Colony". I look up at Mum, who smiles again and sits down, holding her cup with both hands.

"Open it!" Mum flaps, nodding at the package.

I rip at the paper to find thin, white tissue protecting something soft. I scrabble some more, to reveal a cloth square which slowly unfolds into a shirt. But not just any old shirt. An Awesome Shirt. This is one of those shirts you see in medieval movies – puffy sleeves and a lace-up collar, which I can leave open to show off a bit of my chest.

IM: *You might want to borrow Beggsy's beard to shove up there.*

"Whoa!"

"Keep looking!"

I pull out a black square and see it open, like one of those paper flowers you put in water, to form a pair of britches. Black, velvet britches. And then, underneath that, there's a belt, with a skull buckle and a bit to put your sword in.

"Mum! What did…? How did…?" The solar eclipse over my head is passing rapidly.

"I just went to that site where we bought the ears and had a look round. Did I do OK?"

She knows she did more than OK, and I reach over and give her a big hug.

"You going to try them on?"

"Yep!" And then Mum's left eating the cloud of dust that I leave in my wake.

I dash up to my Lair, wrestle my clothes off and get to grips with real-life elf-wear. The trousers go on, followed by the shirt and belt and then the ears. I stick my sword in the scabbard for effect, and then I dash into Mum and Tony's room. I need the full-length effect. It's like someone's changed the channel on the mirror. Instead of the usual picture of a hopeless Geek, my scrawny frame is hidden beneath my billowing shirt and even my legs look pretty good under velvet. The leering skull round my waist adds just the right element of danger and mystery. I'm looking at something much more impressive … imposing, even. A quick slick back of the hair and Bararc Darkleaf stares back at me, with all the Wisdom of the Eldar playing in his eyes.

IM: *And all the ignorance of the Geek telegraphed by his ears.*

Mum appears in the mirror behind me and puts something over my shoulders; it's my cloak. And it's perfect. I fasten the clasp and pull up the hood and suddenly, there's nothing Archie-ish left about me. This must be how Bruce Wayne feels whenever he puts on the suit.

IM: *"Commissioner; is it true that Gotham's criminals are under siege from a giant gnome?"*

"D'you like it, love?" Mum asks, knowing full well I do, but wanting the pleasure of hearing me say it.

"It's brilliant, Mum!" I laugh. "Thank you!" As she giggles with pleasure, I turn round, draw my sword and chase her halfway down the stairs, batting her with my foam weapon.

If I can't have fun in my own life, I'm going to make sure I have fun in someone else's. At least elves don't get caught up in fauxmances.

By the time I've changed back into my jeans, Tony arrives and we all sit down to some shepherd's pie made with soya beans or something. And then it's up the stairs for the usual, but I do my homework and finish the final details on the sword with my ears on. And out of respect for another guy with pointy ears, I get into bed early and break out the *Dark Knight*.

Frank Miller knows how to spring a surprise – this is the final showdown between Bats and the Joker! But Bats doesn't kill him, like he should. He can't – he hasn't got what it takes. So, the Joker does it for him.

The way I read it, it's not because Batman hasn't got the guts, it's because it'd be like destroying a part of himself. The Joker's what defines him and without him around, he'd be nothing. And maybe that's how I feel about Sarah. Maybe the torment I seem to keep putting myself through is what defines me.

And without it, I'd be nothing.

IM: *No change there, then…*

Just as I'm about to turn my bedside light off, R2 squeals from my bedside table. My gloom deepens, as I see it's a text from Clare.

IM: *I have an awfully bad feeling about this…*

Heads up, Cupcake! It's all systems go this end! Ollie's taken the bait, so it's time for me to get single.

Have changed my status – suggest you do the same. Been great dating you! Will keep you posted. See you on the train, your EX-Girlfriend, C xxx

IM: *Phase Three: initiated…*

I climb out of bed, call up Facebook on my laptop and scroll back along my Timeline to find Clare's status update, which tells me and the rest of Facebook that she is "Single". Above the various comments of condolence from her girlfriends, someone has hit the Like button.

Someone called Oliver.

I open up my profile and change my status to the same. But it doesn't feel like I'm part of some brilliant plan. It might've worked for Clare, but all it's done for me is teach me how easily I can lie. And to Sarah and my mates, of all people. I ought to be rejoicing and excited that the next phase of my mission is underway. Instead, I just feel worse than ever.

TWELVE

Friday starts before my alarm clock does. I'm awake and excited: today is LARP Day! And something has fallen into place overnight: I'm single! Which means that I can start getting closer to The Most Beautiful Asymmetrically Eyed Girl In The World™ – but on my own terms. And my terms are dressing up as an elf and going on a dangerous quest with her.

IM: *Isn't there something else you'd rather be doing … y'know … like gouging your eyes out with a spoon? Just a suggestion.*

First thing I do is check my sword: looking good, full of arcane mystery and untold stories. Then I carefully fold up my Elfwear and put the ears in the pockets of my britches. On top of that goes *The Dark Knight Returns*, my iPod and my mobile. That's the Important Bits sorted.

IM: *Robinson Crusoe couldn't have done it better. No, really.*

I hit the bathroom, have a quick shower and grab a roll of toilet paper from under the sink. With a bit of luck, I won't need to use it. I can't imagine, in my wildest dreams, making the announcement to Sarah that I've got to leave the battlefield because I need a poo. No way.

IM: *Nobody seemed to do it in* The Lord of the Rings. *Not even Sam and Frodo, and they walked for months. "Where's Gandalf? There's a Balrog coming!" "See that bush with the pointed hat sticking out of it? He's dealing with one of his own…"*

I hurry downstairs to discover I'm not the first up. Mum's there, surrounded by piles of Stuff.

"Tea?" she asks, already filling a cup. "I've packed your clothes and the cloaks are on the table – all ironed. Your sleeping bag's rolled up next to the tent."

"Wow, Mum!" It seems I have my own little Camping Fairy.

"Well, you'll need to thank Tony; he got the tent out and bought a little camping stove, even though Marvin's taking one. There're pots and pans and plates and cutlery and a torch. I'll make some food for you to take."

I'm speechless. I'd only thought as far as my ears and a foam sword.

"Thanks, Mum."

Once breakfasted, I head off to meet the guys. And to my surprise, Sarah and Caitlyn. The gang are assembled on Hamilton Road, no doubt impatient to get chatting about what the plans are for later.

"Well met, fellows!" I hail them, striding forward as imperiously as I can and raising an arm in salute.

But instead of the round of pseudo-medieval greetings I'm expecting, all I get is a lukewarm set of nods, as their conversation grinds to a halt.

IM: *Checks to see if flies are undone*

"What's up?" It's like I've crashed a funeral. The atmosphere that ought to be thick with excitement and bubbling with laughter is subdued and apprehensive. There's some earnest nodding between Beggsy and the girls, before Sarah and Caitlyn start to walk ahead. The guys flick each other uneasy glances, before, as one, they bathe me in an uncertain gaze.

"You OK, Archie?" Ravi manages, while everyone else checks out the pavement.

"I'm good. What's going on?"

IM: *I smell a disturbance in the Force.*

"Dude – Clare!" Beggsy splutters, clapping a hand to his forehead in exasperation, like some stereotype of an Italian chef.

IM: *This is Archie's Interior Monologue; I'm not in at the moment, but if you'd like to leave a message after the tone...*

Bollocks. In all the excitement of ears and tents and foam swords, I forgot. I'm newly single.

IM: *Easy to forget, given it's your default setting.*

"Uh ... yeah," I nod, my EM scrunching my face up into something that I hope gives the impression of a deep and wounding pain.

"*Dude!*" Beggsy bursts again, stepping forward as though he might give me a hug or something, but finds it too awkward to follow through; his arms do a weird little jerking thing, like whoever's working his strings suddenly woke up, but then went back to sleep again. "What ... I mean... What *happened*?"

I breathe in deeply and then expel a sigh for as long as possible, without actually passing out. Not only does this add to the picture of a Man in Torment, but it buys me vital thinking time. After a few moments, I opt for a version of the truth.

"She – ah – she... There's another guy." It kind of says it all.

IM: *Apart from the hideous lie bits...*

"*Dude!*" Beggsy supersonics. "What a ... I mean... What a *bitch!*" I don't think I've ever seen him so outraged and the sympathetic nods from Matt and Ravi only compound the horrendous feeling of guilt that swirls in my chest, like some sort of poison. "Sorry, dude," Beggsy blinks furiously. "Sorry. I know you liked her and all that..."

"I think now might be a good time to shut up," Matt scowls at him, trying to lighten my load.

IM: "*O, time. Thou must untangle this, not I. 'Tis too hard a knot for me to untie.*" Act Two, Scene Two.

I thank you.

"Archie," Ravi thunders, clapping his hands on my shoulder, "we're your friends. We're here for you. If you need to talk or whatever – just let us know, OK?"

"OK."

While this might seem a bit melodramatic to anyone else, you've got to remember that this has never happened to one of us before. None of us has ever had a girlfriend and none of us has ever been dumped. My Geeky, gracious friends are dealing with this the only way they know how: awkwardly and riddled with clichés. But every kind word and gesture they throw my way only serves to remind me what a two-faced liar I am.

IM: *Cad (noun): old-fashioned; a man who behaves badly or dishonestly, especially to women. See also: Archie.*

Matt swings up alongside me and tentatively pats me once on the back, signalling his sorrow for me and reminding us all that we ought to get to school. We walk on in silence, my friends' heads bowed lower than mine and each lost in their own thoughts, signalled only by the occasional nod or sigh of disbelief.

We hit the gates, where Sarah and Caitlyn are waiting for us, presumably to see if I'm all snot and tears. I know it's wrong, and I need to kill this as quickly as possible, but a part of me is basking in my new role as Heartbroken Romeo.

266

"Guys," I announce, although it feels like someone else has taken control of my body, "I just want to say thanks. But I'm not going to mess up this weekend with my stuff. We're supposed to be enjoying ourselves, right? So, let's forget everything else and get on with it." And then, in a moment of inspiration, I add, in my Declaiming Voice™: "Bararc Darkleaf commands it!" It's brilliant. It's like in the films where they're being shot at and the guy everybody likes takes one in the leg, but tells the others to go on without him.

IM: *But normally, he's not pretending.*

The guys clap me on the shoulder and pat my back, but Sarah links my arm in hers and we walk into school. I feel like a triumphant, treacherous god.

I don't think I've ever felt so fantastic and so bad at the same time. Even though she has to go off to Physics, I can still feel the sensation of Sarah's arm in mine, can still smell her snowflake scent – it's like I'm walking around with her hologram beside me. Beggsy balances the scales for me, though. It's like he can believe my dumping less than I can and, through Biology, he tries to convince me not to give up on Clare.

IM: *Another fly in your evil web.*

"Dude. You've got to fight for her! She's your *girlfriend*!"

"She *was* my girlfriend. Anyway, what d'you suggest? That I Facebook him to death?"

"No, but you could let her know how cut up you are!" Beggsy seems more cut up than I'm supposed to be.

"Why? What's that going to do? It's over."

"Well, what if she doesn't really mean it?"

"What d'you mean?" I ask a bit too sharply, suddenly worried that he's worked out what's really going on.

"You know... What if she's having 'problems'?" He does that air-quote thing with his fingers on the last word.

"Like *what*?" I'm actually starting to get a bit irritable now. I wish he'd let it go.

"You know... What if she's 'riding the cotton pony'?"

"Riding the WHAT?" Beggsy's seriousness combined with his choice of words takes me by surprise and I collapse into a series of snorting giggles. Maybe it's the stress of the whole situation, but the more I realize that I'm supposed to be conducting a chromatography experiment and the more serious Beggsy gets, the less I can keep it together. Within about two minutes, I'm pretending I've dropped a pencil on the floor, so that I can do one of those silent lung-laughs while tears roll down my face.

"Archie," he says, as I finally surface, sniffing and wiping my eyes, "you can't let this dude come between you. She's your *girl*friend, dude."

It's not the word "girlfriend" that suddenly brings me to my senses, it's the sudden realization that I'm surrounded by a group of friends who actually care about me. Sure, I've seen it on the tabletop, when we've been surrounded by ogres and somebody takes one for the team, but this is Real Life. I think I'm just starting to work out the difference. There are no dice in my hand and there's no Dungeon Master to guide me. I'm making my own story as I go along and, right now, this one isn't going so well.

For a split second, I *almost* confess everything to Beggsy. The words are queued up in the back of my throat – I can feel them. But a coward dies a thousand deaths and I've got a few hundred more to go. I swallow the words, hoping they don't fester too much in my gut.

Luckily, by lunchtime, everyone seems to have taken the Command of Bararc Darkleaf to heart and the conversation is back to the LARP and costumes and the rules, which we're all getting a grip on. But, even though I'm chatting and interacting with the rest of them, I feel like I'm on the outside looking in. The film camera in my head does slow-motion close ups of each of my friends, checking for signs of suspicion and mistrust, but all I get is good-natured concern. Sickening, good-natured concern.

IM: *Isn't this the cue to start hiding in tunnels, developing a taste for raw fish and throwing the word "gollum" into daily conversation?*

But the LARP-light at the end of the Tunnel of Lies grows brighter through Maths and Physics and by the time the final bell goes, I've all but forgotten that I'm supposed to be mourning the death of my first relationship.

The walk back home is fuelled by urgency, excitement and mild hysteria. We can't seem to walk or talk fast enough and the conversation goes round in circles as we all make sure we know what we're doing.

"…and you and Ravi can sleep in my tent," I gabble at Matt. "It's a four-man, so there'll be plenty of space and it'll save you guys bringing tents."

"What about you two?" Ravi asks Caitlyn and Sarah.

"We've got a tent, so we're fine, thanks, Ravi." Caitlyn's slowly spreading her field of communication beyond Matt. And Matt seems cool with it, which makes me wonder why I get so uptight when I see Sarah talking to other people.

IM: *Because you're not worthy. And you seem to be on a mission to try and prove it.*

"So where are we all meeting?" asks Matt, ever-practical. "At the Hovel?"

"Um … Sarah's mum phoned Big Marvin and he's coming to Sarah's to pick us up…" Caitlyn's coy announcement prompts a "Woo-oo!" from me and Ravi. Given that they don't even know him, they are being afforded the Highest of Honours.

"What if the guys all meet at mine," I suggest, "then Big Marv can pick us up in one go, and you can check out your *cloaks*…" I suggest.

"Has she done them?" Matt's face is suddenly an intense mask of concern. "Are they good?"

"Of *course* they're going to be good! Archie's mum made them!" Ravi says. I think he would like my mum to adopt him.

"They're *awe*some," I nod. "And they've got hoods!"

"Whoa!" Matt and Ravi breathe in perfect unison.

"Hoods?" Matt double-checks.

"Hoods," I confirm.

"Epic." Two syllables that mean so much more.

I can't help but be distracted by a crest of laughter from Sarah's conversation up ahead – Beggsy must've come up with one of his Americanisms or funny stories. I know I shouldn't, but I feel angry at him. He's managed to get under her skin, somehow. Especially when he starts shoulder-bumping her as they walk along and she

271

starts doing it back. This makes it even worse, because I know that if it was me walking with her, I wouldn't have the guts to.

By the time I get to my house, Mum is clucking and fussing like I'm leaving home for good. The pile of Stuff she had for me this morning seems to have grown.

"Mum! Why do I need *swimming* trunks? It's a camping weekend!"

"You never know!" It's Mum's answer to anything that she hasn't got an answer to.

"Well, *I* do," I growl, taking out the trunks and everything else I think I won't need. Which is quite a lot. "*Matt's* taking a cool box, so I won't need one! And *wellies*? Two nights! I'm only going for *two* nights!"

Eventually, we whittle the pile of Stuff down to a size I'm happy with, then I get changed.

Shedding my school uniform like a snakeskin, I change into a pair of jeans, my skater-style trainers, a *Star Wars* T-shirt (black with the words "Han Shot First" in the classic lettering style) and a hoodie. While I'm dressing up a bit for Sarah's sake, there's also a certain amount of liberation involved in going to a place where you can wear geeky clothes and not get hassled.

When I get back down to the kitchen, Tony's there.

"Packed your wellies?" he asks, chucking me a surreptitious wink.

IM: *Oh, GOD!*

I have a weird vision of me, naked, wearing a wellington boot. And not on my foot.

"No, there's not enough room for them, apparently," Mum chips in, patently not in on the conversation. "And he doesn't think he'll get dirty."

IM: *Brace yourself…!*

"You ought to take them, Arch. You never know when it's going to get dirty…"

IM: *Hull breached! Damage to Engineering and main warp drive!*

I *know* Tony's only looking out for me and I *know* that he thinks he's giving me early membership to the Grown-up Club by sharing Private Man Talk with me, but I don't like it. I don't like it because it feels like he's got a peek into my private life that I don't want him to have. In fact, I don't like it so much that a word flutters around the back of my head: a word that I've worked hard to consciously try and ban from my vocabulary.

IM: *Tosser.*

Luckily, a ding-dong prevents the situation unravelling any further. I open the front door to find Matt, Beggsy and Ravi with their assorted parents and what looks like the remains of a scouting jamboree: sleeping bags, backpacks and camping chairs. But there are More Important Issues to be dealt with first.

"Hey! Guys! Do you want to try on your cloaks?"

While Mum tells Mrs Cameron, Mr Beggs and Mr Guramurthy that it'll be fine to pick their sons up from here on Sunday, me and the guys charge into the kitchen.

"One Ring to rule them all, One Ring to find them, One Ring to Rule them all and in the Darkness bind them!" Tony wails from his chair, getting it oh-so-wrong. He caps off his little routine with some weird movement like he's playing an invisible piano. I guess it's supposed to be casting a spell or something. I mentally cast one back. But the guys just laugh, somehow able to see beyond whatever it is about him that seems to irritate the hell out of me.

IM: *I see a reflection, Archie…*

I pass each of the guys a green cloak. The looks on their faces as they hold them out and take them in are made of pure win.

"Awesome!" Ravi avalanches, while Matt nods with approving intensity.

"Dudes!" Conveys *Best moment in history* "Let's put them on!" Beggsy's like a six-year-old who's just discovered a box full of cowboy hats. And so are the rest of us. We all put on our cloaks and flip our hoods up, before checking ourselves out in the hall mirror.

There's something about a cloak – it creates a subtle shift in the way we stand and carry ourselves. It's as if the heroes that've been locked inside our puny bodies for all these years have suddenly been given permission to flex their muscles. I wish I could wear one every day.

IM: *Alternatively, you could just send Jason Humphries an invitation to kill you. Much less humiliating.*

"Awesome!" Beggsy breathes, his eyes looking two sizes too big. I guess he's seeing what I see – four brave adventurers, swathed in green and noble in aspect, just waiting to discover what fortunes will come their way.

IM: **Looks hard* Nope. I'm still getting four Geeks in curtains.*

We don't get long to admire ourselves. Mum appears to tell the guys that their respective parents are going, so we all file to the front door so they can say goodbye. But we take our cloaks off first. We're not *that* stupid.

IM: *Remind me again what you're doing this weekend…?*

As three cars pull out of the drive, they're almost immediately replaced by a honking horn and loud music: Big Marv's arrived.

In a lilac VW camper van. With flowers painted

on the sides.

IM: *Not quite Shadowfax, is it?*

"Ha-haaa!" Big Marv turns off the engine and leaps out. "All aboard the Skylark!" I have no idea what he's talking about but, in Big Marv's Geeky way, it sounds like it ought to be cool.

"Oh, Marvin! Is this yours? It's great!" Mum is already touching the camper van like it's a UFO or something. "Can I have a look inside?"

"Ha-haaa! But, of course! And while you do…" Big Marv turns to face the rest of us, "…we shall store your essentials!" He slides open the side-door for Mum and we are greeted by the sight of Sarah and Caitlyn sat across a small table in the back of the van.

"Aha!" Big Marv declaims. "Sprites and faeries attend within!" The girls start laughing, partly in delight and partly because they're just working out how nuts Big Marv is.

Sarah looks stunning. She's in her full Goth make-up: pale skin, smoky eyeshadow, dark lipstick and her hair has been brushed back so it sticks up, like an inky crown.

IM: *Or a burnt hedgehog. Just sayin'.*

She's wearing skinny black jeans with a white, loose-fitting T-shirt that shows a picture of an angel sitting on the ground, her wings unfurled and apparently weeping, chained by one ankle to a post. It's impossibly sexy.

Even Caitlyn looks a bit different. When Sarah's around, she doesn't figure on my radar. But now it's almost like I'm seeing her for the first time.

IM: *Not that you're shallow or anything.*

She's wearing her hair down, which kind of softens the length of her face. I also can't remember seeing her smile, but she is now and it's a clear, open one that lifts her features. I see where Matt's coming from – she's pretty, in a bookish kind of way. Caitlyn would never be a Goth or anything like that, but it's enough of a transformation for Matt, who stares at her just a bit too long for it to be a casual glance.

IM: *It must be like getting a cheeky wink off a Ringwraith.*

While the girls are showing Mum what the inside of Big Marv's camper van has got to offer, me, Ravi and Matt help stack our gear in Big Marv's top-box. We manage to get all our stuff in, save a couple of bags of treats that we elect to have on the journey.

"I want one!" Mum laughs, stepping off the van.

"Alas! We must away!" Big Marv bows to Mum and walks round to the driver's side. "And who will be joining me at the helm?"

"That'll be me," Matt mutters awkwardly. "I get travel-sick."

"Then, let us fare forward, Questers!" Big Marv hoots. Matt gets in the front and our guide starts the engine. The rest of us squeeze in next to the girls, but Beggsy gets pole position, next to Sarah. It's kind of annoying – he's become a Sarah-hog – he always seems to be as close to her as he can possibly get. It's probably just the novelty of being near a girl who doesn't laugh at you as soon as they look at you. At least being opposite her, we can talk and I can enjoy worrying whether those are her legs I'm touching with mine.

IM: *If they're not, you've just developed a fetish for table legs…*

"Ring me when you get there," Mum says, as she closes the door and mouths "Love you!" through the window. I do a big, panto-style eye-roll because everyone has seen my mum telling me she loves me and the girls are making "Awwww!" noises. It's all in fun, but it reminds me that I'm still not quite the Man of Mystery I'd like to be.

"And welcome to the Magical Marvmobile! Ha-haaa! Next stop: Ailae!" Big Marv's over-the-shoulder enthusiasm is infectious and as we drive through the streets of my home town, we pepper him with questions about what we're doing.

Big Marv tells us as much as he can about the LARP, which goes on for about half an hour, punctuated by medieval laughter and obscure references to films or books. It's the kind of talk we Geeks thrive on. According to Marv, the players are divided into teams or "factions" and we are now part of Big Marv's faction. It's not too far off our Games Nights: while there are scripted events that happen at certain times throughout the day, like raids on the camp by orcs and goblins or puzzles to be solved, the various factions help to create further storylines by interacting with each other, in character, throughout the weekend. It's the equivalent of Geekri-La. The only downer is that because it's our first go, if we die, we die.

IM: *It's a big game of Let's Pretend. With ears.*

But we soak it up. We soak it up like big, Geeky sponges. Big Marv delivers it all like a medieval bard, drawing us in and weaving the history of the imaginary world, the characters and the battles; even the girls seem interested. And as we listen to him rattling away in his Bombadil patter, it starts to feel like a *real* adventure.

Time passes and the early evening sun wipes through the van's windows as we drive, framing Sarah in a continuous stream of golden parallelograms. Ravi and Beggsy begin an argument about the worst Doctor in *Doctor Who* and I'm free to chat to the girls.

"What're your character names going to be?" I ask, wondering if I can at least offer my gaming expertise in this department.

Sarah's eyes glitter with mischief and pretend reproach. "I would have thought you'd have been able to guess that one!" she sort-of tells me off.

IM: *Sounds of tumbleweeds and a gate squeaking in the wind*

"Uh…"

"Nox Noctis!" Sarah hisses in an exaggerated whisper. "Nox Noctis – Mistress of the Night!"

Nox Noctis is the name I gave to her character when Sarah came to my house for an ill-fated game of Dungeons & Dragons. My mind ought to be flooded with sexy images, probably involving thigh-high boots. But it's not. Instead, I feel like I've just had my soul cleaned and it's brighter and lighter than it ever has been. I feel like there is no past and there is no future; there is only This Moment™.

IM: *In a van. With a bus-load of Geeks. Looking to dress up and play at being wizards. And who said romance was dead?*

"Well, it *is* an awesome name," I reply. I think I might be flirting,

IM: *Checks data banks* No information available, Captain.

"Caitlyn's got a good name!" Matt's obviously been keeping one ear on our conversation. His comment makes Sarah squeeze Caitlyn's arm and do one of those

"Aw" faces that makes her nose crinkle.

"Oh yeah? What is it?" Beggsy butts in.

"It's Mirella Thistlebark," Caitlyn replies, surprised at the attention she's getting. "I'm a healer."

"Ha-haa!" laughs Big Marv into the rear-view mirror. "Most excellent! We will need a healer, since our last one was killed by Rat Ogres! We must protect Mirella Thistlebark at all odds!"

"Rat Ogres? Dude! Anyone bring any cheese?" Beggsy starts doing a weird squeaky growl and pretends to gnaw on Sarah's arm. Much to my disgust.

"Land ho!" Big Marv shrieks from the front cabin. "Almost there!"

We all take a look out of the windows, just in time to see the "Welcome To" sign that heralds the village we'll be camping near. Once through the village, we hit a number of winding country lanes, all high hedges and cracked tarmac.

"Look!" Beggsy's pointing up ahead. We crane our necks to see a little, yellow, hand-painted sign, saying "QuestFest" in Ye Olde Handwritinge pointing off to the right. This leads us on to a dirt track that cuts its dusty way between two fields.

"Is this a farm?" Sarah asks Big Marv's back.

"Ha-haa! It is, indeed! The adventure is held on some farmland not two minutes from here!"

We drive further, coming up to the farmhouse then hanging a left into a field that has obviously been designated as the car park. Big Marv swings the van into a space and turns off the engine.

"Ha-haa!" he yodels, getting out of the van and stretching his legs. "Those are your toilet facilities, Questers." Along one side of the field, there is a line of what look like ten plastic TARDISes.

IM: *Those? Those things? Toilets?*

I can practically feel my digestive system shutting down at the mere thought of it. But the girls are bursting, apparently, and make their way through the cars to the Portaloos. While we're waiting for them, me and the guys help Big Marv get the gear off the roof. Then we head towards a gap in the hedge that lines the back of the car park. Just before the gap, Big Marv stops and gestures towards the field beyond, dropping something from his washbag in the process.

"Questers! Welcome to … Ailae!" With a final, joyous laugh, he picks up a tube of toothpaste and steps through the hedge into another world.

THIRTEEN

Walking into the campsite *is* like walking into another world. Already groups of tents are springing up – and I'm not talking the usual tent-shaped tents like the one I'm carrying and already feeling inadequate about.

IM: *Could this be the first recorded case of canvas envy?*

The LARP tents are like proper wigwams made out of proper wigwam material with round front flaps or colourful medieval-style octagon tents with pointed roofs. Some groups of tents are fenced off with black windbreaks joined together, creating little villages within a larger community. And some of the windbreaks have Elvish inscriptions painted on to them, while others are festooned with twigs or fake foliage. These, Big Marv explains, are the homes of the various factions: the Dark Elves (Drow), the Cat People (Felinetta), the Celts (Cessair) and us lot: the Tribe. There is even a gateway formed from poles outside some of the tents, skewered with skulls and severed heads. Rubber ones.

IM: *For added authenticity.*

This is all too much for Beggsy, who starts hopping up and down, tugging at Sarah's shoulder and pointing out various things – campfires, cauldron-style cooking pots, an anvil and some shields. I know it's cool, but I wish he'd leave her alone. Matt just stares at everything as we walk, as though he's trying to burn it all down with his eyes and hovers close to Caitlyn. Sarah, however, is also bubbling with excitement, fuelled by Beggsy's near-hysteria.

"Awesome!" Ravi rumbles. "But where is everyone?"

"In-game!" Big Marv answers, pointing down the slope to where distant shouts are coming from. "Alas, we are late and the Quest has begun!"

He's right. It's kicked off already. In the bottom corner of the field, past a small lake and bordered by hedges, there's a battle in full swing. The crowd is a clash of colours – some guys have gone for the muted, *Lord of the Rings*-style outfits, whereas others have gone for bright reds, blues and yellows.

IM: *Fifty Shades of Geek.*

And there are the bad guys. In true baddie style, they're wearing black and packing maces and clubs and battered, circular shields. Even from this distance, their green faces give them away: they're orcs.

"Dude!" Beggsy squeals. "It's real! Look! They're really doing it!"

They are. Swords are clashing…

IM: *Silently. Ah, yes – the sound of foam on foam!*

…spells are being cast…

IM: *By people who appear to have no self-consciousness at all...*

...and monsters are being slain...

IM: *Which means that they lie down for a bit and then walk off the battlefield, looking a bit sorry for themselves. The attention to detail is astonishing.*

For a moment, it *is* ridiculous. But it's also exciting and weirdly beautiful. My eyes go into slo-mo and the battle looks for all the world like a colourful, chaotic ballet. I can almost hear the *Lord of the Rings* theme in the background.

IM: *You can. Ravi's whistling it.*

A figure at the edge of the battle-ballet suddenly looks our way and starts running up the slope towards us. He's about the same age as Big Marv, with short, dark hair, thick stubble and a beautiful-looking sword that I envy the instant I see it. That and the black leather body armour he's wearing, embossed with some sort of Celtic design and studded with glittering, silver rivets. And the billowing black shirt he's got on underneath, capped off with studded, leather gloves. And let's not forget the black leather bucket boots.

IM: *And the lip-ferret. Don't forget the lip-ferret.*

His moustache is something I doubt I'll ever be able to grow – thick, black and curled at the ends. It's like a miniature hedge over his mouth.

"Lord Gyrus!" Big Marv cries, dropping everything

in his arms and embracing the Man in Black.

"Lawmar!" Lord Gyrus responds and then does a grim look. "Your arrival could not be more timely; the forces of darkness are among us and we sorely need more warriors in our ranks." Then he stops and puts his hand up.

IM: *Maybe he needs a wee.*

It's the sign to show he's stepping out of character. But just so we know, he says it. "Out of character: first battle of the night, mate. It'd be a shame for you guys to miss it. Dump your gear outside my tent and go and get changed inside. The girls can change in my quarters and I'll do your weapons check."

"Excellent!" Big Marv beams. I'm not sure if he's Big Marv or Lawmar at the moment. "Questers! Give up your weapons to Lord Gyrus, who will check they are game-safe. Make haste! We must meet the enemy in battle!"

A tidal wave of excitement crashes over the group and we hand our swords and Beggsy's axe over to Lord Gyrus, who gives them a quick squeeze. He hands them back, and gives Caitlyn a spare dagger, telling her she might need it. Then we trot after Big Marv to an octagonal tent with a red flag outside it. Inside, it's even better. It's a huge open space, scattered with floor cushions and faux fur rugs. At one end, in front of a partition that the girls go behind, there's an ornate wooden chair, draped in furs and with a pile of rubber skulls either side of it. And there's a low table in the middle, decked with stuff: leather-bound books, writing quills, bottles with different-coloured liquids in, a small treasure chest, gold coins – pretty much everything you'd expect to find if you woke up one day and found yourself in your favourite fantasy novel.

With the girls' dignity protected, we drop our bags and start pulling our costumes out. There is a lot of giggling as our clothes come off and when we spot Big Marv's TARDIS boxer shorts as he changes a few feet from us. The giggling turns to semi-stifled snorts when Matt asks us if we think they're bigger on the inside than they are on the outside.

The transformations begin. I'm first past the post and as I put on my ears, I get a small cheer from the guys and a Vulcan salute from Matt. Matt's next, but his costume has more of a cobbled-together feel about it: black jeans and a T-shirt. But the cloak helps. Next up is Ravi, who looks great as the cleric, Jh'terin. He's got his hands on a puffy-sleeved shirt, too, and has doctored an old suede waistcoat to act as a jerkin. And then there's Beggsy. Actually, he looks pretty good – he's got a long jumper on that's been sprayed silver to act as chainmail, with a thick leather belt in the middle. And it's not the plastic Viking helmet that sets me off…

IM: *The plastic, historically inaccurate HORNED Viking helmet…*

…he's painted that really well. And it's not the wellies, either. It's the beard – the huge brown beard that almost reaches his waist. It's not quite the Gimli he was looking for.

IM: *More like Sam Gamgee peering out of a Wookiee's arse.*

"Dude!" *Conveys hurt at the hysteria of a friend* "I think it looks pretty good!"

"You look like you've been mugged by an Ewok," Matt comments, which sets the rest of us off.

"Come on, boys! Stop messing about – we've got a battle to win!" It's Sarah's voice and I turn to be confronted with a sight that would make Mr Freeze hit a sauna.

"Ah! Maidens fair – be welcome!" Big Marv announces, struggling under blue robes.

My jaw almost hits the ground. Strike that: it does.

IM: *Houston, we have a problem…*

For more than a few seconds, my lungs forget what they're supposed to do and all I can do is try and keep my eyes from dropping out of their sockets. She's wearing Mum's green cloak…

IM: *And a corset.*

…with a black velvet skirt that stops just above her knees…

IM: *And a corset.*

…knee-high boots with turn-down tops and velvety

gloves that stop halfway up her upper arms.

IM: *CORSET!*

And a corset. Because it's Sarah, I'm *really* trying not to look, but my peripheral vision won't let me off the hook. While I'm soaking up the bruised beauty of her Gothic make-up – my eyes are busy telling me that it looks like she's had a bum grafted to her chest. I hate myself for my baseness, but I just can't seem to blot it out. For a few, precious moments, it's just me and her in here – everything and everyone else fades away.

IM: *My, these "Hero Pants" are tight…*

Thanks to the cover of my cloak, I'm able to slip a hand in my pocket, adjust the angle of my extending lightsabre and trap it under the waistband of my undies. It hurts, but it's better than nothing. I'm not the only one goggling. But instead of just standing and staring, like I do, Beggsy walks over in some weird, slow strut, nodding appreciatively.

IM: *Young Santa: The Pervert Years.*

"Sexy *lay*-dee!" he smarms, producing a laugh from Sarah, before she tells him how great he looks, too. He steps in to give her a hug, and she returns it, but cautiously – probably not wanting to mess up her costume. I know he's my mate, but I can't help thinking he's enjoying it a bit too much. But Sarah, being Sarah, gives us all hugs which, weirdly, seem a bit less cautious. Even Matt, who doesn't do physical contact with other humans, gets one. But Matt's only got eyes for Caitlyn, who does a humble curtsey, showing off her autumnal robes, which produces an angular smile from his generally expressionless face. Only Ravi maintains his dignity, telling the girls they look beautiful with an ease that I wish I could muster.

We cap it off by comparing our weapons. Everybody's done a good job and Ravi's gone as far as putting some runes on his blade. Sarah's glued some crystals to her hilt, giving it an arcane, magical look. We swish them around for a minute or two, accompanied by theatrical grunts and war cries.

"To battle, Questers!" Big Marv booms. His outfit is blue velvet – a robe with long wizard sleeves and gold cuffs; a dark blue, Gandalf-style hat, nicely bent at the top; proper, curly-toed wizard shoes and a staff that's taller than he is. It's made of foam and latex, but painted to look like silver, capped off with a metal-looking dragon's claw at the top, which is clutching a round, blood-red crystal. Made of foam.

"Wow, Marvin! You look amazing!" Caitlyn gushes from underneath her hood. Marv raises a hand in reply.

"I am Marvin no more! From this point – unless you are out of character – I am Lawmar and you are your characters. The game begins!"

As we're filing out Sarah turns to me, her eyes

shadowed by her hood. "Nice ears," she says and I can see the corner of her mouth curl up playfully. You know when Popeye eats his spinach or Scooby gets a Scooby Snack? Well, that's what I feel like. And, thankfully, there's a battle in which I can get rid of the surge of energy that pinballs around my system.

As soon as we're ready, Lord Gyrus leads us at a trot to the top of the slope.

At the bottom of the field, there's a small gate, through which a swarm of about twenty orcish figures are charging, shouting and waving their rubber swords. Already some of the good guys have rushed in to meet them in combat, whooping and hollering their battle-lust.

IM: *Or just the joy at leaving their Geeky lives behind them.*

Amid the war cries and the screams of death and injury, the air is thick with people shouting "Single!", "Double!" or "Quad!" as they call out the damage their weapons are capable of inflicting. Magic users are getting ready to use their arcane powers. You can tell because they have to shout "Summoning Magic!" before they can do a spell. It's a bit like when the Power Rangers used to shout "Mystic Force!" or whatever it was, just before they did something cool.

IM: *"Geek Power!" doesn't quite have the same ring to it.*

It's time to get myself noticed.

"Orcs!" I growl. "Come on!"

Unsheathing my sword from my belt, I start to run. Beggsy's at my side, his beard threatening to smother him, while Ravi's on the other, bellowing for all he's worth. Matt and the girls are behind us, waving their weapons and running wildly. It's beautiful. Who else could I do this with? I'm proud to be a Geek.

IM: *Somebody has to be.*

As I reach my first orc, a valiant battle cry bursts from my lungs: "Baraaaarrrc!" It may just be a guy in a rubber mask but I'm in the TwiLARP Zone right now: he's a slavering monster with a cruel-looking scimitar and I'm just the elf for the job. He takes a swing at my head, but I parry and take a swipe at his left side. The orc blocks my attack and, hooking his sword under mine, sweeps my blade away from his body, coming in for a deadly cut to my neck. I duck and come in again for his side, forcing him to step back.

IM: *Get in there, Bararc! Show this orc some manners – elf-style!*

I keep up my attack, swinging for his head. He blocks. I go for a leg and make contact, shouting "Single!"

IM: *Probably true of ninety-nine per cent of the people on this battlefield.*

The orc gives a scream of pain and staggers back, so

I come in again, hard. He blocks my swipe to his left arm, but has to step back again. And then something happens: the orc suddenly looks behind him, at where he's stepped back, lifts his heel in a very un-Uruk-hai way and holds up a hand. I freeze, panting.

"Cowpat," the orc says through his rubber mask. "There's a cowpat here. D'you mind if we move over a bit?"

"Sure." We move, crab-like, about five feet to our right, with the orc checking the ground around him.

"OK," he says. "Sorry about that." And puts his hand down.

I re-enter the Zone without any trouble at all. Within seconds I'm hammering away at my foe and scoring two more singles, watching in grim satisfaction as he drops to the ground with a final scream.

IM: *Eat foam-latex, orc scum!*

I spin round, in case any more green-skinned goblins want a piece of me, but the invaders are being forced to retreat through the gate from where they came. A slap on my back announces Ravi's arrival. He's got his hand up and a huge grin on his face.

"Wow!" he laughs. "This is AWEsome! Did you kill yours?"

"I cut his legs off, I think. You?"

"Yeah! He got me once, but it was only a single! I can't believe how epic this is!"

As we laugh and walk to find the others, I realize that I feel fantastic, like I've just purged myself of something. For fleeting moments, I *was* an elf, fighting a real battle and free from the tyranny of self-consciousness.

IM: *You can add "dignity", while you're at it...*

We find Sarah and Caitlyn kneeling beside Beggsy, who's lying spreadeagled on the grass. Matt's standing by them, glowering to himself.

"Hey!" I pant. "What's up?"

"The mighty Damli took a mortal blow to his beard. Caitlyn's healing him." I love Matt's sarcasm. Especially when it's not directed at me.

"Hey, shut *up!*" Beggsy protests. "It was a poisoned weapon! I'm dying here!"

"Well, I think you've been dying long enough," Matt retorts.

"Rules are rules," the wounded soldier snipes back. "It says five minutes, so I'm going to lie here five minutes!"

If I didn't know him better, I'd swear he was just milking it to be surrounded by girls in corsets and cloaks.

IM: *At this point, your argument is invalid.*

We wait the required time until Beggsy has recovered enough Beard Power, or whatever it is that dwarves rely on, and then head back to camp to put up our tents.

By the time we've finished, it's getting dark, campfires are being lit and the smells of cooking start to flirt with our stomachs. Thankfully we're saved from having to cook anything by the generosity of the other campers and, pretty soon, we're sitting round a fire, tucking into stew.

As we sit and chat, still dressed in our costumes, we get introduced to other LARPers. Even though everybody's out of character, the conversation still remains wonderfully Geeky – but Sarah and Caitlyn do manage to find a foothold. While Matt, Ravi and Beggsy end up in a conversation with Mark, the bespectacled werewolf, about the evolution of Dungeons & Dragons, the girls end up chatting to Mally, a beautiful blonde elf, and Bastet, a cat-lady, about how they got into LARPing in the first place and why it's a Good Thing. Even Kev, the shy assassin, comes out of his shell to tell us it's helped his self-confidence.

I can't think of many other places where you could have these conversations with a bunch of grown-ups and be taken seriously. And, looking around at my Geeky mates chatting to each other and the firelight dancing across Sarah's face, I can't think of anywhere I'd rather be. It's the Geek equivalent of Paradise.

IM: *The Garden of Geekdom?*

Big Marv, silver goblet in one hand and a bacon roll in the other, pulls up a camping chair next to us.

"Questers!" he booms. "How are you enjoying yourselves?"

We all agree that it's great and that we're having a really good time.

"You are most gracious," Marv nods. "And, in keeping with your parents' wishes, we must agree a time at which you retire. It would weigh heavy on me to deliver their children to them in a state of exhaustion. It is nearly ten of the clock, would that be acceptable to you?"

We agree that ten of the clock is probably a good time, which pleases our necromantic shopkeeper-chum and he thanks us, before throwing the topic of tabletop wargames into the conversational melee. I do my best to guide Sarah and Caitlyn through the terms and try and explain why Invulnerable Saves are a good thing but, in the end, we start chatting about what might happen tomorrow. The furthest we get is Caitlyn deciding that we should all have breakfast at their tent.

Ten of the clock comes knocking soon enough. By this time we're all quite tired, what with all the orc-bashing, so we get ready for bed and, with a chivalry that seems only to announce itself when you're wearing cloaks, we walk the girls to their tent and then head to our own.

Ravi and Beggsy take one compartment and me and Matt take the other.

"What d'you think?" I whisper, once we're zipped up in our sleeping bags.

"About what?"

"About the LARP?"

There's a rustle as Matt turns over on to his side. "I think it's possibly the weirdest thing we've ever done. But it's awesome."

"Yeah." I can hear Ravi and Beggsy rustling in their room. "How d'you think the girls are with it?"

There's a moment's pause while Matt considers this in the darkness, gently underscored by the sound of campfire chat.

"I think they like it. I don't see how they couldn't."

"Hope you guys aren't getting *too* friendly in there!" Beggsy's voice cheerfully smashes through the quiet. "Know what I'm saying?"

"Go to sleep, Beggsy," Matt volleys back. "Maybe you'll get lucky and meet the man of your dreams."

"Ha-ha."

Once our conversation stops and we settle down, I can hear the sounds of the campfire. Conversation drifts into stories and stories drift into laughter and laughter drifts into gentle singing. But I'm not drifting into sleep, so I find my torch and plunge into the *Dark Knight*.

About an hour after Hypnos, the God of Sleep, has finally done his thing, Bladderos, the God of Wee-Wee pays me a visit. According to my mobile phone, it's just after midnight and all is quiet.

IM: *Maybe you could get away with going in a bush?*

I find my torch and unzip the compartment's flap as quietly as I can, listening intently to Beggsy and Ravi's breathing and Matt's nasal snore. Then I unzip the front entrance. It's amazing but, against the backdrop of silence provided by sleeping in the Great Outdoors, even the slightest sound seems magnified. However, my friends stay asleep and I tiptoe behind the tent, in search of a good place to go.

IM: *At least if you do hear a werewolf huffing, it's going to be a real one. Wearing glasses...*

Gotta choose my spot. I don't want to wake anyone with my midnight widdling. There's a hedge behind our tent – the one that divides the field from the car park, but there are other tents too close to it for comfort. I creep along its border, towards the entrance, passing Sarah's tent as I go. Involuntarily, I pause and kill the torch, my senses heightened to see if I can hear anything. Nothing.

Then there's a rustle. I freeze.

IM: *Not that you're a stalker or anything.*

Caitlyn's voice whispers through the canvas. "Why don't you just tell him?" she's asking drowsily.

At the mention of the word "him" and "why don't you just tell", my heightened elf-hearing suddenly kicks in.

I stand, breathing silently through my mouth, straining to pick up every nuance in their conversation, looking for a clue as to whether it might be me that she ought to just tell whatever it is.

"You *know* why," Sarah mutters back. She sounds grumpy and tired.

My heart sinks, even though it might not be me they're talking about at all. There's another rustle of sleeping bags as somebody turns over, then a pause before Caitlyn resumes her sleepy interrogation.

"You're just being paranoid. Is it because you like him?"

My heart leaps again.

"Of course I like him. He's a friend!"

And sinks once more.

"You know what I mean. Do you *like* him?"

But my answer is the crack of a twig that I stand on. As the girls go silent, I go rigid.

"What was that?" Sarah whispers urgently.

"Probably an animal or something," Caitlyn mumbles, obviously unconcerned.

"Shall I go and see?"

IM: *NOOOOOOO!*

Without waiting to hear Caitlyn's reply, I creep quickly away, doing the stretchy steps I perfected at Dad's house. In a rare moment of clarity, I keep the torch off, so I don't attract any more attention than I need to. The last thing I want is to get stopped by an insomniac Drow or something.

IM: *Or Bastet looking to use the litter tray.*

The grass in the car park is just starting to get damp with the chill of night and I'm grateful for my trainers. I just make out the ghostly obelisks of the Portaloos against the hedge so I head on, listening out for signs of any other nocturnal toilet-ninjas. Just as I hit the end cubicle, I notice that there are lights on in Big Marv's camper van – he's sitting across the table from Lord Gyrus, both still in full costume and a bottle of wine between them, probably discussing Important Game Stuff. But they're far enough away not to hear or see me, so I quietly open the door and go in.

Peeing by torchlight is a new one on me; I'd never realized how much steam's involved. Bladder empty, I kill the torch and slip out. A quick check shows me that Big Marv's camper van lights are off, so I take the longer route back to the tent, through the walkway we first came in on. I don't want to get caught by Sarah or she might put two and two together and make "eavesdropper". But I wish I knew what she and Caitlyn were talking about. Part of me really wants to believe it might be me. But there's another part of me that doesn't dare entertain the thought – it's too big and too much like something I don't deserve.

Back at the tent, I creep back inside and zip myself into my cocoon.

FOURTEEN

Tomorrow arrives a bit later than it should. I wake up to find that everyone else has got up and gone, which pisses me off. Grumpily, I check my mobile, to find that it's nine o' clock and hurriedly get dressed, ears and all.

Blinking in the sunshine, I hit the TARDISes again, before heading to the girls' tent. The camp's slowly showing signs of life as the smell of bacon settles in savoury clouds over campfires and cooking stoves, and the world of Ailae begins to get its act together.

"Keep still!" Caitlyn's overly articulate voice cuts through the ragged laughter that drifts between the tents. I round a corner to see the gang sat outside the girls' place. Matt and Ravi are cross-legged on the ground eating porridge, while Sarah and Caitlyn are kneeling either side of Beggsy, who's on a camping chair. Beggsy's got his head tilted back, while the girls appear to be crowding over his stomach.

"Hey, guys!" I'm surprised at how croaky my voice is. It must be all the battle-shouting.

"It's awake!" Matt declares. "We were just wondering if we should find a handsome prince to come and give you a kiss!"

301

"Ha ha. You could've woken me."

"There's porridge in the pot, mate. Go for it." Ravi nods at a camping stove.

"Cheers, Rav. You guys sleep all right?"

"Apart from Beggsy farting all night, not too bad."

"Shut up, Ravi!" Beggsy protests from his chair. "That wasn't me!"

"What're you doing?" I ask, sorting myself out some breakfast. Beggsy just scowls and lets out a huge sulky groan in response.

"We're braiding his beard," Sarah answers, in a way that suggests that her client hasn't been that cooperative.

"Why?" I laugh. "What for?"

"Ap-*parently*," Matt drawls, "the mighty Damli's beard keeps blowing in his face, which is why he nearly got killed yesterday..."

"That orc would be dead if it hadn't! Easy! I'm The *Begg*ster!"

"Keep *still*!" Caitlyn's starting to sound hacked off, now.

"*Gimli* never seemed to have a problem with it," Matt fires back, chucking me and Ravi a sly smile.

"Well, that's because *Gimli* had braids in his beard! Which is what I'm having done!" Beggsy splutters from the grass.

With a final huff of frustration, Sarah stands up.

"There! That's all you're getting! Come on, Caitlyn. We're finished!"

They sit back to reveal their work. It looks infinitely better and they've braided in some coloured beads to give it some weight. But it's not Beggsy's beard that captures my attention – for the first time ever, Sarah is make-up free. And the sadness that was peeping out of her eyes in Art is there, on her face. I guess I wouldn't spot it if I hadn't seen it before, but, like her bum-chest, now that I've seen it, I can't *stop* seeing it.

Without her make-up on, a bit of Sarah's readable, like small print suddenly come into focus; at last, I can see what she's thinking. And she's as scared of the world as I am.

IM: *Check out her bum-chest – that'll be less humiliating for both of you.*

I catch Sarah's eye and she must get a sense of what's going on in my head because she suddenly announces that she's got to finish getting ready and disappears into the tent, followed by Caitlyn. Me and the guys spend the next few minutes discussing what we think's going to happen today and listening to Beggsy tell us exactly how he's going to bring down his next foe, now that his beard is no longer an obstacle.

IM: *Braid them to death?*

Caitlyn emerges first, looking fresher-faced, but not that much different. Sarah comes out looking perfect, but now that I've seen her face in the buff, I realize that it's *too* perfect; she's hiding the parts of herself that make her interesting. Her make-up doesn't look so sexy any more, it makes her look a bit lost.

"Ha-haaa!" Big Marv bounds over the guy ropes with an agility I wouldn't have expected from a grown-up dressed in full wizard regalia. "Who here can read Herb Lore?"

IM: *Everyone, surely! Isn't it a GCSE subject?*

I'm pretty sure I put it down as a Skill, but I check my Character Sheet before sticking my hand up, like I'm in school. Just as Sarah says, "Me; I can."

IM: *This day is made of win!*

"Of course! An elf and a sorceress!" He leans in conspiratorially. "I am preparing a potion, but I need some particular herbs... Perhaps you would be so kind as to collect them for me from the forest?"

"Sure," I answer, but then decide to throw in a bit of role play. "But I shall expect payment."

Big Marv/Lawmar nods sagely. "It goes without saying. Bring the herbs to my tent and we shall agree a price."

"I think we should agree it in advance," Sarah says, in a hard voice.

"Very well." Big Marv unties a pouch from his belt and counts out some plastic jewels. "This should be more than enough for your trouble." Sarah holds her hand out, but Big Marv puts the payment back into the bag. "On collection," he says, before turning and going.

"Shall we?" I ask.

"I think so," she replies.

"And what are *we* going to do?" Beggsy whines.

"Go and find some *lay*-deez to impress with your beard," I laugh. It's a bit blunt, but I need some time on my own with Sarah; I need to see if I can connect with her, like we did in Art.

IM: *Bom-bom-BOM-bom...*

As we walk through the camp, we point out all the weird clashes between the world of Ailae and the world we're supposed to have left behind: cat-people listening to the news on their radios, elves texting on their mobile phones and armoured warriors conducting conversations with swishes of a toothbrush. Two worlds have collided, but I guess you never get to fully leave Real Life behind.

We walk across the field towards the forest; the conversation is light and easy and, once again, I'm in a little golden bubble. But the difference this time is that

I'm more aware of Sarah than I've ever been before. While I might be dazzled by the way she looks, at last I'm not blinded by it any more.

IM: *Your eyes can betray you, Archie; don't rely on them. Reach out with your feelings...*

It does feel as though I've got something like the Force on my side. But I mustn't give into any more fear or lies or my journey to the Dark Side will be complete.

IM: *Darth Archie? Doesn't quite chill the marrow, does it?*

Despite the morning sun, the forest is dark and silent, lit only by dusty beams of sunlight that cut between the trees. It's also not the friendliest terrain; there are rocks, bits of glass, old cans and bottles lying around. As we wander deeper into its embrace, a silence forms between us. All my systems are on Red Alert, waiting for one of us to break it.

But I don't, in case I say the wrong thing.

IM: *Like "I was going to have a wee behind your tent last night, but I heard you talking and changed my mind." That cover it?*

It's Sarah who does it, with a gentle sledgehammer.

"How are you feeling about Clare now?"

The question takes me by surprise. As I scrabble for something to say, Sarah takes my silence for Inner Turmoil.

"It's OK. You don't have to talk about it, if you don't want to."

"No … it's OK…"

IM: *Flips through Dummies' Guide to Girls* How long are we supposed to be in mourning? Is forty-eight hours long enough? Too much? Too little?

That's the problem. I just don't know. If I'm over it, then that might suggest I'm callous and if I'm not, that might suggest I'm still into Clare.

IM: I'm sitting this one out. You're on your own. *Sound of back door slamming*

"I think I'm working out how much we didn't know each other," I manage falteringly. "Which is a shame, but I think it's better to know now…"

"…before you got in too deep?"

"Yeah. That's it. Before somebody…"

"…gets hurt?"

"Yeah," I laugh, partly because of the delight I feel at her finishing my sentences and partly because I think I've just worked something out. I risk it. "You seem to know a lot about this…"

"Ah!" Sarah smiles, like she's just been caught out. "Yeah… Long story…"

IM: Remember, Archie: a Jedi can feel the Force coursing through him…

"A boyfriend?" I'm channelling so much sensitivity,

I think my midi-chlorians are working on overdrive.

"Something like that. Before I came to your school."

"Right… Not a fun experience, I'm guessing."

Suddenly there's a muted thump on the tree behind me and something drops on to a pile of broken stones with a clatter. We freeze, before I turn round.

"What the hell was that?" I mutter.

"Look!" Sarah's pointing to what looks like an arrow, except there's a rubber ball where the pointy bit should be.

As I bend to pick it up, another one smacks the tree, just missing my head.

"What the…?"

"They're LARP arrows, Archie! We're under attack!"

Great. Just great. Here I am, *finally* about to make open, honest contact with a girl I really like and somebody's shooting blunt arrows at me.

IM: *Could be Cupid's just aware of your low pain threshold?*

As we crouch down and peer between the trees, Sarah takes a tumble sideways.

"Shit!" she hisses. For a moment, I'm shocked; a swear word coming out of her mouth is like Yoda suddenly flashing his willy.

"What?"

Sarah holds up a block of black, broken plastic.

"My heel!" she growls back. "It's snapped off!" And just to make sure that we know we're pinned down, two more arrows thump against the bark behind us.

"Is that bad?" My knowledge of women's heels is fairly limited.

"I can't walk in them like this!"

"Take them off?"

"I'm not wearing socks! I forgot them!"

IM: *Stretch out with your feelings, Archie…*

I know what to do. And for once, there's nothing behind it other than the desire to help someone.

"Hang on," I whisper, wrestling with my trainers. "Put these on!"

"What?"

"Put my trainers on! It's cool: my socks'll get me back to camp!" I tell her. "Hurry up!" I can see figures darting between the trees up ahead. Orcs.

Thump. Thump. Two more arrows. Thump. Another one. The orcs scatter between the trees, gaining ground, getting closer.

Sarah pulls off her boots and puts my trainers on. I've only got time for a brief laugh at how big they look, when there's a roar from the trees and four orcs hurl themselves out of the shadows and come charging at us, all gnarled faces and glittering swords. I rise up and meet them, in a silent symphony of foam on foam.

IM: *You could make the noises like your dad did…*

The orcs are relentless, arriving like a green-skinned wedge. I swing wildly with my blade, keeping them just out of reach. In the background, I can hear Sarah building up to cast a spell of some sort. I swipe again and the orcs move back as one. But as my sword completes its journey, I'm left open on my left side and feel the tell-tale thump of latex against my side. The orc responsible calls the damage and I do my bit, reacting with a cry of pain.

"A mighty fist from the Netherworld: KNOCKBACK!" Sarah's arm punches forward as she completes her spell and, on command, the orcs stagger back as though buffeted by an unseen, magical force. In keeping with the rules, I stagger forwards, as though I've been caught in the blast too and then I let out my second cry. Only this time, it's a real one.

I drop my sword and fold to the ground as a hot bloom of pain floods my right foot. But the orcs, recovered from their battering, start back on the attack, roaring their orcish rage – the battle's still on. Thankfully, I remember the rules and put up my hand; the orcs stop.

"You all right?" the orc closest to me says, lowering his blade.

IM: *They never did this in* Lord of the Rings!

"I think I've cut my foot!" I gasp, gently pulling my sock off to reveal a shard of glass twinkling amidst the pool of blood.

"Go and get Marvin," the orc says to one of his buddies and then, to me: "Don't pull it out. Wait til Marvin gets here – he's our first-aider."

I feel such an idiot. Here I am, dressed as one of the Eldar, clutching my foot and making pathetic "Ow" noises.

Sarah kneels down beside me. "I'm so sorry, Archie. It's my fault."

"Gah! It wasn't your fault!" I mutter, possibly hamming up the level of pain that I'm actually in.

"But if I hadn't worn these stupid boots!"

"They're not the best for combat," says the orc, squatting down. "You should've worn wellies or trainers."

"It's our first time," I mutter, with surprising aggression. I think I might be defending Sarah's choice of footwear.

Big Marv arrives, removes the glass and cleans my wound, before patching me up with a plaster and a bandage. Actually, my battle-damage isn't that big at all, but it hurts enough to give me a heroic limp. As we get back to camp, Big Marv tells me to sit out of battles if it hurts too much. But there's no way I'm missing a Geeky second – this is too much fun.

IM: *Sings* Gather round, ye children of yore,
As I sing the song of a wound most sore…

Sarah sits me in the camping chair outside my tent and gives me one of those looks that involves a half-smile and a gentle shaking of the head.

"That was a really lovely thing you did back there," she says after a moment, giving me my trainers back. Which I make a rather painful display of putting on.

The phrase "You're worth it," rattles around my mouth, before I swallow it – it's too cheesy and I don't want to scare her off. The Art-class connection is building up again – I can feel it. So I just settle for, "It's what we elves do."

IM: *Real cool, Leg o' Glass.*

"Dudes!" Beggsy's panting arrival quashes the chance to chase the moment any further.

"What's up, Beggs?"

"There's a bunch of Drow turned up at the camp! Dunno if they're good guys or what, but they've got prisoners! Better get up there – it's getting weird!"

"Archie's cut his foot," Sarah starts, putting on her slightly less-sexy trainers. "Can you walk?"

"Dude! D'you wanna stay here?"

"Of course I can walk!" I sigh. "It's not that bad!"

IM: *Swoons* He's SO brave!

The Drow have got it going on. They stand in formation, heralded by the clunking of their awesomely impressive armour, which is all plated mail and must have been seriously buffed before they got out here. All the Drow have white hair, even down to the goatees that some of the men are sporting, while every inch of visible skin is a lurid blue – even their pointy ears. Anyone who knows their Dungeons & Dragons lore knows that these guys are Dark Elves and not to be messed with. And they also don't like us regular elf-types, so I put my hood up as I limp to join the guys. Just in case.

Big Marv seems to have taken on the role of spokesperson for the camp and is doing his best to calm things down. The Drow are arguing that we're in their way and Lawmar/Big Marv wants to know who their prisoners are. The prisoners look like a bunch of ragged peasants, hemmed in by the ranks of about twenty Dark Elves. According to the Drow, they're traitors of some sort.

"We ought to do something," Ravi mutters under his breath. "This doesn't feel right."

"I know what you mean," I murmur back. "It'd be good if we could talk to the prisoners – find out what's going on."

"What would you do if this was one of your Games Nights?" Caitlyn asks.

"Create a distraction," Matt answers immediately. "And one of us sneaks round the back."

"Great! So how do we distract them?" Sarah's back in the Zone.

"An insult would do it," Ravi says slowly. "The Drow are a pretty touchy bunch, if I remember rightly."

"Yeah!" Beggsy bubbles. "Something about them being spider-lovers!"

For those of you with lives, Beggsy is referring to the Drow religion – they worship a giant spider, called Lolth. It all makes perfect sense when you're sat round a table, rolling dice and moving little miniature men around a map.

I pull out my character sheet and give it a once-over.

"Guys, I've got a Sneak ability, so I'll go round the back – what's the signal for Sneaking?"

Matt and Ravi reply by putting a hand over their mouths. It's Geeky, it's a way of helping everyone else know what you're doing and suspend their disbelief but, most importantly, it's a rule.

IM: *And Geeks love rules.*

"And who's going to do the distraction bit?" I ask, putting my sheet back in my pocket.

"It'd come best from a dwarf, wouldn't it?" Ravi says.

"What?" Beggsy splutters. "Why me?"

"Because they're *elves*," Ravi replies, using that intonation that turns his statement into a question and communicates his irritation all at the same time.

"Go on, *Begg*ster; you'll be fine," Sarah cajoles him. And it seems to work.

"You guys had better give me some back-up," he scowls, before pushing his way through the crowd. I put my hand over my face and limp towards the rear of the platoon, dutifully ignored by everyone who sees me. As I get round the back, I can see that the Drow have arranged themselves in a triangle formation, but with no base to the two ascending sides.

A sudden flare of voices from the front of the triangle lets me know that Beggsy's begun his elf-baiting. I limp, as quickly as my throbbing foot will allow, into the huddle of prisoners, before taking my hand off my mouth. In a beautiful example of what role play is all about, three of the prisoners act as though I've just appeared from nowhere – all jumpy and shocked.

"Greetings," I whisper. "I am Bararc the elf, no friend to the Drow. Who are you and do you need help?"

The prisoner closest to me taps the shoulder of one in front and nods my way. The other prisoner looks around, nice and shifty, like there's a real threat, and then presses something into my hand before indicating with a sharp flick of the head that I should make myself scarce. I stick my hand over my mouth again and start to withdraw. Just as I'm nearly out of the prisoner pen, something big goes off at the front; probably Beggsy getting carried away. At the same time, a prisoner in the middle shouts "Now!" and they start to scatter, running for their lives. A couple of the Drow guards turn to try and stop them, but the adventurers in the camp aren't having any of it.

IM: *It's foam-time!*

As I turn, a Drow spots me, whipping out his curved sword, a snarl cutting across his cobalt features.

"Elf!" he spits, before taking a couple of quick slashes at my head. I manage to get my sword out and up just in time, blocking his attack. As he raises his blade for another hack, I swipe across his chest, missing as he jumps back.

We separate, panting, but keep our swords trained on each other. I realize that it's pointless going for any body blows as he's protected by a lovely silver breastplate. My best bet is to go for his arms or legs.

The Drow takes a swipe at my stomach, obviously having worked out that I'm packing nothing in the armour department. I stumble back, bumping into someone who's running away from someone else. It's a momentary thing, but it gives my enemy the chance he's looking for. With a cry of "Single!" he wallops me across the stomach. In keeping with the game, I cry out as if in agony and drop to one knee, holding my sword up to ward off another attack. But he obviously knows what he's doing; in one swift movement, he changes his grip on his sword so he's holding the blade, before swinging it like a giant hammer at my head. Instinctively, I block it, but it's just what he's after: his cross-guard hooks nicely over my blade and with a swift yank, I'm defenceless. Taking a traditional grip on his sword, the Drow delivers another foamy wallop to my midriff. I cry out once more and fall back on to my thigh.

IM: *You can't die yet! It's only Saturday!*

But if he gets one more in, then I'll be hanging up my ears for the rest of the weekend. The Drow has no pity. He grips his sword in both hands, raising it above his head, ready to deliver the killer blow.

"Single! Single! Single!"

The Drow jerks in time with each shout and then falls forward, revealing a much shorter and hairier figure behind him. It's Beggsy.

"Dude! Saved ya!"

"Thanks, mate! Thought I was a goner!"

"It's all in the beard, laddie!" Beggsy grins, doing his best Gimli impression. "It's all in the beard!"

And then he turns away, looking for someone else to

introduce to the taste of cold, hard latex. I limp to the sidelines to get healed by Caitlyn and watch the action unfold. Matt does his best to protect her as she lays her hands on me, but he's not a natural swordsman – it's like watching an angry windmill. Ravi's a bit better, but not by much; the cool-minded mathematician in him takes a back seat and he charges forward into the crowds, wobbling his sword around and occasionally hitting something. Damning my foot, I spot Sarah's sword flashing as she fights alongside Beggsy. Maybe it's because he's using an axe but he looks pretty good, swirling his weapon in heavy, sweeping arcs and bellowing "Single!" with practically every swipe.

IM: *Maybe he's trying to tell Sarah something...?*

I think, unfortunately, I'm just about to solve another Moustache Problem.

Ten minutes later, we're all back at the camp, listening to Beggsy recount the Taunting of the Drow.

IM: *Soon to be a major motion picture.*

"...no – the *best* bit," Beggsy splutters, already having told us three other best bits, "...the *best* bit was when I..."

"Shut up, Beggsy," Matt gripes. "What about you, Archie? Did you find anything out from those prisoners?"

"Oh, yeah! They gave me something!" I pull out a paper package from my trousers and open it up. Inside there are two tiny bottles, one filled with a red liquid and the other with blue. "What d'you reckon these are?"

IM: *"Eau de Geek". Guaranteed to repel all women in a twenty-mile radius.*

"Don't know, but there's something written on the paper," Ravi points out. We all look at it. There, written in some nicely archaic handwriting are three words: "Baelroth is coming".

"Who's Baelroth?" Caitlyn asks, obviously expecting the four Geeks to have a ready answer. But we don't. None of us have ever heard the name.

"We should show this stuff to Big Marv," Ravi offers.

"Good idea," I nod. As we set off for his tent, I can't help but overhear Sarah telling Beggsy that she thought he was brilliant. OK, so it does sound like a mother pacifying a kid, but I can't help feeling that the Moustache Problem is growing. It's been growing under my nose all along; I've got a nagging suspicion that he likes her.

Like *"likes"* her.

We find Lawmar/Big Marv doing some magic over one of the camp's wounded. It seems we took a few casualties and one or two bit the dust. When we show him the paper, his face becomes uncharacteristically grim.

"This is heavy news," he breathes, going all Obi-Wan for a moment. "Baelroth... I haven't heard that name in a long time."

"Who's Baelroth, then?" Sarah asks.

"Baelroth is a Greater Demon of the Underdark, which would explain why there have been so many assaults against our encampment. The orcs and the Drow are his minions. As are the undead."

"Undead? AWEsome!" cries Beggsy.

"And what about these?" I ask, holding out the two bottles. Big Marv's face brightens under the brim of his pointed hat.

"Ha-haa! These are potions – elixirs of power. The red one is a Potion of Fearlessness – whoever drinks it will be able to withstand the presence of even the most fell creature! And this one..." he takes the blue bottle and holds it up to the light, "...this one is most precious. It is a potion to Heal Greater Wounds. Even someone on the threshold of death can be restored to full health with but a drink from this bottle."

IM: *Can it make Geeks into Normal Human Beings? Just asking.*

"Caitlyn should have that one," Matt interjects. "She *is* a healer."

"Most wise," Big Marv intones. "And who shall

have the other?"

"Archie – I mean, Bararc, should." Ravi says diplomatically. "After all, he got it."

"There will be a luncheon served in our camp by Mally," Big Marv booms. "After that, I think it would be pertinent to arrange a camp meeting to share the news of Baelroth. Until then, you should say nothing to anyone. Oh, and Mister Beggs," – at this point, Big Marv's out-of-character hand comes up – "that was a most excellent example of role-playing earlier. Most fine." And then he sweeps away.

As we walk back to our tents, Beggsy lapses into story-telling mode, regaling us with what the best bit was. While my friends laugh and jeer in the appropriate places, I find myself watching him with new eyes – every word he speaks and every move he makes seem designed to attract Sarah's attention.

One of my best friends has become my rival. We both like the same girl.

At the gang's insistence, I'm plonked in a camping chair outside my tent, with my foot up. Maybe it's being out of character or maybe it's the adrenalin wearing off, but it's starting to sting a bit. The girls hit the TARDISes and

I've suddenly got an opportunity to put my suspicions to the test.

"The girls are totally buying into this, aren't they?" I throw it out like a piece of bait and wait to see if Beggsy's going to bite.

"I think they're really enjoying it," Ravi nods, as though the thought's caught him by surprise.

"They probably do it all the time," Matt jokes and a ripple of laughter rolls around the group. Beggsy laughs, too, but he doesn't add anything. Either he's spotted the bait or I've misjudged him. I decide to try a different tack.

"Looks like you were wrong about Sarah, Beggsy."

"What d'you mean?" He answers quickly; perhaps a bit too quickly. But I need to be sure.

"Her imagination *is* as good as yours."

"Dude! That was just a way to get her to come – the girls," he adds quickly. Maybe too quickly.

"Good call," Ravi grins.

"Leave it to The *Begg*ster!" Beggsy replies, neatly moving the focus of the conversation. But I'm not done yet.

"You and Sarah seem pretty tight." I make the statement light and careless, but I think I see his face flush. Hard to tell, given he's still a bit red from all the running around.

"They're part of the gang, dude!" If it's a deflection,

then it's a neat one; he's answered as though I was talking about both the girls, not just Sarah.

"And more use than you've been so far," Matt adds sarcastically, unwittingly interrupting my line of questioning.

"Ha-ha." A muffled R2 squeal from the tent makes me twist in my chair. "My phone. Could somebody get that for me?"

"Could be mine," Beggsy grins, standing up. "Great minds think alike! I'll have a look."

There's a lot of muted under-canvas scrabbling as he tries to locate the offending droid.

"Lurking within tent," Ravi says suddenly. He's been thinking about this one.

IM: *Should've kept it that way.*

"Ravi – that's not even a joke!" Matt's face is screwed up in disgust. "It doesn't work on any level at all!"

As the repartee rises, Beggsy emerges from the tent and just stands there, staring at the air in front of him.

"Was it mine?" I ask.

Beggsy blinks a couple of times before slowly turning his head to look at me, as though he's not sure if I'm really there.

"Uh, no," he mumbles distractedly, his voice suddenly deep in his boots. "It was mine... I need to pee." And he walks away, like he's in a trance.

"What's eating him?" Ravi frowns. "Is he OK?"

"Probably his Olds; you know what they're like." We all nod sagely at Matt's wisdom; Beggsy's Olds don't really get their son's Geekhood; they seem to have had an imagination bypass.

IM: *But maybe it's something else…*

Lunch only serves to fuel my paranoia. It's not Mally's burgers – they're delicious. It's the way Beggsy doesn't meet my eyes or engage in conversation. Not even with Sarah. But there's a welcome distraction as Big Marv calls the camp together. Standing on a cool box, he addresses the crowd.

"Questers! It has come to my attention that a shadow is about to fall on our camp! Few of you will know the name "Baelroth", but those of you who do will know the seriousness of the situation." Cue shock-and-horror acting from a handful of individuals who, it's pretty safe to assume, know the name."

IM: *Unless they've just worked out where they are and what they're actually doing…* "Gah! I'm dressed as a cat-person! What have I done with my life?"

"This is surely our darkest hour. But we must prepare! We will not simply roll over and die!" Cue cheering from pretty much everybody. "I suggest that we put the time we have to good use and reacquaint ourselves with the skills that will serve us best! Those who wish to may train under Maedoc, our most skilled fighter!"

IM: *Who studied for years under the Sponge Ninjas.*

At the mention of his name, a guy in his thirties with a sandpaper beard, a huge belly and dressed as a Celtic warrior, makes his way to the front of the crowd and replaces Big Marv on the cool box. He speaks in an Irish accent that seems to take a tour of most of the British Isles and ends up somewhere in France. Maedoc tells us that anyone who wants to "really learn how to foight" should find a partner and meet him at the top of the slope in ten minutes.

"What d'you think, guys? You up for it?" The idea of getting some proper fight instruction is too cool to pass up, in my humble opinion, no matter how much my foot stings.

"I'm in," Ravi nods.

"And me," Caitlyn agrees and Matt takes his cue from her, saying he's in, too.

"Yep," Sarah says. "*Beggster?*"

"Uh ... yeah," he nods. And then again, like he's suddenly decided something, "Yeah."

We sort out the pairs: Matt and Caitlyn are pretty

obvious, but then it all feels a bit awkward deciding who goes with Sarah. I want to, though I don't want to make it look too obvious, but Beggsy's got other ideas.

"Come on, Archie. You and me."

IM: *Bum.*

Not wanting to blow my cover, I follow him up the hill.

"Ears versus Beards!" I call after him. But he doesn't respond, he just keeps on walking, like he's trying to put some distance between us and the others.

About twenty other LARPers rock up and Maedoc divides us into As and Bs, facing each other, while he barks instructions at us in a variety of accents. Down the other end of the line, I can see him giving Matt some extra attention, much to my red-headed friend's obvious discomfort. Sarah and Ravi are laughing in the sunlight, exchanging blows in slow motion. And I'm fighting a dwarf. It's not fair.

"Come on, then," I half-sigh, raising my sword and putting my left leg forward, like Maedoc's told us to. "Let's do this thing!"

But Beggsy's axe stays by his side and he tilts his head, looking at me sideways from under his helmet and behind his beard.

"What's going on with you and Clare?" His voice is flat and steely.

IM: *Produces Book of Lies* Ah ... *here we are: page forty-three, I think.*

"What do you mean? She broke up with me, mate; you saw it on Facebook. Now, come on – get your chopper up!" But as the words leave my mouth, I know I've made two mistakes already: under questioning, you should never call your questioner "mate". It signals that you're desperate to keep them onside.

And I've been too quick to change the subject.

My lies are starting to smell.

IM: *Thought maybe it was nerves...*

"How can she break up with you if you were never going out?"

I can almost feel my ears wilt. With the helmet and the beard hiding the rest of his features, all I can really see are Beggsy's eyes. And they're full of flint.

"What are you talking about? She dumped me! Now, come on – let's get fighting!"

IM: *Be careful what you wish for, young Padawan learner...*

But I've done it again – the smile that my EM boots up is riddled with guilt and I can feel the cold blanch of sweat across my face. And my mouth's working too fast, like the quicker I lie, the more likely it is to be believed.

"Bullshit, Archie." Beggsy's beard puffs away from his lips as he spits his contempt.

IM: *Mission compromised! Agent down!*

But the orchestra in my head is on strike. This is too serious; I've been exposed as a liar by one of my best friends. I know I ought to shut up or tell the truth, but my brain panics and sends my mouth in for one last pass.

"Beggsy..." Another mistake: you don't use first names unless you're trying to buy time. "You *saw* what happened..." And another: I'm trying to suggest that his powers of perception might be skewed. But the shame in my face is spreading and I can feel it circle my eyes, like the lies are etching wrinkles round them.

"Bullshit, Archie," the beard spits again. "The message was on *your* phone. I saw it. It was from Clare."

"You read my *text*?" It's another classic from a drowning man – the Righteous Indignation card. But the dwarf in front of me doesn't break his stride.

"She wanted to know if Sarah had *fallen* for it, yet; whether your 'plan' had worked." Even the gate-squeak of his voice doesn't lessen the gravity of his statement. I can't hold his stare any longer. All I can see are horns and beard.

IM: *You've been caught out. Leave it there.*

But I can't. I try and snatch something – anything – that'll buy me a way out of this.

"It's not like that. It was..."

"So you still like her, then. Sarah." The beard's

showing teeth and it ruffles as his breathing gets harder and there are little nods coming from under the helmet, which tell me that he's getting angrier.

"If you just hang on a minute…"

Beggsy's axe thwacks against my shoulder.

"Just answer me, Archie. You still like her?"

"Yes!" I snap. "I do, all right? Happy now?"

But Beggsy isn't happy. He swings his axe again, whacking my other shoulder.

"Why did you have to lie about it?"

"I didn't! It was just…"

IM: *Bad move, Brainiac.*

The dwarf's had enough.

"Why. Did. You. Have. To. Lie?" Each word brings a blow swinging towards me. The first one connects but my instinct kicks in and, stepping back on my throbbing foot, I start to parry them.

"I don't know! I just did, OK?"

But the only answer I get is a series of quick and deadly blows that send me back even further, parrying with my sword up and then down and then jumping painfully out of the way as one cuts across my stomach. One comes in at my head and I duck – anything to keep my distance from his relentless, swinging axe head.

IM: *Which is made of tempered foam.*

Oh, yeah.

I stop and lower my sword, letting the spongy, impotent thwacks rain over my body. Once Beggsy realizes that it's going to take him millions of years to erode a wound into me, he stops and his axe falls to his side. He stands there, glowering and panting, his beard riffling like a hairy sheet on a washing line.

"Beggsy," I gasp. "I lied. I'm sorry. But I like her."

The beard undulates once more, as Beggsy lets out a ragged breath.

"Yeah," he rasps. "And so do I." And with that, Damli, Lufur's Son, turns away and walks towards the forest.

IM: *Nice going, Elf-boy.*

I watch him go, feeling guilty and angry and stupid. I should've seen this coming a mile off: the shoulder-bumping, the seat-hogging, the playful banter… It was happening right in front of my face, but I was too caught up wallowing in my own mire to notice. Of *course* he likes her.

Even the cry of "Incoming!" from the camp doesn't move me. I'm like one of the trolls in *The Hobbit* – caught in the sunlight and turned to stone.

But inside I'm all fizzing, fearful panic. What's he going to do? Will he tell Sarah what I've done and then make his move?

IM: *Don't judge by your own standards, Archie. Beggsy's one of the good guys.*

Beggsy disappears into the woods and I turn my head towards the rising shouts in the camp. Between the tents, I see flashes of action. Ragged, tattered zombies lurch at the questers, who hack at them with their weapons. The zombies go down, but in true undead fashion, they keep getting back up. Somewhere, I hear Ravi's voice thundering out his Turn Undead spell and then there's a cheer. He's going to be busy.

"Archie!" Sarah's beside me and I feel a sickening lurch in my stomach; this is all going wrong. "What happened? Where's Beggsy gone?"

"He went into the forest," I mutter miserably.

"What for? I saw you two arguing; did you have a row?"

"Something like that."

"What about?" Sarah sounds peeved that I haven't answered her directly.

"Nothing," I blurt. "I don't know."

"I'll go and see if he's OK. You coming?" She can't stand to see anyone upset and alone. It's like Beggsy's just run out of Art class, crying.

"No. I don't think it's a good idea."

My face must be communicating my depression, because she puts a hand on my arm. "It'll be all right," she says sincerely. "You and Beggsy are such good friends. Nothing can get in the way of that."

IM: *Yeah, right.*

"Go and kill some zombies," she adds, before following in Beggsy's bearded footsteps. As I watch the forest swallow her up, my heart sinks. Beggsy's going to spill the beans and Sarah won't ever talk to me again. I'll have lost one of my best friends *and* the girl I love. This is officially The Worst Day of My Life.

IM: *There's always tomorrow. Plenty of time for things to deteriorate...*

I limp back to the tent, staying away from the zombie massacre and putting my hand in the air, so that everyone knows I'm not playing.

I fall into the tent, sliding my hand around the ground sheet until I find my mobile. And there it is, the text that is the instrument of my doom:

Hey, Archie! The plan worked! Well, it did for me... Got together with Oliver & feeling loved up! How about u? Has Sarah fallen for it? C u on the train! Clare x Your EX-girlfriend! ;)

IM: :(

There's even a winky face to drive the stake right into my heart.

IM: *Assuming you have one.*

Lying on my sleeping bag, I clap my hands over my

eyes and let out a loud, long, frustrated groan. I am such a twat. Such a huge, treacherous, deceitful, lying twat.

IM: *"Tosser," please. Let's get the terminology right.*

Yep. I'm a Tosser. My journey to the Dark Side is complete. Pretty soon, Sarah won't be speaking to me, my friends will disown me and I'll be sat on my own, in my room, painting miniatures that no one'll ever see.

IM: *Like Sméagol living under the Misty Mountains. Only lonelier.*

"Archie! Archie!"

Ravi sticks his face into the tent and I sit up, immediately on Red Alert in case he's bringing more Bad News.

"Yo, Rav. What's up?" My EM paints something half-heartedly on to my face. I think it's supposed to be a smile.

"Where've you been? We've been looking for you everywhere!"

IM: *This is probably the bit where they execute you.*

"I've been here."

"Oh, yeah!" Ravi laughs.

"So, what's happening?"

"Baelroth's coming!" he rumbles. "You've already missed one battle and now there's like a ton of demons coming and Baelroth's behind them! He's immense! But you can't get close to him!"

"Why not?"

"He's got some power to frighten everyone away! You've gotta come! The whole camp's being torn apart! We've got to get the gang together and *do* something!"

But I don't know if I can face it. I'm just revving up an excuse about my foot hurting, when Ravi chucks something else into the equation: "Have you seen Beggsy and Sarah?"

"No," I mumble. "No, I haven't."

So, they're not back yet. An image of the two of them sharing a bearded kiss in the forest floats into my head. Maybe it was him she was talking about in her tent – he's a friend, she likes him, they get on. Maybe she needs someone in her life who can make her laugh, like Beggsy does. Someone honest. Not someone who will lie and cheat and deceive to get what he wants. Like I do.

IM: *But you have to know.*

I do. I don't know whether I've turned into some sort of masochist, but it seems that my Misery Department™ has always got room for a little bit more. If Beggsy and Sarah are together, then I'll do an impression of being happy for them. I'd rather have them in my life as a two-headed reminder of my uselessness as a human being than not at all.

"Come on, then," I sigh. "Let's go."

By the time I've limped to the top of the slope to join

Matt, Ravi and Caitlyn, it's carnage. There are bodies of villagers strewn across the battlefield and bat-winged demons are locked in combat with the survivors. But what's really causing problems for the good guys is Baelroth. Ravi's right, he's awesome.

They must've got the biggest guy they could find and stuck him on stilts, because he towers over everyone. He's got a wicked pair of wings and his skin is burning red. Where his minions are guys wearing half-masks and make-up, they've blown the budget on Baelroth's mask – it's a crimson, fire-ravaged skull with horns sticking out of every available space. Even his clawed feet have horns and his tail could well double up as a mace. In one taloned hand, he's got a cruel-looking trident and in the other, there's just what you want your Greater Demon to have: a three-tailed whip.

"Bloody hell," Matt mutters, looking and sounding more like Ron Weasley than I think he knows.

A bunch of the good guys take a run at him, but Baelroth bellows, "Fear! Fear! Repel! Repel!" and, in line with the rules, they have to stumble back about three feet. No one can get close.

"Look!" Caitlyn's pointing to behind where Baelroth's looming. Hidden behind a tree at the edge of the forest, her sword at the ready, is Sarah.

"Is she nuts?" Ravi booms. "She'll get totalled!"

Suddenly Big Marv puffs his way up the slope to join us. "A grim day, Questers!"

"Yeah – and look over there!" Ravi rumbles. We follow his pointed finger to the edge of the forest that's closest to where we are. Hugging the undergrowth is Beggsy, all beard and horns, weighing up his axe in his hands – and slowly getting closer to the winged demon-on-stilts.

Suddenly Sarah makes a break for it, running up behind Baelroth, her sword raised and ready to strike. But one of the Lesser Demons spots her and shouts a warning to his magma-coloured master. Baelroth turns and, with a mighty sweep of his trident, bellows "Quad!"

Sarah drops to the ground.

"Oh my God!" Ravi thunders. "She's down! She's dead!"

"Not quite," Big Marv twinkles. "If someone had a Potion of Greater Healing, they could restore her…"

"I have! I have a potion!" Caitlyn shouts like she's just had an ice cube dropped down her back. "But how can we get it to her?"

"It would take someone possessed of a fearless nature," Big Marv says, his eyes full of excitement, as Beggsy suddenly roars his way towards Baelroth, his braided beard blowing around him. He looks like a hero ought to – selflessly charging into battle, although the odds are stacked against him. The Greater Demon sends him tumbling back with a bellow and slowly starts to stalk towards him, flicking his whip. Beggsy gets back up and puts himself between the demon and Sarah's lifeless form. Just like real heroes do.

"And," continues Big Marv, watching the action unfold, "you only have sixty seconds before she is lost forever…"

IM: *What's that up there? A shape on the evening clouds? Could it be … the Bat Signal?*

All the frustration, misery and deception of the last few days suddenly boils up in my head. Baelroth is suddenly everything that's wrong with my life: he's Jason Humphries, he's my dad in York, he's Clare, he's my stupid lies and he's Beggsy and Sarah. Right now I need to channel the surge of emotion that roils from my stomach into my veins. No one puts my friends down on the ground.

IM: *No – that's your job.*

I'm going to kill me a demon.

"Give it to me!" I yell. "I've got the Fearless Potion!" I pull out the bottle, take a swig of the contents and grab the Healing Potion off Caitlyn.

"Go!" Ravi yells and I charge off, haring across the grass, spasms of pain lighting up my bad foot as I run. But I don't care.

IM: *Dinga-dingding-a-ding-a-dinga-dingding…!*

I race across the field so fast that I barely notice one of my ears blow off. Out of the corner of my eye, I see a Lesser Demon trying to intercept me. We meet on the run, our legs drumming out different rhythms as he tries to catch me one with his club. I throw myself to the left, but then I come in again, slashing at him with my sword.

"Single! Single! Single!"

The Lesser Demon drops forward, his momentum carrying him on to the ground in a rolling tumble of wings and snarls.

"Beggsy!" I bellow. "Yours!" As I crash past him, I toss the phials into his hands. "The potions! Blue for Sarah! Red for you!"

"Fear! Fear! Repel! Repel!" shouts Baelroth, from underneath his rubber mask.

"Fearless! Fearless!" I roar back, as he strides to come and nail me. But I'm running like an express train and no force on Earth could stop me now. I raise my sword and, ducking a sweep from his trident, get one in on his legs.

"Single!" I shout as he does a bit of tottering and howling. I risk a look to my left – Beggsy's pouring the Healing Potion into Sarah's mouth.

But there's no time. As he pivots round on one leg, Baelroth's tail cuts a perfect scythe across the grass, taking my legs out from underneath me, with a deafening "Single!" As the world turns upside down, I briefly wonder whether he's got a microphone in his mask. Rolling on to my back, I see the shape of Baelroth blot out the sky as he glowers over me. His whip comes down and I roll again, just getting out of the way.

Suddenly there's an arm on mine, pulling me to my feet. It's Beggsy.

"Sarah…?"

"She's good."

"You?"

"Fearless," he smiles grimly.

Baelroth takes a couple of strides towards us, sizing up which one he's going to eat first.

"I never thought I'd die fighting alongside an elf," Beggsy growls in his best Gimli voice. It's an olive branch – a sign that he hasn't grassed me up to Sarah and that he wants us to be friends again. And I know what the reply is.

"What about fighting alongside a Tosser?" I smile, with genuine remorse.

"Aye. I could do that, laddie," he grins back and, in perfect unison, we both raise our weapons and charge forward, yelling as we go.

IM: *Wipes a tear away*

Beggsy's in there first, swiping his axe across the

demon's legs, but Baelroth steps out of the way, bringing his trident down hard. But my bearded friend raises his axe with two hands and meets the blow above his head. Using the shaft to push the trident away, he comes in for another hack at the demon's side.

"Single!" he squeaks.

I come in on the other side, slashing at the other leg, but missing. I swipe again and connect.

"Single!"

Baelroth roars and spins, his wings swooshing over our heads. This time, I see the tail coming and jump it, but our horned adversary uses the momentum of his turn to bring in his trident in a sweeping arc and he completes his three-sixty. For a moment, I feel like a genuine, bona-fide hero. And then I feel the dreaded impact of foam across my back.

IM: *AAAARRRRGGGHHH!*

"Quad!" Baelroth blares.

"Archie!" As I fall, I see Sarah standing. A quick round of "Fear! Fear!" et cetera from the crimson demon sends her tumbling backwards and I finally allow my head to sink into the grass.

"Single! Single! Single!" I open one eye to see Beggsy hacking away at Baelroth's back. The demon's obviously got a few more lives up his sleeve than most, but he drops to his knees and does a baleful wail. This seems like an open invite to the surviving warriors from the camp, who surge to Beggsy's aid, taking Baelroth down in a flurry of foam weapons. I guess I'll never know who delivered the killing blow, but I do know that, amidst all the singles, doubles and quads that are dealt out, I hear Beggsy's rusty, man-boy voice shout, "And this one's for Bararc!"

The post-battle stories fly thick and fast. Beggsy is a living legend and I'm a fallen one. Apparently, "The Bane of Baelroth" will be told around campfires for generations to come.

And, as Beggsy is clapped on the shoulders by warriors twice his size and has his head patted by passing cat-people, I kind of hope that he has asked Sarah out and that she's said yes. They're both my friends and nothing should get in the way. Not even me. But, if they *are* together, they're being very low-key about it. The most I see them do is share a meaningful look, followed by a big hug. Something must've happened; something must've been said – and it must've worked in Beggsy's favour. There's no other reason I can think of that he'd be my mate again. Matt, Ravi and Caitlyn are blissfully unaware of this tapestry being woven in front of them;

they're too busy learning LARP demonology from Big Marv.

The crowd finally releases the bearded hero and he stumps over to me, a proud grin on his face.

"Well done, mate," I smile back at him. "Beggsy the Brave."

"Well, you helped!" he counters. "Archie the ... the..."

"Arsehole?" I offer up.

"Ha!" he laughs. "I can't think of anything else!" There's a brief pause, as we allow the chuckles to drain from our bodies.

"Sorry," I mutter, shaking my head as my Head Cinema™ does a rerun of my recent behaviour. "You know... About the lying and stuff."

"Dude! We're cool. We're friends, right." It's not a question and it makes me feel better.

"And ... you and Sarah...?" I can't help myself. But I have to know.

"We're cool, dude. No worries."

Just as I'm about to ask him if it means they're an item, another crowd of celebrating warriors drag him away. Although I'm glad we're back on track, I still want to know what's going on. It's more than that: I *need* to know. But I guess it'll have to wait for a quieter moment.

IM: *Bladder to brain: we have reached full capacity!*

I hit the toilets, feeling a bit out of it, like my brain can't handle the conflict of relief that I'm done with my stupid mission and disappointment that Sarah seems to be completely out of my reach. In a numb daze, I Point Percy at the Porcelain ©Beggsy.

Once I'm done, I wash my hands and step out into the afternoon sun.

"Archie." It's Sarah.

"Hey."

"Hey."

If awkwardness had a shape, it would be exactly the same dimensions as the space that's between us, because I know what's coming and I've got to try and prepare for it like a grown-up.

"Beggsy's brave, isn't he?" she says finally, chucking a look over her shoulder towards the camp.

IM: *Here we go. Brace yourself. Impact in ten seconds.*

"Yeah," I chuckle, as best I can. "Beggsy the Brave! What a dwarf!"

IM: ...*nine*...

There's another silence, only this one's got spikes.

"You know he asked me out today?"

IM: ...*eightsevensixfivefourthreetwoone! BOOM!*

"I kind of guessed he might." I'm really trying to hang on to my newfound feelings of benevolence, but they're starting to slip through my fingers. I silently damn my bearded buddy for his good fortune.

"He didn't say anything?"

"Not as such. He told me he liked you and I just assumed he would ... you know ... 'do the deed'." My EM works harder than it's ever done before and resurrects the rotting cadaver of a smile. "But that's great! Really great."

IM: *Sound of a single party trumpet*

"I said no."

Someone just pressed the pause button. I swallow, taking in the information. Beggsy asked her out. She said no. And Beggsy's still gooning around like nothing ever happened. Man, that *is* brave. But I know what he'll do; he'll hoot and laugh and shriek all the way home in the van and then, when he's home, alone in his room, he'll let it swallow him up. He's a bigger man than me.

IM: *And he's a dwarf.*

"Wow. What happened – I mean, why?"

Sarah's eyes falter, falling from mine ever so briefly. And even when they're back on target, there's something unsure about them, like she's rolling a D20 for the first time.

IM: *Against her Courage, by the looks of things. With a plus two modifier.*

"I told him I couldn't because I like him as a friend. But nothing else."

IM: *"Friend"* = *"in your dreams"*.

"OK."

"But there's another reason…"

"Uh-huh."

"I told him I couldn't because I like someone else." She rattles the words out like they'll cause her pain if she keeps them inside any longer. "I had to tell him the truth. *Because* he's my friend."

IM: **Drum roll like the one before somebody has their head chopped off*

Her eyes change again – it's fear. I can see fear in them. She's vulnerable and she doesn't like it. Whatever particular drawbridge is being let down, it's a big one and it's taking her a lot of effort.

IM: **Still drumming*

"But it's more than that. I've made a connection with that person; he's seen the real me."

"And … do I know that person?" I might be being stupid here, but I want to make sure the path I'm feeling with my feet isn't lovingly made from quicksand.

Sarah takes a deep, slightly irritated, breath. Keeping that drawbridge down is costing her a lot. Probably more than I know.

"It's you, Archie. You."

I thank God I've just been for a wee or, right now, I might be an elf with soggy Hero Pants. Sarah likes me.

More than likes me. It's me. Not Beggsy or Chris Jackson or anyone else. It's me. My head suddenly feels too light for my body, like it might float away. For an instant, I experience the bright, white, blinding light of Complete Happiness.

"God, you're making this hard!" The words nervously topple out of her mouth. "Archie, I'm asking you out."

"But I thought…" I thought we were just going to be friends. I thought she didn't see me that way. My thoughts must be telegraphed through my face because Sarah swallows and smiles uncertainly.

"Archie, I've learned a lot about you in the last few days. And I think you understand me. It's like you don't even have to try – you just *see* me. But not the me that everyone else sees."

There is a silent detonation in my head. In the space of about five seconds, I see me and Sarah holding hands for the first time. I see our lips tentatively pressing together. I see me giving her the first bunch of flowers she'll ever get and that I'll ever buy. I see us laughing. I see us having Sunday lunch with Mum and Tony. I even see her coming to York for a weekend.

IM: *Isn't this the bit where Elrond showed Arwen that there was no point marrying Aragorn?*

And then I realize that, throughout this Future Montage, there's been something missing: my friends.

And then Beggsy pops into my head and I think about how much we've been through together, and how quickly he's forgiven me despite all my deceit and double-dealing. And then I know what friendship's all about and how much I need my friends around me and why I'll never lie to them like that again. And, as all these thoughts crash into each other, they form a single syllable that springboards off my tongue, without me even thinking about it.

IM: *Resumes drumming*

"No."

IM: *Sounds of guillotine dropping*

I can't believe I've just said that. I can't believe what I've just done. My head feels like it wants to explode; I can practically feel the cracks starting. But it's The Right Thing To Do. For once, I know it.

"I can't," I blink. "It wouldn't be right. Beggsy ... he's my mate ... one of my best friends..."

Sarah's eyes change again – the drawbridge goes up and that beautiful, invisible barrier is reinstated.

"No," she blinks back. "You're right. Friendship like you two have is too important to risk."

"I reckon." My voice is a rasp; it's the sound of a future that will never happen.

"Well..." she breathes, conjuring up all the fake sunshine she can muster. "I'd better go and help Caitlyn..."

"Right. No problem. See you in a bit."

I stand and watch her walk through the bristled grass. Once she's out of sight, I finally exhale. My breath carries a ragged, mournful groan with it, like pieces of my dreams escaping into the wind.

This has got to be why Batman always looked so grim. If he's got to go around doing The Right Thing all the time, then he must have a hole in his soul the size of the Sahara. No wonder he dresses up like a bat. I let out another miserable sigh, falling slowly against the TARDIS door behind me. Which opens. And I tumble back, on to the toilet. The door swings shut and I sit there.

IM: *Like a constipated gnome.*

For a few minutes, I remain there, my head utterly empty, my eyes shut. Then I stand and look into the mirror above the sink. A one-eared elf looks back at me. I can't believe I've done this. I really can't believe it. I've just turned down The Most Beautiful Girl In The World™. And then, something boils up out of me. It starts as a tremble in my feet, works its way up through my legs and stomach and causes my arms to shake as I grip the sink. A shudder lurches through my shoulders and into my throat and then I'm suddenly bellowing a long, despairing, frustrated vowel at my reflection.

As I sag against the sink, there's a knock at the door.

"Just a sec!" I gabble, snapping out of my madness.

"Dude?" It's Beggsy. "Are you OK in there? What the hell're you doing?"

In spite of myself, I start to laugh as I open the door.

"Nothing. Just…" I can't finish the sentence – it's all suddenly funny.

"Dude! Thought maybe it was the burgers…!" Even Beggsy's starting to laugh now – though I'm not sure either of us really knows why.

"No," I splutter. "What … what's up?" I'm actually weeping now, clinging on to my friend for support. For some reason the thought of him thinking that my screams were the result of a digestive problem is, right now, the funniest thing I've ever heard. As I laugh, I can feel all the tension and the lies and the disappointment leaking away, replaced by a sort of comforting weariness – the exhaustion you feel when you've just done The Right Thing. "How did you know I was here?" I sniff.

"Sarah said she'd seen you going to the toilets."

"So, what's going down?" I ask again, sighing loudly through occasional flurries of mirth.

"Dude!" Beggsy bounces. "Looks like Baelroth was just the beginning – there's a load of minotaurs headed for the camp! It's all hands on deck!"

"But I'm dead."

"Big Marv says he'll bend the rules just this once and

sort you out another character – but we've got to hurry!"

Beggsy's concern and forgiveness and everything else that makes him my friend suddenly light a little firework inside me.

"Me and Sarah," I say, out of nowhere. "Not going to happen."

Beggsy looks at me for a moment, an expression of sympathy making his beard droop slightly.

"Same," he smiles sadly. "Wonder who the other guy is?"

"The other…?" And then I get it. Sarah didn't tell him it was me she liked. And because I'm not going out with her, he thinks we've both been turned down for somebody else. "Yeah," I nod. "The other guy." It might be a lie, but it's a lie I can bear to tell, because having Beggsy as my friend is that important to me. "Guess we'll never know."

"Probably that werewolf in the glasses," Beggsy jokes wearily.

"Ha."

"Dude!" he announces finally, as though he's just been switched on. "Let's go and kill some monsters!"

"Yeah," I agree. "It's what we do best." And, side by side, we jog through the grass towards the field, clutching our foam weapons. Friends. Friends til the end.

IM: *And Geeks to your core.*

THANK YOU

I think I've learned that your first book is the one you throw your heart and soul into and the second one is where you try and bring your brain into the equation. Without the editing skills of the ever-patient and ever-buoyant Jane Harris and her tireless team, this book would be about three times as long. Thank you, guys!

I'd also like to thank the wonderful and altruistic army of bloggers and reviewers who have been so supportive. If I could make medals, you'd all get one.